Big Bad Ed

by David Kaufman

DORRANCE
PUBLISHING CO
EST. 1920
PITTSBURGH, PENNSYLVANIA 15238

Dorrance Publishing Co
585 Alpha Drive
Pittsburgh, PA 15238
Visit our website at *www.dorrancebookstore.com*

ISBN: 978-1-6480-4522-6
eISBN: 978-1-6480-4487-8

PART 1

When I was a child, people would call me Edward. But I grew sick of Edward and told them to call me Ed. Soon enough it caught on. My two younger brothers would tease me by calling me Edward anyway. Their names were Henry and Cleet. They always had my back and I felt happy when I was with them. They were always fighting with each other like little brothers do. But they knew not to get me riled up. Otherwise they wouldn't be talkin' dirty for a while. We'd pull pranks on each other all the time. I remember one time, Henry threw a bucket of cold water on Cleet while he was sleeping. Ever since then, that boy kept his bedroom door locked. I would've done the same. Our mother kept us under control. If one of us went out of line, we'd be asking for a beating; and boy she'd beat us real good. Usually I was the one in trouble because I'd get violent real fast. I had gotten into a few fights at my school. Wasn't gonna let anyone talk bad about me. I lost my first fight. It was with a big kid who was at least a couple years older than me. I was seven or eight at the time and was just too damn small. The teacher saw the shit getting beat outta me and didn't do nothing 'bout it. From that experience I figured I should learn how to defend myself. So I practiced using a better stance and throwing better punches. After a while I started becoming faster and stronger, and it felt good. Soon enough I was in another fight. It was with a kid who called me a little wimp, so I called him… I called him something not very nice. That ticked him off and he threw a few punches at me. He was quick, but was a bit smaller and wasn't all that strong. I told him my momma hit harder than he did, which ticked him off more and he kept on fighting. I didn't wanna lose that fight or I'd look like a fool. I made sure to keep my face protected and strike him at the right opportunity. I think he had the same idea as me, so we didn't hit each other that much. That fight ended in a draw. Both of us decided to go our separate ways and that was that. I was just glad I could hold my own. I told my brothers they would need to stick up for themselves as well, and to not take crap from nobody. Respect was important to me. It was what my father taught me and my brothers. Henry and Cleet would tease other kids, but knew not to push it. Else they'd end up getting in fights like me. But we all knew right from wrong. Back then I believed in whatever my parents told me. I never doubted them. They meant a lot to me.

My brothers and I thought we'd have a job working' on a ranch, or a factory somewhere. Our mother wanted us to be lawyers or maybe even doctors. My father worked in a factory, and we all thought it was a decent life. I wanted to be like him. He spoke in a deep voice, taking his time while he spoke. In the end however, he lost his mind. And I'd say the same thing happened to me when I grew up. Problems started when the war started and my father was drafted into the union army. Momma told me that many more men were going to die, and it wasn't clear which side would win. I was just hoping they wouldn't draft me. Life was harder for us since less money was coming in, so I tried selling hats I made out of animal skins. I didn't make that much, but it was nice to help out my family a little. An older boy saw me selling hats one time and we talked for a while. His name was James. It turned out he worked at the same factory my father worked at. James said it wasn't easy work, but he didn't have a choice. He was living with his uncle, who didn't help out very much. James told me to keep up what I was doing, and that I might make a living off of selling hats. But I doubted it. I figured I might as well follow my father's footsteps. At the end of our conversation, James invited me back to his house. I wouldn't normally hang out with someone I barely knew, but he seemed like a fun person to be with. So I went over there, and once I got inside, the air was filled with booze and cigarettes. James stayed away from smoking, but enjoyed drinking; said he could hold his drink properly unlike his uncle. His uncle was sleeping on the couch all sweaty, smelly, and nasty-looking. The house wasn't too bad with James taking care of it. He just did his job and tried to enjoy life as much as he could. For him, it was by hanging around town 'n meeting new people. Later I introduced James to Cleet and Henry. My brothers took well to James, and we all got along. Eventually James became a friend of ours. We played cards, told stories, sang songs; those were some good times. There was one time James showed us a couple revolvers he had stashed in his bedroom. My brothers and I never fired a gun before, and my brothers were eager to play with them, which led to shooting them. We all took turns firing shots in the woods and shooting targets. At one point, we started having competitions where a bottle would be thrown up and we'd try to shoot it as quick as we could. I got the hang of it quickly and shot those bottles like it was nothing. One time James decided to challenge me by throwing up four bottles at once, and I shot them all in the blink of an eye. I felt like the fastest gunslinger out there and that no one could mess with me.

Life was better with James. He was someone I could always trust. As we all hung out more often, drinking came into play. James offered me some whiskey and I thought I'd take it in one shot like a real man. Instead I threw up after drinking half the glass and swore off it. James said I would eventually get around to it. The thought of it made me want to throw up. Henry and Cleet tried the whiskey and liked the taste of it. They only had a little. Not too much or Momma would have caught them, and they'd have been in the shitter for weeks. I on the other hand, stayed clean. My brothers teased me for it, but I felt it lead to nothing good. Unfortunately it did. One time my brothers were having too much fun drinking beer for the first time and things started getting wild. I was talking with James and my brothers went out in the woods somewhere. Cleet took one of the revolvers and asked Henry to shoot a bottle from the top of his head. I didn't know how much they'd been drinking. I should have stepped in. Henry was a bit drunk and his aim wasn't the best, so you can figure how that one ended. Cleet was buried in a cemetery not too far from our home. We didn't tell our momma the truth. We told her he was with Henry when they got mugged by a man, ending with Cleet shot dead. We wanted to say what really happened, but we just couldn't. She wanted "Cleet's Killer" brought to justice, but of course, would never see that happen. I'm sure it was the hardest time of her life since our father would likely die in the war and her youngest son was dead. As the next few weeks passed, our momma was harder on us. She'd get mad for the smallest things, like "walking too quickly" or "talking too loudly." Even getting mad at God, cursing him for what he was putting her through. We both felt accountable, and we sure as hell were. Henry and I were there for each other, hoping Momma would be okay and Cleet was in a better place.

A few days later, I was doing chores around the house until someone knocked on the door. It was a postman who gave Momma a letter about my father. She started weeping. She couldn't read it, so she asked me to. As I opened up the letter, my heart felt heavy…and cold. I started reading it to myself, but to my surprise, it said my father was alive. He had just fought in the Battle of Gettysburg where the Union won against the Confederacy. My father was being hailed as hero for killing many Confederate soldiers and saving the life of a union soldier. It ended saying he would come back home to visit for a few days. I started telling my momma, who's face turned from devastation to joy and relief. At that moment I almost cried. My father told me to never cry, so I wouldn't let that happen. I couldn't wait to tell Henry. It would make him feel better after what had happened with Cleet. I don't think Henry could ever forget about it. That guilt followed him everywhere. Henry was outside hanging some clothes up. He seemed to be okay. But I could tell he still felt broken.

When I was telling him the good news, he said "Well that's great then." Didn't say anything after that and continued with his chores. Later on I went to visit James and said that Henry wasn't doing so well. He had been a lot quieter than usual and only talked to me a little bit since Cleet's death. James however, didn't seem so devastated.

He said, "I'm sorry, but sometimes these things happen." I told him that I still wanted to be his friend, but no more booze, and that all of us were too young to be drinking. Then James changed the subject and we started making small talk.

Then his dirty uncle barged in the house yelling "You gotta clean this place up boy!" James shook his head and started chuckling.

He said "No matter how much I try to clean up around here, the old man makes it a mess the next day." We both went outside and took a walk to get away from his uncle. I told James about my father, and he was happy for my family. He reassured me that if there was anything me or my family needed, he would be there for any of us. James said my brothers and I felt more like family than anyone in his family. I asked him who else was in his family besides his uncle. He said that his parents were in prison for theft, and that he had been living with his uncle for the past ten years. James told me to enjoy being with my family and to be there for Henry. I told him I would.

A few days later, I was eating breakfast with my mother and Henry. My mother was in good spirits, more hopeful than she had been in a while. I don't know why, but I asked if she thought father might be different.

She replied, "He will probably have some stress and anxieties from war but that he will get through it." Momma told me how hard the war had been. The Battle of Gettysburg was the bloodiest battle so far. I was glad my father fought for a good cause. It wasn't right for people to be kept as slaves. Colored folk were people too, and deserved freedom. Momma told us that President Lincoln would be delivering the Gettysburg address in the coming weeks. It was supposed to be an uplifting speech, giving motivation to the Union cause. I wanted to see it, but I had to stay here and help Momma out. Then a knock came. My mother walked to the door and opened it. I followed to see who it was. As soon as Momma opened the door, I saw it was my father. Momma was in shock and gave him one big hug. Henry and I joined in. It was honestly the happiest moment of my life. My father was excited and had a lot to share. I had many questions for him, but didn't want to ask him too many questions about the war. That would have been overwhelming. He said he was unscathed from war, feeling thankful and very lucky. Of course, he asked where Cleet was. Henry went to his room and I followed. I closed Henry's bedroom door and tried to help Henry relax. He was breathing heavily, not knowing what to do. I held his hand and told him everything was going to be alright. Our father called us back into the living room. He looked devastated, saying he should have died instead of Cleet. In that moment, I looked over to Henry, wondering what he was thinking. Maybe he would tell our parents what really happened. I think he wanted to, but instead said nothing. If I was in his position, I don't think I would have told the truth either. My father said he needed some time alone with Momma, so Henry and I went back into our rooms. A few hours later, our father asked us if we wanted to go fishing. We happily agreed and got our fishing gear right away. I was excited for it, and Henry was too. It had been a long time since any of us had gone fishing. So I didn't expect that we'd catch any big fish; just a few small ones. The three of us took a walk down to the nearest pond. I still remember playing there with Henry and Cleet when I was really young. We would try skipping rocks and catching small fish with our hands. There was one time I'll never forget. Cleet was chasing after this frog he found minding its own business before he scared it off. Cleet must have been like five or six at the time. That frog ended up jumping into the pond and getting away.

Of course Cleet jumped in the pond right after it screaming, "I'm gonna get getcha!" Henry and I were laughing so hard. But when Cleet got so deep in the water, he started to struggle. My dad was nearby and started to notice what was happening and swam over to save him. My father brought him to shore, and Cleet was just fine.

My father was upset with all three of us saying, "If you boys ain't careful, one of you is gonna get killed!" Henry and I remembered him telling us that; and I'm sure my father remembered too. I guess we weren't careful enough. I should have looked after those boys a little more, or at least told them to watch themselves. I know Henry felt guilty about Cleet's death. But I did as well, and that never went away. When all of us got to the pond, there was no one else around. The view was beautiful…it almost looked like it could've been heaven. The only part I didn't like was the frogs and toads croaking so much. After a while, it gave me a headache. When we stood at the edge of the pond, we started throwing our fishing lines in the water. None of us were saying anything. Usually my father would be yapping away about how he used to catch bigger fish, but something felt off. I couldn't stop wondering what my father was thinking. It seemed like he was trapped in his own head. Not paying attention to what was going on around him, just staring off into space. Henry had a tense posture and didn't look too comfortable. I didn't know what to say to Henry or my father because I didn't want to say something that would upset them. So I focused on my fishing line when suddenly my father was trying to say something. The way he was speaking however, was strange. I wasn't even sure what he was saying. All I can remember was there a lot of stuttering and mumbling. It was something about how his old man used to catch fish. Then he paused for a long time, lasting about ten seconds. Then he tried to finish what he was saying, but couldn't. Normally my father had no problem saying what was on his mind. Even when he came home, he was speaking just fine. I looked over at Henry, but he had his head down. So I put my head down as well.

After a few minutes passed, my father said, "Sorry boys, I-I-uh…gotta leave." Just like that, he left us. My brother and I had no idea where he was going. Henry looked at me confused. I looked at him the same way. We decided it was best to go back to the house and wait for our father to come back feeling better. I figured I would at least tell Momma what was going on.

When we got back, our mother looked at us with a worried face, asking us, "Boys, where is your father!"

I replied, "I don't know." I told her he was probably heading into town since he started walking in that direction.

Momma was upset he left us like that, and started to weep saying, "He wouldn't just leave you boys like that." I told her he was speaking very strangely, and that it might have had something to do with the war. Or maybe he was upset Cleet died. To be honest, I still don't know what happened to him. But what started happening to him, eventually happened to me. At the time, I believed things would be fine. That he just needed to brush things off. My mother started getting worried and told us to stay in the house. She was going into town to look for him. Later that evening, both of them were back. My stumbled in drunk as a skunk and Momma tried to keep him upright. He was barely able to stand, let alone walk. Momma asked Henry and I to get father a wet rag and a glass of water to help with a severe headache he was having. Father started getting angry at Momma, yelling at her to leave him alone. He said he was fine and just wanted peace and quiet. This time he was speaking fluently, but his words were slurred since he was drunk. I put a glass of water on a table next to his chair, and Henry gave the wet rag to my father.

In a panic-stricken voice she said, "You boys best get to bed, your father ain't feeling well." We did as she told. I went straight to bed and tried to fall asleep. About ten minutes later, I heard a loud smack that made my eyes go wide open. Momma started crying and my father was yelling at her. I felt my heart swell up as I realized he hit her. He never hit her before, even when he was drunk. Sure, he would get angry at her, but he wouldn't go that far. I closed my eyes and tried to forget what was happening, pretending things would go back to normal. The next morning, they thankfully did. I woke up and went to the living room. My father was reading the newspaper, so I asked what he was reading. He said it was about the war, and how it was now in favor of the Union. He asked me if I was working on my writing for school. I got cocky and told him I could write a whole novel if I wanted to. He smirked like he always did and told me to try writing poetry before writing a novel. He said that writing poetry helps describe the emotion and creativity within oneself; and that it helped him by providing comfort during the war. I asked if he had any with him. He said he had some in his suitcase, so I asked if he could show me. But he became agitated quickly, saying his poems were only for him. I figured he had a few poems in his suitcase. But I wouldn't dare go near it. Clearly it was very personal to him. I walked over to my mother who was making breakfast. Right away I saw a bruise on her right cheek.

I asked if she needed anything and all she said was, "No." It made me upset to see her like that. She worked hard to keep everything going. She didn't deserve that. I wanted to ask my father why he did that to her. But I just couldn't find it in myself to ask him that. Instead I asked if he knew James, since they had both worked at the same factory. He answered that he might have heard that name before but wasn't sure. I wanted to ask him earlier, but if Henry heard anything about James, it would bring him back memories of Cleet's death. Those two didn't speak since the accident. Henry didn't blame James; he just didn't want to be friends anymore.

The next few days were quiet and went by quick. During that time, I watched my father's behavior carefully. There were a few instances where he would take longer than normal to respond, and wasn't in touch with what was happening around him. There was one instance where Momma asked him to say grace before we ate supper. For a few seconds he stared blankly, not paying attention to anything.

Momma had to shake him to get his attention, and he responded "Oh... right, I-I'll start the prayer." I found this very worrisome. It seemed he wasn't getting much better. At the time I was too naïve; I should have killed him then.

He left the next day to receive awards for bravery in combat and some other stuff. In the end, it never meant a whole lot to anybody. After everything was said and done, he would have to do things normally like everybody else, which he was struggling with. At least he'd get to see the Gettysburg Address, which was a big deal back then. Back at the house it was me, Henry, and Momma. That was alright with me since all that my father brought was problems. He didn't even say goodbye to us and just left like it was nothing. I looked around to see if there were poems he left behind, but he took his suitcase with him. I wanted to read them; it was all I could think about. I asked Momma about them, but she told me to let it go.

As life continued, Henry started to become his old self again. He was hanging out with his friends, reading his books, and telling his jokes (even if they weren't funny). I hoped the same would happen for our father. Momma kept telling me I needed to get a job one day, so I could live a decent life. Having a job was all that mattered to me during that time. I wanted to make my parents proud and be the man I had to be. Things weren't going well for my family since money was tight. It was hard just to get enough food on the table. Clothes were starting to get worn, and Henry was getting sick, coughing quite a bit. The way things were going I thought we'd end up living like James' uncle. James did say he was there for me, so I sought for his help. When I arrived at his house, James was sitting on a chair on the front porch. With him there was another boy around his age sitting across from him. James saw me approaching from a distance, so he smiled and waved. His friend also started to wave. I waved back, quickly walking down to the front porch. I hoped James could help me find a part-time job or something. I knew doing some job wouldn't be fun, but it would beat trying to sell hats. Unfortunately that wasn't going very far. Whatever advice James offered, I was all ears.

As I approached them, James' friend said, "Hey there kid. Are you the one they call Ed?"

I replied in a deep voice, "Yes I am tough guy."

We started chuckling and James offered me a beer but then stopped and said, "I forgot you don't drink; especially not after what happened to your brother."

In that moment, I changed my mind and said, "It ain't gonna kill me, so why the hell not!"

James said, "Alright then, let's get him a beer!" His friend introduced himself when we got inside. His name was Joe. He was taller than me and James, had a few zits on his face, and looked like he wouldn't take crap from no one. I knew I wouldn't wanna pick a fight with him. James said his uncle was out buying a few things, and that he'd be gone for a while. He asked me how my family was doing and that he missed seeing Henry. I told him things weren't going well with my father, but that Henry was doing alright.

James said, "It was my fault the accident happened. So when Henry is older, tell him that every drink is on me."

I responded, "I think for now he's just taking it easy." James nodded and was glad me and my brother were doing alright. But I had to be honest, I needed help finding a job or a better way to make money. I couldn't stand seeing momma struggle to take care of us and do nothing about it. It was hard without my father helping out. So I told them how things were. James said that jobs in factories didn't have the best conditions. Saying the workplace was dirty, causing men to get sick. Worst of all, the boss didn't even care about it. My father never told me that, and I suppose he was lucky since he never got very sick; at least not physically. Joe said that he worked on a ranch, but was fed up with sweating all day and working to the bone. I didn't think that life was for me. Then James brought up an interesting idea, saying there was somebody we could easily scam. It was a man named Pete Evans, who was known for scavenging real treasure maps and finding real treasure. Although no one believes he ever found much, since he lived in a tiny run-down house by himself.

Joe said, "There's a rumor he's got a bunch of cash hidden in that house, and he has it for safe keeping." It sounded far-fetched to me, but I decided to follow along with James' scam. He told us to stay put as he went to his room to get something. He came back with a treasure map that looked intriguing, filled with detail. It was surely impressive.

I asked "What we were gonna do with that map?"

James replied, "Make some money boy!" Joe chuckled and I chuckled along. "It's a phony map but a damn convincing one." said James. Then he picked up a case full of beer, saying it was gonna come in handy. We all went outside and James loaded everything onto his wagon. It had one work horse looking to be in good condition. That was something I wanted my family to afford. Me and Joe climbed up in the back of the wagon and James got in the front, taking the reins. We started moving, and James started talking about the plan. He told us we were going to convince Pete the treasure map James had led to a lockbox containing gold worth quite a handsome sum. He said about 150 dollars or so. James said we could sell it for around 40 to 60 dollars. The case of beer would be used to get Pete drunk to increase the chances of him falling for it. I started thinking about momma and how angry she would be seeing me doing something like this. I had never committed any crimes or nothing. But I realized this was a real opportunity; something that needed to happen. The plan to scam the guy seemed a little far-fetched, but James was confident we could pull it off. He told us it wouldn't get violent, and to try to act charming. I told him I was good with shooting, but not so much with acting. Joe said to act natural, and that as long as we give off the right impression, we'd make some good money. I asked them if they'd done this kind of stuff before. They said just a few times, nothing big. James said this would be the biggest one they would be attempting, and that he was glad to have me along.

James said to me, "We're doing this for you…for you and your family." I felt touched by that. It really meant a lot to me. And it sounded like Pete Evans wasn't spending much of his money anyway. Figured someone should put it to good use. Joe didn't talk much. I wondered if he was thinking or was staring off. I asked him if he knew Pete Evans.

He replied, "Nah, never met him. Sounds to me like a decent feller, just a little odd."

"I hear the man's a hermit. Most folk don't know too much about him." said James. Later I started getting tired. So I crossed my arms and rested my head against the wagon. It wasn't very comfortable, especially with all the bumps in the road. But I fell asleep anyway.

James yelled, "Wake up kid! We're almost there." I sat up straight and Joe had the case of beer in his lap. He told me to just act casual and to not look tense. I felt ready. It was either me or Pete, and my family mattered more than some damn hermit. James stopped the wagon several feet away from the house, and we started walking up to the front door. We all walked calmly up to the front door. Then bam!

He burst out with a shotgun pointing at all three of us, saying, "The hell you want! You boys look no good to me!" None of us had brought any guns, so there was not much we could do but run.

James however, kept his composure and simply asked, "How you been sir?" I was impressed James had guts like that to stare death in the face like it was nothing. If I had a revolver on me he'd have dropped already; wouldn't wanna take too many chances. I guess James saw things different. Pete said that things were alright and asked him once again what we were doing there. James told him we wanted to make a deal and that he might be interested in. I had to hand it to James; he had a certain finesse and charm about him that could convince someone to do almost anything. As he was talking, Pete started to lower his gun and put it off to the side. James gave Pete the map and said the map was from a gang of outlaws, who hid the money there for safe keeping. He asked Pete if we could come in and get to know each other for a bit. At first the man was hesitant, but agreed to let us in, saying it was pretty lonely with just himself. Pete was a pretty skinny feller with a squeaky sounding voice. It didn't seem like he was really all that tough, just a bit skittish and nervous. When we got inside, it wasn't as bad as I thought it would be. The place didn't look like shit nor smell like shit. Joe handed Pete over a beer and he snatched it right out his hand. It looked like he needed one, and in a way, I kind of felt bad for him. I was beginning to wonder if he even had that much money. But he was gulping down every bottle we gave him. James started telling some jokes and we were all laughing quite a bit, especially Pete. At that point he was definitely drunk. James then encouraged me to try one, saying I needed to loosen up more. But I told him it wasn't for me. James got a little angry, pushing me to at least have one. I told him I'll never be a drinker, and that all it did was kill my little brother.

James said, "If you say so." and focused his attention back to Pete, who looked like he was about ready to pass out. With a little more convincing, James was able to rip him off. Making 100 dollars! Later, me, Joe, and James walked out and went back to his house. On the way back I asked James what that map led to anyways.

James replied, "Who knows." I asked him where he got it, and he said to not worry about it. James apologized for snapping at me about drinking, saying it didn't even matter. I told him it was fine. And we left it there. I couldn't be mad at James because I got to keep all that money, just like he promised. It was hard to believe someone I didn't even know for that long would do such a thing.

I asked him why he did this for me and he said, "I like to help my friends out. Besides, you need that money. So don't spend it all in one place." James was a good kid and I was grateful to have him as a friend. None of my friends in school would have helped me out like that. I don't think they even cared that much about me. Aside from that, what James did with Pete wasn't the nicest, but it was necessary. Joe and I started talking more on the way back and got to know each other better. He still didn't say much, but we did both like card games. He said that one day we should play some poker. I told him I wasn't too familiar with poker, but we both liked blackjack. And that one I knew how to play.

Later that day I went back to my house, only to have my mother screaming at me to the top of her lungs which wasn't like her. Normally she kept a calm composure. She asked where I had been and why I hadn't been studying for school. I told her I was studying for classes with one of my friends, but of course she didn't buy that. I told her that I started making some good money shining shoes for people, but didn't tell her I had 100 dollars. Otherwise she would have thought I robbed a whole bank! She was happy to hear it, but then had me sit down and told me not to get too close to Henry.

"The boy's dying." she said. "I took him to the doctor a little while ago and they said he has TB." We weren't able to afford medicine. I told her I would try to find something that could slow it down or help out. But she believed he was a goner. And I figured the same. I decided to go out right away and try to at least find something. When I got to the doctor, I told him I was

Henry's brother, and asked him if anything would help. All he said was to pray for him, and I told him that wasn't good enough. I had the money and was willing to pay anything to keep my brother alive. The doctor told me he gave him some medicine and said the best thing was for him to take things easy. I did buy some rags and a canteen filled with cool water for him. I got back to the house and knocked on Henry's door. He asked who it was and told him that I had something that might help. When I walked in, the sight of Henry really hit me. Some cool water and rags weren't going to make a damn difference. Henry didn't look like he would last much longer. Then he leaned towards me, telling me something that hurt me more than anything.

He said, "You shouldn't have let me and Cleet drink anything. Us boys were too young and foolish. It seemed like you didn't even care that much. You're just as much to blame as I am." I told him it wasn't like that, and that I didn't think Cleet would've ended up dead. There was a moment of silence between us.

I added, "You're the one that pulled the goddamn trigger!"

Henry said, "I'll tell that to Cleet when I see him in heaven, or maybe I'll just go straight down to hell." Then Henry started coughing profusely, with his voice getting weaker and weaker. I told him, "I know I'm not perfect, but nobody is. I promise you I'm gonna take care of momma and make sure father is ok. Just stick with us for as long as you can."

Henry slowly nodded his head and told me, "Just be careful, Ed." He rested his head and closed his eyes. Then I knew he passed. He was buried next to Cleet. It was nice seeing them next to each other. I hoped they were both looking over me. I knew they were, and I think they still are now. My mother was able to handle Henry's death a little better than Cleet's. I couldn't imagine what it must have been like for her. Without those two, I felt a lot lonelier. No more pranks, laughs, or even arguing. I missed all of that, but I still had my mother. We did talk to each other, but the house was much quieter, and it was hard to get used to.

Momma asked me to come with her into town to pick up a few things. Normally Henry would go with Momma, but I was happy to join her. The town wasn't very far from our house, about a five-minute walk. Momma said Henry told her about my friend James, saying he was a bit older and not much else. I knew James was there for me, but I needed her just as much. She wanted me to carry supplies, and to provide some company. As we were walking together, she told me I should try to find a fun hobby. Suggesting I should try writing stories, or learning an instrument. I told her I always thought about playing the harmonica, which seemed like a fun instrument to play.

With that, she said, "Well then, let's buy you a harmonica! I wanna hear you play!"

I told her, "It'll take a while to get the hang of. But hey, if I'm really bad, people might pay me just to stop playing!" She chuckled and told me I could learn with my father. I said, "In that case, let's get two! I got enough money to afford it." She said okay, and we walked down the hill leading into the town. Momma went and got some food ingredients for supper and soap for laundry. I went to the general store to see if they sold a harmonica. They only had one available; unsurprisingly a cheap little thing. Cost about five cents. I was happy to at least have one. Having something fun to do would bring joy to our lives, and we needed some way to cope with the loss of Henry and Cleet. At first, I didn't think of learning any songs, just wanted to get sound out of it. I put it in my pocket and caught up with Momma, who had purchased everything she needed.

On the way back, Momma was telling me, "Your brothers are angels now, and they are always watching out for us."

I told her, "I know. I pray for them every night, and I promise to be the best man I can be."

Momma smiled and said, "I know you will." It felt like we were connecting more than ever before. I just hoped things would be the same with my father.

Life went on with me and Momma for a few more weeks. I was staying out of trouble and helping her around the house. Since my brothers passed, I had to do all the chores. So I was pretty busy being the man of the house. One day I was sweeping the floor and Momma was knitting when we heard a knock on the door. I opened it and my father was back and this time for good. He still seemed out of touch, just like the way he was at the pond. He said hello to me, but showed no emotion or expression.

I said, "How have things been?" I never got a response. My father sat down on the chair with his head down. He was completely stuck in his own head.

Then he looked up at Momma and said, "I've been discharged from the military."

Momma looked happy and said, "Well, that's fantastic! I know you've been through so much. Are you gonna keep working at that factory?"

Big Bad Ed

My father seemed strange, saying nothing for the first few seconds as if he wasn't going to respond, then he suddenly replied, "Yes, I am. Arthur Williams is still running the place. I start work there in a few days."

"Well you don't sound too excited for it!" said Momma. Then my father said he needed something to drink.

I said I would fetch him some water, but he said, "No, I mean like some whiskey or rum or something."

Momma said, "You just got home! Do you have to get drunk now!?" He then went over to Momma, putting his arms around her. He told her he was sorry and that he's been going through something. Momma then asked what it was. He whispered something in her ear that I couldn't make out. Then he gave her a kiss and left the house, presumably to go drinking. When he walked out, I asked her what was going on with him.

She replied with, "He said he couldn't tell me. So I can't say for now." My father came back late that night; we started to think he wasn't going to come back.

As he drunkenly walked in the house, he started yelling, "They're gone! They're gone! They're finally gone!" I went with Momma as she ran up to him in her nightgown.

She frantically asked, "What are you talking about dear!?"

He replied "The voices...they've finally stopped! I don't know what the hell is wrong with me!" He started whimpering, something I had never seen before. I wasn't sure what to think of it. Momma walked him into their bedroom and told me to go to sleep. I did as she said and went straight to bed. All I could hear was her talking to him and calming him down. I couldn't fall asleep that night.

The next morning, I was getting ready to go to school. Momma was in the living room having coffee. She didn't get any sleep either. She told me not to talk to my father for now, and to just focus on school.

I wanted to ask him what it was like watching the Gettysburg Address but instead I replied, "Yes ma'am," and headed out the door. I didn't talk much while I was in class. The teacher even asked why I was being so quiet. I'd normally at least crack a few jokes in class. I told him it was nothing, and he moved on. School went by quickly and I headed home right after school finished. Momma was sweeping the front porch and I immediately asked how father was. She said she took him to the doctor and they had given him something to calm down. Apparently, he was doing better. But he still wasn't normal. For the next couple days, we gave him some space to relax and put himself together. Soon he had to go back to work; and I prayed he'd be able to do that. Momma was nervous too, and wasn't sure how much any medicine would help him. She told me he could still do simple tasks, but was having a hard time with communication. Still, he worked in that factory for over ten years. And he was a Civil war hero. They wouldn't fire him just like that. In just one day, they did. I came back home seeing Momma crying with her hands covering her face. My father had his arm around her, trying to comfort her. She told me the news in a small, quiet voice. I got angry and said it wasn't fair for them to do that to us.

My father said, "They thought I was…acting strange. I'm sorry. I'm trying my best and I'll figure something out."

"Tell us what's going on instead of staying silent!" shouted my mother.

"I can't!" my father shouted back. I went into my room and tried thinking about something else. I didn't know if my father could get another job. Those people working at the factory just threw him to the side like that! Just shows all of them are heartless. My parents started arguing which turned into screaming, and then my father turned away and walked out of the house. I knew where this was going. Momma stayed and took out the sweater she was making and continued knitting.

She said, "This is supposed to be for your father, but he probably won't even wear it." I didn't know what to say, so I went to my room and sat on my bed. I didn't feel like practicing my harmonica, so I started studying for one of my tests. I figured I would have to carry most of the weight for us to survive.

Once again, my father barged in drunk and momma was still in the living room, still knitting that sweater. I was in my room and could hear my father saying something slurred, but I couldn't tell what he was saying. At that point, Momma snapped. She couldn't take it anymore. I had to cover my ears because she was so loud. I tried to not think about it. But I could still hear her. Her screaming was becoming more intense. She must have felt nothing but anguish because of everything that was happening. I was beginning to think that she might leave him, and I supposed I was better off with her. The yelling was going on for a few minutes. My father wasn't saying anything. All of a sudden, I heard a loud bang! I knew right away it was a gunshot. I don't know what made me do it, but I decided to go into the living room. I saw Momma dead on the floor, with a bullet in her head. My father was standing with the gun in his hand and immediately turned to me.

He shouted, "She was turning into a demon! I had to stop it!" I stood there frozen. He then put the gun to his head and said, "I'm sorry, Ed." He pulled the trigger and dropped to the floor. Everyone in my family was dead. All I felt was emptiness in the pit of my stomach. It didn't feel like it was real, but it was. I walked past the corpses, trying to not look at them. Once I got outside of the house, I slammed the door shut. I felt my best option was to go to James, so that's what I did. I started running and never looked back.

PART 2

Two weeks passed by, and I was living with James. I didn't have to do any chores around the house. So that gave me lots of free time to practice the harmonica. I was starting to play a few tunes, but the notes were coming out choppy. Still, I was proud of how far I got with it, if only I could show my family. But I had James, and at this point it felt like we were brothers. I don't think his uncle even noticed me. The man was asleep for most of the day, and spent the rest of it drinking. I would say hi to him, and he would mumble something back that I couldn't understand. Eventually I got used to it.

There was a small room I had to myself. It was a mess at first, littered with dirt and dust everywhere. James helped me clean it, and we at least made it look half decent. I wasn't sure whether or not I should've returned to school or tell the law about what happened. James said they probably would have put me in some orphanage, which would feel like a prison. People around town would wonder about my parents, and the law would eventually find their bodies. I tried to stop thinking about my parents and thought about school. Was it worth going to? How far would I have gotten? I knew I never wanted to become a doctor, but I wanted to please my parents...so much for that. All I ever liked from school was fighting; I didn't actually want to be whatever momma wanted. What I wanted was to do what was right for me. James was still working at the factory that my father worked at and I asked him if he had seen my father when he came back from the war. James told me he never saw my father but that he did hear about someone yelling and cursing at the boss, who was named Arthur Williams. James said he was a large man with a big belly and a well-groomed goatee. James always kept a calm composure. Even after I told him what happened with my parents. That whole time I was in shock. It felt like I was in an alternate reality. But all of this was real and James was someone who could sympathize with me. He told me he was sick of working at that factory. Saying he wasn't making enough for the work he was doing. This made me realize that our society is corrupt. The government doesn't care about its people, and Arthur Williams fired my father, leaving him with no job. If the government cared, they would have had some kind of program to help someone like him dealing with mental illness. Instead they threw him to the side like he was garbage. I figured it was the war that messed him up. A war he did not want to be a part of. They did nothing for him after he gave them everything, and I knew this was wrong.

I sat on the bed inside my room thinking about all of it, when James came inside and pulled up a chair. I told him how upset I was with the way things were. I was massaging my forehead, trying to ease the headache I was having from thinking for so long.

Then James said, "Look Ed, I have a plan to get enough money, so we can leave this house and start a new life someplace else. Just you, me, and a couple other buddies of mine, and we'll all be a family." I asked him what it was, and he told me he wanted to rob his boss Arthur Williams.

"You should be the one to rob him because I can't have him recognize me. I quit today, so now there is no turning back. I know you want to do this. I need to do this." said James.

I nodded my head and replied, "Well, let's do it." James brought me over to his gun case and pulled out two revolvers, giving one to me. He also pulled out two bandanas, also giving me one. "Keep these in your room for now. We'll do this at night, when Arthur will be in the factory all alone. He keeps a bunch of money in his office. You're gonna go in there, threaten him, and take as much money as you can. I'll watch the front entrance in case somebody is around." said James.

I replied, "Ok. I'm sure he has enough to spare."

James gave me a pat on the back saying, "Get some rest. Clear your mind for a bit. I need to do the same." Then he went outside as I sat on my bed. I couldn't believe we were going to do something like this, but I didn't want to just get buy, I wanted to live a life I could be proud of. James and I knew this was the first step to getting a better life.

As nighttime came, James called me over to the front door. I was lying on my bed, thinking about where we would go after we got the money. I knew James had it all figured out, like he always does. I met him at the front door, and he pulled out a lock pick.

"This is what we'll use to get the front door open. Just act real tough and scary; he'll give in pretty quick." he said. We headed out the door and walked towards the factory.

As we started walking I asked, "What's going to happen with your uncle? We're not bringing him with us are we?"

He replied, "Of course not. He won't give a damn that I'm gone. He'll get kicked out of the house by tax collectors and will be homeless for the rest of his miserable life. I couldn't care less." I didn't blame James for saying that. His uncle was only a burden, and was always upset with everything, no matter what James did. Good riddance I'd say. It was chilly that night. The breeze was blowing fast, so much so that it was hard to hear the crickets chirping. I kept on thinking of what I had to do. Just go in, threaten the man, and take his money. James warned me not to fire the gun, since it might alert someone nearby. It wasn't just about the money though. This was personal to me. Arthur Williams fired my father, and that is what caused him to kill my mother. At least that is what I believed back then. I didn't want it to be about revenge, but it was in the back of my mind. It didn't take long to get to the factory. It was only a few minutes from James' house. I had never been in there before, so I was curious to see what it was like inside. I imagined it would be pretty dirty from what my father and James told me.

I asked James, "How well am I going to be able to see in there?"

He said, "There will be a few lights on. Arthur will be on the second floor in his office. It's where he is every night." Soon enough, we saw the factory. My heart started pounding, so I took a deep breath and focused on what I had to do. It was either this, or nothing. There were no guards or anyone else hanging around the front entrance. So we walked up to the front door, and James pulled out his lock pick.

He said, "Keep watch in case anyone approaches." I stood there, looking around on all sides. There wasn't a soul in sight. It wasn't too long before James got the door open, and we walked right in. Inside it was cold. The air was thick, and there were rats roaming about. Slightly better than what I had imagined. It was a big place, but James told me to follow him slow and quietly. I followed him into the factory for a bit, until he pointed to one room that had lights on.

He said, "That's where he is. Make sure he doesn't notice you while you're walking up. Get right in there with your gun out and take him by surprise. I'm sure he'll piss his pants. Oh, and here is your bandana. You know how to put it on right?"

I put it on quickly and said, "I know what I'm doing. We'll be done with this in no time." Then I walked over to the stairs and started slowly walking up. As I was going up, I pulled out my revolver, which did have a few bullets. I slowly walked to the door, and started loading my gun. I wanted to be ready in case he tried to pull a fast one on me. I saw the door was just slightly open, so I walked to the front and took one last deep breath. I kicked it down, and he was behind his desk right in front of me.

I had my gun pointed at him yelling, "Mr. Williams, you're gonna give what money you got in here! And don't try anything funny, or I will kill you." My hand was shaking while holding the gun. My nerves were starting to take over, but I had to be the one in control.

He looked surprised, not scared at all, and said, "You got some nerve coming in here like this kid. Who are you with?"

I replied, "No one. It's just me and you."

"Look, this is not something you want to do, it's not gonna lead to anything good for you. And if you choose to rob me, you're gonna learn that the hard way. If you turn back now, I'll let you go and we can pretend this never happened. How does that sound?"

I cocked back the gun and said with an angry voice, " I ain't playing around old man." Then he knew I was real serious, so he pulled out money from his desk and put it on the table. I went over and took it; looked like it was a few hundred dollars. That would be a good start, but I wanted more. So I asked him, "What else you got?"

He said, "That's it, now get the hell outta here."

I didn't like his tone towards me, so I told him, "I swear I will kill you right now and won't think twice about it." That got him to comply. He pulled out more and threw it over.

He said, "That's everything in my desk."

I said, "Good. Now I'm gonna search the cabinets and see what else you got for me." I kept my gun pointed at him as I searched the drawers but only found some paperwork, no money. After looking everywhere in the room, I felt satisfied, and told him I was finished searching the room.

"Then leave now and don't ever think about coming back." he replied.

I responded back saying, "I said I was finished searching the room. I never said I was finished with you."

He asked, "What do you have against me? I don't think I've ever met you before."

"You knew a man named Fredrick Miller." I said.

"Yes, I did. He started going crazy and wasn't fit to work here anymore."

I replied, "So you're just gonna dump him like that?" My teeth were gritting, and my eyes were staring into his. "He was my father. And now he is dead along with my mother. All because a stuck-up bastard like you wouldn't help him. You threw him away like a piece of garbage. And you know what…you're a piece of garbage!" I started pulling the trigger, shooting him four times in the chest. It happened fast. And just like that, he was sitting on his chair dead. I had the money stuffed in my pockets, and I knew we had to get out of there. James definitely heard those shots, but no one else was around. So I knew we were safe for now. I quickly went down the stairs and James rushed over looking confused and panicked.

I told him, "I'm sorry. I lost control of my anger. It got the better of me."

"Is he dead!? Why did you shoot him?" he asked.

"Yes, he is dead. I… I couldn't stop myse-"

"That wasn't the plan Ed! Dammit! Now they're gonna want to find us for killing him!" James started walking very fast out of the factory and I followed right behind him. James was angry with me, and I knew I made a mistake. I honestly couldn't believe I killed him. It felt like I didn't have control of myself. It kind of just…happened, but it felt good.

James and I ran back to his house. His uncle was there, drunk as usual, and yelled, "W-What the hell have you boys been up to?"

"Nothing to worry about." James said. I walked with James into his room. He was being pretty quiet, and I hoped he calmed down a bit. He sat on his chair and took a long sigh.

I said, "I'm sorry James, I really am. No one saw us, so they won't know it was us."

"Yeah, but they're gonna suspect it was us. We'll probably have a bounty on our heads. And they'll really want to find us now that Mr. Williams is dead." said James.

I replied, "But they don't know for sure that it was us. So just relax."

"Whatever. Leave me alone right now. Tomorrow, we're gonna leave with Joe, and another guy you haven't met. But try to keep your finger off the damn trigger, or you'll get us all hanged." said James. I went back to my room and tried to forget about what just happened. I couldn't imagine what Momma or my brothers would have said if they saw me kill that man. Momma surely would have disowned me, or maybe not. It's not like I would ever find out. But that was all the past. I had a new opportunity, and it seemed I already made things go bad. I hoped James wouldn't kick me to the side, because I relied on him to be there when I needed him. He was almost like a father to me. If any lawmen came after us, I'd shoot em'. Shooting was something I knew I was good at, and I wanted to show James that I was a valuable asset. I prayed that very night that things would go in the right direction, and that I would find a real purpose in life. However, I was starting to realize that my purpose was gonna involve a lot more robbing and shooting. And I couldn't think of a finer purpose than that. It fit me. But I didn't see myself as a bad person. I saw myself as a person living on his own terms, which I knew was true freedom.

That night I passed out on my bed. I was still wearing my old PJs from a few years ago. Soon enough I knew I'd have to throw them out, since I was growing more every day. I didn't sleep with the blanket because it was always so damp in that house, especially with cigarette smoke in the air. I couldn't wait to leave that place. As I lay on my bed, I imagined being on the road and seeing beautiful sights. What an adventure that would be. Those thoughts kept me up for most of the night, so I didn't get much sleep. The next day, I woke up to James calling my name. I shouted back that I'd be there in a few minutes. I could hear him talking to a couple other kids; one of which sounded much older than James, and it wasn't Joe. I got myself ready, put my hat on, and walked into the living room. I saw Joe, James, and another kid who was bigger than the rest of us.

James said, "Morning, killer. Come take a seat." As I sat down, the new kid introduced himself. He told me his name was Buck. He was thin, and very tall. I was by far the smallest one in the group. After all, I was the youngest.

Buck asked, "I hear you killed the "Big Boss Man, huh?"

I replied, "I shouldn't have done it, but he had what was coming to him."

Buck said, "Well, remind me not to get on your bad side Mr. Ed. I heard you've been through a lot."

"It feels like I'm just getting started." I said.

James jumped in saying, "We are just getting started. We're gonna steal some horses at Joe's ranch and ride outta here. Then we'll make a camp somewhere and figure out the next step."

"What is the next step?" asked Joe.

James replied, "I don't know yet, but I'm gonna figure it out... Now I know you boys are tough, and strong. I trust all of you, just like you all trust me. We'll definitely go through some rough patches together, that's for sure. But I know you all have my back. So I'm proud to say us boys are a gang, a gang of outlaws. We all know the government has too much power, and it's not fair for folk like us. Some will bow down to the system like the sheep they are, and others, will fight back! So we're gonna need guns. No question about it. But what we have right now is a lot of heart. That's who we are, just folk trying to live free from government oppression!" James sat back down and stopped talking. In the back of my mind, I knew that robbing and killing over and over would lead to big trouble for us. Back then I didn't want to think about that, but I was ready to fight for freedom. There was no other way.

"By the way Ed, we made some coffee. It's up on the counter. Help yourself!" said James. I walked over and poured myself a cup. I only tried coffee once, and I wasn't a big fan of it. But I knew I was gonna need it. We had a long day ahead. There was some bread on the counter, and I saw a can of jelly, which James couldn't get enough of. I combined that together, and it wasn't like what Momma used to make, but it filled me up enough.

Buck said to me, "James told me you could really shoot! I'd like to see that in action."

James responded saying, "There will be plenty of time for that; just try to keep your gun holstered Ed! I don't want every mission to turn into a shootout."

"That's fair enough." I replied.

James said to everyone, "We're gonna have to sneak past the ranchers quietly. And I mean quietly!" Then all of us will get a horse and try to be as quick as possible." If they see us and start shooting, then Ed will surely take care of them. But it shouldn't come to that."

I said, "What about the horse you have now?"

James replied, "That old thing? Just as tired out as my uncle. They'll keep each other company. We need new, fresh horses, ones that can ride fast for a long time. This is the right move; one that'll get our feet in the ground. Now it's gonna be a long walk, but after we got those horses, we won't need to walk a whole lot no more." Everyone started getting up and we went right out the door. James' uncle was busy snoring the whole time, and that was the last thing I heard when I left that house. It was time to start a new life with a new family. I figured I was probably the best shot out of them all, but I knew I had to be careful. We all wanted this done right.

One the way there, Joe was chatting with James and I was chatting with Buck. The two of us were getting along well fast. He told me that he ran away from home when he was real young and was barely able to scrape by. He was homeless for most of his life until he started working at the same ranch as Joe. He told me how badly the other ranchers treated him and Joe.

Buck said, "I never got along with some of the guys there, but Joe was a true friend to me. Now he's become my brother. So is James. And I'd like to call you my brother as well; but maybe my little brother for now. Don't worry, you'll grow up pretty soon. One thing you should know is to never get on my bad side. I've beaten many men, and even choked a feller to death just for pissing me off. So don't think you're a big man just yet."

I nodded my head and replied, "I just wanna do my job, and do my fellow brothers right." I put out my hand for a handshake, and Buck gripped my hand, giving it a tight squeeze. His grip was so strong, it felt like my hand was going to break. I was a little afraid of him, but it seemed like I was on his good side. So I intended to keep it that way. He started talking about how his parents verbally and physically abused him. I was sure glad I never went through that, but what I experienced was nothing nice. And I couldn't erase that memory. I had my revolver with me and a few rounds on my belt.

I said to Buck, "It would be nice to get a new gun, maybe something more powerful." Then Buck pulled out his Schofield revolver. It sure was a beauty. Much larger than the small revolver I had.

He said, "This will kill just about anything in one shot. Not something to play around with. I've even killed fully grown grizzlies in one shot with this thing. I'll let you shoot it one day."

I replied, "I'll be looking forward to it. And soon I'll have my own arsenal to choose from. I'll be unstoppable."

Buck laughed and said, "Don't get too cocky there. If you really want to be a 'big bad gunslinger' one day, you'll have to earn it. So for now, just try to not get yourself shot."

I said, "I understand Buck. I'll learn." Buck felt like an older brother to me, even if he was a little rough around the edges. It felt weird feeling like a younger brother. It was like my whole world turned upside down. But I was happy, and I felt safe in James' newly formed gang; which was really just family at this point. After walking a few miles, we started getting close. We were all sweaty from walking in the hot sun. But James told us to focus and listen to his directions when we got close enough to the ranch. I didn't want to feel nervous, but I couldn't help it. My heart was pounding even harder than it was inside the factory. It may have seemed simple and easy to Buck, Joe, and James. But for me, it felt like I was walking straight into hell. And I wasn't sure if I was going to make it out. Still, I pretended to act tough, and hoped James knew what he was doing. We got to the top of a hill, and James told us to get down. We all got flat on our bellies; James and Joe pulled out binoculars and looked for how many men there were.

"I only see three guys. How 'bout you Joe?" said James.

"Same." replied Joe.

"Let's just do this already. It's now or never." said James. He then told us to get up and move quietly, so we slowly walked over with our heads hung low. We were coming from behind the stables, so no one would see us coming. As we got closer, I could hear the ranchers talking. They had no idea we were coming. We all lined up at the back of the stable. James and Joe went around the left side; Buck and I took the right. Buck peaked around the corner and saw the ranchers weren't paying attention to the stables. So he cued me over and I went around with him. As we got to the front, we saw a bunch of healthy-looking horses lined up. Buck knew how to handle them. He calmly whispered to them and let them sniff his hand. James and Joe were doing the same thing. I looked out in case anybody might've seen us. Besides getting shot, the next thing I was worried about was a horse bucking me off, but Buck gave a little bit of corn to feed to a smaller one. I put it under the horse's mouth, and the horse ate it right away, which made me feel a little more confident. I went up and started to pet it, and I think it might have liked me. Then, James and Joe slowly opened up the gates for the horses they wanted. I told Buck that that horse was the one for me. Buck had a satchel with reins for us to put on, so he handed me a pair and told me to watch him do it. He attached the reins on the horse in front of him, making it look easy. I was about to try myself, but he changed his mind and put them on for me. I'm sure he figured this wasn't the best time to learn how to do that. I wasn't that big, but I was able to mount up; James and Buck did the same. Then Joe started to mount his. I guess he picked the wrong horse, because it began rearing and making some loud squealing noises. We all began quickly walking our horses out of there as Joe tried his best to calm it down.

"Find another horse, Joe! Those men are gonna come looking over here." James whispered to Joe. I could hear one of the ranchers asking if someone was there. Then I could hear them running over.

"Just get on the back of my horse!" James said to Joe. Buck and I started trotting off; James and Joe were together on the same horse. James was light, but Joe was big and built, so the horse wouldn't be able to go that fast. "Just go! We'll catch up with you boys!" James shouted to us. Trotting felt okay, but then I gave it a kick to go faster, and I hoped to God I wouldn't fall off that thing. Or it would have been over for me. Fortunately, I got the hang of it quick, and followed Buck into a wooded area. We got to a point where he told me to stop and get off my horse.

He said, "Let's just wait here and hope they were able to get away."

"I didn't hear any gunshots. And that horse did seem pretty strong." I said. A few moments later, we could hear a horse running fast, and I heard James' voice.

"Buck! Ed! You around here?!"

I shouted back, "We're over here!" I heard the horse slow down and come over to us. The horse had James and Joe. As soon as they got over to us, they got off the horse. It looked pretty tired. I could only imagine what it would be like riding that thing with just me. It was the second biggest horse in that stable. The one that rejected Joe was the biggest. We wanted four horses, but having three was not bad either.

"We got away from them pretty quick. By the time they knew what was going on, we had already gotten away." said James.

"Are they coming after us?" asked Buck.

"Maybe, but let's rest here a moment, and then we'll keep moving towards the next town. As long as we're all in one piece, that's the main thing." said James.

"So I guess we got one more horse to find, huh?" I asked.

"We will, eventually. For now, you and I will ride the big one here, and Joe will ride your horse." said James.

"No you know what? We need another horse. I'll go back, lasso one, and bring it back here." said Buck. James didn't agree with this, and told him it was too late for that. Buck insisted however, that he could handle himself just fine. And that he could shoot himself out of any situation.

James said, "We can always find another horse pretty easily, and by now there will be a bunch of men guarding those horses. Don't be stupid." Joe started feeding the horses some crackers, and the horses started to calm down. It seemed we were bonding with those horses well and started to feel like they were a part of the family. I sat down against a tree and took a deep breath. I had the feeling that God was with us, and believed in us. So no matter what was happening, we'd make it out alright.

James told me to get up and mount the larger horse with him. I was too small to be able to get on, so Buck had to pick me up and put me on top.

"You still got some growing to do young Ed. Don't worry, you'll mount this one on your own soon enough." said James.

"Yeah, hopefully!" said Buck. I sat on the back behind James, and we started trotting towards a town called Clover Hill. None of us had been there before and it was a long trip away, and we didn't even have saddles. James said we'd buy everything we needed from that town. So for now, all we had was the clothes on our backs, a few revolvers, and some brand new horses. We would still need tents, medicine, and a lot more food. Most importantly, we needed some rifles, which we planned on purchasing at the gunsmith. Being on the horse wasn't my favorite thing. My groin was still sore from when I made my horse start running. I was sure the saddle would feel a lot nicer, but in the meantime, I had to buckle down and hope we wouldn't run into any trouble. Fortunately we didn't. The trip for the most part was pretty quiet. We all needed a breather after all that action, so having a peaceful trip felt nice. I almost fell asleep and would have fallen right off. Luckily I caught myself. And that horse was pretty high off the ground, so falling from it would have surely broken a bone or two. Our horses were walking on a dirt road, and saw other civilians riding on their horses.

A few of them said hello to us; one of them asked me, "Where is your horse at?"

I responded with, "Unfortunately, I don't have one just yet." I was thinking about just buying one. Either that or steal another one. But I didn't want us to get into too much trouble. James and I were in the front, but I couldn't see a thing past James' head. When more people started to pass us by, I figured we had to be close.

A few moments later, James yelled to us, "I see the town! We'll hitch our horses by the trees." Clover Hill was nice to look at. It was small, but had a lot of people moving around. James took us to an area with some small trees and we all got off our horses. Buck got out a few pieces of rope and tied the reins of all the horses to a tree.

I was excited to walk around town, but James said, "I need you to stay put, and guard the horses Ed. It's not like we're going to be here for too long."

I told him, "C'mon James, I was sitting on that horse for quite a while. I need to do something interesting."

James replied, "Well someone has to stay with the horses, and you're the youngest one. So for now it's your job."

I said 'Ok then, as you say, boss." James shook his head and walked with Joe over to the general store. Buck went to the gunsmith. I was stuck with the horses, and one of them just started taking a shit.

It wasn't too long before Buck started walking back. He looked like he was ready for war, carrying four rifles with one in each hand and two on his back.

As he got closer I asked him, "What kind of rifles are those?"

Buck replied, "Does it matter? They'll shoot pretty good, got a decent amount of ammo too." He handed me one. I knew the names of a few guns, and the one he gave me was a Henry Repeater. It was truly beautiful. By the end of the day, I had to try it out. Buck told me he would show me how to hold it and reload it, and that we would use them for hunting. I asked him what kind of animals we'd hunt.

He mumbled, "I guess whatever we end up finding… Hey, it looks like Joe's coming over." Joe asked Buck to help carry some supplies over, so they went off to James, and I remained at my post, holding onto the new repeater. It wasn't loaded at all, but it sure made me look tough. I was standing there for only a few minutes when they all came back carrying as much as they could. The three of them dumped everything by the horses.

"Ed, put the saddles up on the horses. We have a few more things to get. Joe, help him out with that. James and I will get the rest." said Buck. They went back towards the general store to get the rest. Joe gave me a saddle for the small horse, which didn't have a name yet. Eventually I wanted to give all of them names, and figured I'd mostly ride the small one. So I hoped I could pick the name for it. Joe helped me get the saddle on. Wasn't very complicated; it was just putting the strap on that felt kind of awkward. Joe never talked to me a whole lot. He was always quiet though, even with James. That's just how he was, but I wanted to get to know him better, and see what he was really like.

I asked him, "You have any idea where we're gonna set up camp? I mean, we should probably secure the area first; make sure there's nothing dangerous lurking around."

"I don't know. That's gonna be up to James. He is the leader, I guess. One thing at a time. Now put one of these handbags on. You'll need it. And we got a few tents. Let's get them on the back of the saddle." he replied.

"How many tents do we have?" I asked.

"Two." he said. A few minutes later, we had all of those supplies loaded up. We had some medicine, clothes, horse food, and some food for us. Then, we saw James and Buck. But all they had was a drink in their hands. "Is now the right time to be drinkin'?" asked Joe.

"It's always the right time to be drinkin'." said Buck.

"Boys, let's get on out of here. We're gonna set up camp a little ways away from here. Not sure where exactly, but we'll eventually find the right spot." said James. We mounted up and started heading into the wilderness. Once we settled down, we could finally relax for a bit and have our own home, even if it wasn't much of a home.

As we went into the woods, Buck said, "Someone's got a fire going not too far from us." None of us said anything. Then Buck said, "They might have something for us."

"Don't worry about it. Better if we mind our own business." said James.

"Well, I'm sure he has a horse we could use. So I'm going over there. I'll be back in just a minute." said Buck. Just like that, he went off. James couldn't stop him. We all just sat on our horses, not saying anything. About a minute later, we heard a gunshot, and all the birds started squawking and fleeing the area. Soon enough we saw Buck coming back with another horse he had a lasso around.

"Jeez Buck. Who did you kill, some poor man?" asked James.

Buck replied, "Yeah, some feller with a nice lookin' horse. I went up to him and said 'Hello.' And that was about it."

"You should have at least said thank you." said James.

Joe said, "You're cold Buck. You really are."

Buck replied, "Well, the world is a cold place. But at least we got that forth horse." I know Buck wanted to help the gang, but I felt he went a little too far. James and Joe felt the same way. They both had an annoyed look on their faces.

But James simply said, "Well alright. Now we're gonna have to move out a lot farther." We kept going, trying to put distance between us and that dead man.

A few hours passed, and we came across a decent-enough-looking spot. It had a flat area that was perfect for setting up the tents.

James said, "This'll do. I think we've found our new home boys!" After hours of travelling, we finally got off our horses and began setting up camp. James told me and Buck to look for some thick branches so that we could build a hitching post for the horses. Buck told me to follow him. We started walking, and all I thought about was that gunshot. Buck didn't think twice about it, but it was something I couldn't erase from my memory. It didn't take long before we found a few good sturdy branches.

Buck pulled out his knife and said, "Just wait there Ed. I'll cut the branches off and you'll help me carry them. We just need three. Then we'll use the hammer we bought to nail them together." Buck was quick with his knife. He was able to cut those branches down fast. He didn't have to climb up for the first two branches. He was already pretty tall, so for him it was easy work. We needed one more, and I saw one that looked perfect. It was on another tree, but it was way up high. I told Buck he would have to climb to get to it.

Buck said, "No problem, just give me a minute." He grabbed onto the smaller branches and got his footing right. He was standing on top of a smaller branch, which I hoped would be able to hold him. He quickly cut the last one off and it landed right in front of me.

In a matter of seconds, he got right back down to the ground and said, "Now how about you take the two smaller ones. I'll take the bigger one." He then pulled out his knife again and said, "Beautiful lookin' thing, ain't she?"

I replied, "It looks like that could cut a man's arm off in one strike."

He said "It can, and one day that might happen to someone that looks at me funny... I'm just kidding. My guns will take care of anybody that crosses me."

I took out my gun and said, "That's why I got this lil' thing."

He chuckled and said, "Atta boy. Just don't get too cocky now." He picked up the big branch and said, "C'mon, let's get back to camp." We started heading back, and when we got there, Joe was nailing in the second tent. James was sitting on a log having a drink.

As soon as he saw us he said, "Good job, boys, let's start putting it together. Ed, take that brush and clean off the horses. They've been travelling for a while and got dirt everywhere." I took the brush and tried to get as much dirt off as possible, giving me some time to think of good names for all four horses. The small one was female, so I wanted to name her Dolly. She was a beige colored horse, still pretty young. She wasn't the fastest, but she was always nice to me. As I brushed her, it felt like we had a special bond. Something I hadn't felt with the other horses. After I finished brushing all of them I turned to James, who was almost finished with putting in the hitching post. I asked if they needed any help, but James told me they had it. Joe came over and started feeding the horses pieces of an apple.

I asked Joe, "What do you think about naming this one Dolly?"

He said, "I think that horse is gonna be yours, Ed. I think Buck is gonna want the one he stole off that poor man."

"You feel bad about that, huh?" I asked.

Joe quietly said, "I think Buck will end up getting us all killed. I never liked him very much. But James seems to be okay with him... What do you think?"

"He cares about all of us. He just wants what's best. But Buck is right; the world is a cold place. And sometimes bad things need to happen. That's the way it is." I replied. Joe slowly nodded his head and continued feeding the horses. I asked him which one he wanted.

He said, "I'll probably take the brown one. Might name it Pepper, I don't know." The brown one was the second biggest horse we had. The biggest was the black one; didn't surprise me at all that that would be James' horse.

A while later, the hitching post was built so we could finally attach the horses to it. We had the basic tools we needed to survive. James even bought some soap, so at least we wouldn't smell like animals. It was getting late, and nightfall was approaching.

James said, "Hey, let's get a fire going. Buck, get some of those rocks over there and make a little fire place. Buck started putting the rocks in a circle, and James brought over a few sticks he had found earlier. Once the fireplace was set, Buck pulled out his lighter and got the fire started.

He then pulled out a cigarette and said, "Feels like I haven't had one of these in forever." Three of us sat by the fire, while James brought over a spoon for each of us and some canned food. Buck was having a smoke; it seemed to calm him down quite a bit. He was always tense, and looked like he could snap at any moment. But I got used to Buck being Buck. That's just how he was.

James said, "Who wants peaches and who wants yams?"

Buck replied, "You think I care? I just want to eat something. But I'll take the yams, never liked peaches." I got the peaches, which didn't taste too bad. We were all happy to finally be settled down. Just the four of us joking around, laughing. It was a good time.

At one point, James said, "The big black one is mine, as I'm sure ya'll know. We each got our own horses. Small one is Ed's, brown one is Joe's. And Buck's, is from that kind man that lent it to him."

Buck took a big puff of his cigarette and said, "And I am forever grateful."

Then I asked James, "So what are you gonna name the big black one?"

He replied, "Not sure yet, but I'll think of one. I'll think of a good one." I was thinking of pulling out my harmonica and playing a little, but I was getting real tired, and was ready to soon fall asleep. James told us that Buck and I would share one tent, while Joe and James shared the other. The tents had a decent amount of room, so we wouldn't be in each other's personal space. That can of peaches I had was pretty satisfying.

"Tomorrow we'll do some hunting. We can use the repeaters, and get some meat in our bellies. But tonight, we rest up. Joe and Buck know my last name, but I never told you Ed."

"What is it?" I asked.

James said, "Mulligan. James Mulligan. And this is gonna be called the Mulligan gang. What do you think of that?"

I replied, "I'm in. I'll do whatever I have to for us to be okay."

"Good. I'm proud of you. You've come a long way Ed." said James. I knew that we would be robbing, and probably killing. Folks were gonna here about us and fear us. This was our way of life, and we were just getting started.

PART 3

Ten years passed, and as you could imagine, me and the gang went through a lot. I was now twenty-two. Felt good to finally be considered a man. Although, it felt like I had to be a man ever since Momma and my father died. Overall I liked being in the gang. We'd travel from town to town, find camp somewhere, rob, and repeat. We've been doing that for a while now, and so far the robbing was mostly pretty easy. Buck, Joe, and James were still there, but now we had two other people with us. One was a woman named Isabella. We called her Bella for short. The other was an older feller named Harry. Both of them had gotten along great with the rest of us. All of the horses were still with us, plus one more. James never came up with a real name for his horse, which was starting to get old but was still riding well. He just called it "The Big One." We found Bella three years ago while travelling. We stopped at a small town, and Buck was the first one to meet Bella outside of a bar. She worked there as a prostitute. Buck and Bella hit it off pretty well, and soon fell in love with each other. We all liked having her around. She was sweet, but also tough. She knew how to handle herself, would never show any fear. She'd help us cook, clean, all the chores we didn't want to do. She was a white girl with curly blonde hair. When Buck found her, she was quite a bit underweight. It was clear she was having a hard time. So she started living with us, and soon became fit mentally and physically. It was nice to have a woman in the gang. Us boys would normally find a hooker when we'd get horny. But Bella was more than that; she was a lost soul longing for a purpose. Being in this gang was her purpose, and she fit right in. She spent the most time with Buck, and he was aggressive towards her, but they got along well enough. They were always there for each other.

We found Harry on the side of the road a year after finding Bella. He was homeless, and was a bit older than Buck. He told us he was in his late 30's; said he wasn't sure what his exact age was. Harry looked depressed and lonely. We could all tell he needed some help. He told us he was kicked out of his home, because he wasn't getting along with his two brothers he was living with. His wife died a long time ago, and he didn't have any kids. Everyone in his life abandoned him, and it didn't seem like there was much hope for him, that is until he found us. He was bitter and angry with the way society treated him, leaving him to rot and struggle just to survive. So he had no problem giving folk, especially rich folk their just desserts. We would never rob the poor, since we knew they had it hard. But the wealthy kept all the money for themselves, not giving a damn about folk not as fortunate. James would tell this to us time and time again. We all knew this was wrong, and it was our mission to fight against it. James' parents were poor, which is why they had to steal. One day James told me how lawmen came into his house and took his parents away. He knows they were both sent to some prison far away, and were either still there or died. Then his uncle got custody of him, and clearly James didn't grow very fond of him. James would always motivate us and remind us of why we had to keep on fighting for a life worth living. We all knew this was the only way, and we had to keep going. There were six of us now. And we were always ready to do some dirty work.

We were in the state of Illinois, camped in the wilderness in a rural area with a few small towns. A lot had changed in America. The Union won the Civil War, freeing the slaves and uniting the country. Big cities were growing, and railroads were being built. People could travel everywhere across the country now, and the government was taking more and more land away from the Indians. The Indian population was having a hard time. They were being pushed around by the government, and there was nothing they could do to stop it. A lot of them had been moved to reservations, but there was one Indian tribe a little ways away from our camp. There was no talk of them attacking anybody, so we didn't worry about them. Industry was expanding, and we were ready for whatever life had to throw at us. We had robbed a lot of stagecoaches, which was always easy for us. But one time when I was fourteen, James and I did a stagecoach robbery that didn't go as planned. We spotted this particular stagecoach travelling down a dirt road, with a couple riding in the front of the stagecoach. It was just them; no one else was around. James and I moved up from the big hill we were on and took cover behind a rock. James had a revolver, and I had a double barrel shotgun. I loaded it just in case one of them pulled out a gun. The stagecoach was getting closer, and James said to jump out when their stagecoach was about five meters away. As it came closer, I gripped the handle of my shotgun tightly. I hoped I wouldn't have to use it. James said to only take what we needed. I guess he didn't want to completely screw them over. As I heard the couple talking, it sounded like they were an older couple, but I wasn't sure. I supposed it didn't really matter.

A few seconds later, James said, "Let's go!" So we came out onto the road with our guns pointed at them. They really were an older couple; the old woman looked terrified. The horse was startled and began rearing.

I tried to calm it down by softly saying, "Relax, you'll be alright."

Then James said, "Ma'am, sir, this is a stick up. We're not gonna hurt ya, but we need some money. Can you lend us some?"

The man said in a quivering tone, "We'll give you money, just put the guns down." Out of nowhere, his wife screamed and I pulled the trigger. It was an accident, but her head was shot clean off. She fell off the side of the stagecoach, and so too did the old man. The shotgun blast hit him in the chest.

"What the hell was that!?" yelled James.

I replied "It was an accident. I-I didn't mean to."

"Well maybe I shouldn't have let you use a shotgun then. It looks like the old man is dead, and the old lady is definitely dead… DamnEd." said James. Before this happened, the only person I killed was Arthur Williams. I felt like he deserved it. But I just brutally murdered an old couple. Even though it was an accident, it felt gut-wrenching. Eight years later that memory still haunted me. I couldn't erase it from my mind.

Now we were planning on robbing a stagecoach that would be well guarded. The coach was supposedly carrying a ton of cash, and a couple government officials. James heard about this stagecoach while talking to folk in a town. I had robbed many stagecoaches since the accident happened. But this one was going to require all of us. Everyone except for Bella, since Buck was afraid she'd get hurt or killed. But the boys and I knew what we were doing. We had a solid plan, which was to ambush the stagecoach from the trees on one side. Then have me, Joe, and James go after them on horseback. We wanted to take as many of them out as quick as possible.

James told us, "We'll start shooting, and before they know it, they'll all be dead like that!" This work was always risky, but we didn't have any other choice. We haven't had anybody get shot just yet. That's because we knew what we were doing, and had enough ammunition to take on an army. We were more than ready. The stagecoach was supposed to come around tomorrow. The five of us would head out by morning. For the time being, all of us were at our camp taking it easy. It was the late afternoon, and I was sitting on a rock, away from everyone else.

James came over to me and said, "This'll be easy Ed. Don't overthink it."

I replied, "I know it will be easy. I just want to find some peace of mind. Think it would be best if I was alone for now."

James said, "No problem big man. You do what you need to." James liked calling me big man quite often. I was just an inch or two taller than him and Joe. Harry and Bella weren't as tall, around five foot eight. Buck however, was still the tallest. And when he got angry, he would be the nastiest. About a month ago, Buck and Joe got into an argument which turned into a fight. Buck was getting nasty with Joe, which happened from time to time. Buck started calling him "Old Slow Joe," and Joe quickly got fed up with it. I was washing some of the clothes while their bickering was going on.

Joe told Buck, "Watch what the hell you say to me because I can be even nastier than you are." I was surprised to even hear Joe talk back, especially to Buck. I think it was because James and Harry were off somewhere, and the only other person there was Bella. She kept her head down trying to ignore it.

Buck snapped at Joe and said in a deep, low voice, "I could kill you right now. Is that what you want!?" They were an inch apart staring each other down.

Then I heard Joe say, "You're really just a coward. And you're too ashamed to admit it." In less than a second, Buck slapped Joe across the face. And he didn't hold back. That slap was so loud I almost felt it. Joe fell on the ground, and slowly got back up.

Buck yelled, "Now off with ya! Don't you dare insult me like that again you sack of crap!" Joe quickly walked away and never spoke about it. He certainly wasn't going to say anything back to Buck anymore. James and Harry never heard about it. We all decided to let it go. I thought Joe would have had a little more fight in him. Since he was a big built guy, but Buck was even bigger, and stronger. He always got his way.

Since that fight, things in the gang were different. Joe and Buck avoided talking to each other, but the rest of us got along well, especially with Harry. At the end of the day, he just wanted to kick back and have a good time with everybody. He played the banjo, and was a master at it. He had his banjo with him when we found him. It was sitting right next to him, and looked to be well kept. He said it was like a son to him. He named it Napoleon. That banjo might have well been the seventh member of our gang. Harry played it almost every night, and I liked it. It sparked the mood, and the only person that didn't like it as much was James. He didn't hate it too much; he was at least able to tolerate it. Sometimes I'd join him with my harmonica, which I always kept with me. We played a number of tunes together. But the two of us never really bothered with singing. Bella could sing, but was shy about it. I thought that was a shame, since the rest of us sounded like dying hyenas, which was not an exaggeration. That night, however, I didn't want to hear any music. I just wanted to rest my mind, so that I could stay focused on my job. But of course, I heard Harry yapping away with Buck and James anyway. Then I decided I might as well join them. I came over and sat on the log.

James asked, "How long have you been sitting on that rock? I don't think you've moved for two or three hours."

"I was trying to, uh…meditate I guess. I'm feeling alright now." I replied.

James said, "You have always been an interesting feller, but you just don't stop getting stranger." Buck and Harry laughed, and I shrugged my shoulders. I asked them what they were talking about.

Harry replied, "Talking about how I used to cheat at blackjack and poker. It got me some decent money."

Then Buck said, "We should play a little poker. We haven't played that for a while."

James started saying, "I don't think now is the time. Because when we play poker, we eventually start drinking. And we need to be ready for tomorrow. Sorry boys."

"I understand boss." Harry replied. Then, Buck insisted that we just play a little Blackjack, since there was really not much else to do. James gave in, and the four of us played for the next couple hours. I wasn't much of a blackjack player, so I never one at these things. I didn't really care. For now, it just passed the time. It was good for us to at least have a little bit of fun. Harry put his cards away, and James pulled out two cigarettes and a lighter. He handed one to Buck and asked if me or Harry wanted one. We both said yes and James quickly lit all four cigarettes. Everyone including myself would smoke and drink. Took me a little while to get into it, but eventually I came around. It was inevitable. As we all chit chatted, it was starting to get dark. Harry told us we should do at least one song, with everybody.

James said, "Yeah, we'll do that after we rob the stagecoach. Not now. It's not the right time."

Then Harry replied, "It'll just be for good luck, I mean, we have to get our spirits up right now."

"I think he's got a point." Buck added. Bella came back to the camp after taking a long walk.

"What you boys up to? Asking God for forgiveness for your sins?" she asked.

Buck replied, "Yep, that's what we've been doing all day, and now we're going to become priests." She came up to us and sat on Buck's lap like she normally would. Joe was lying down a few meters away from us.

Then James shouted, "Joe, get over here! We're not complete without you." Joe slowly got up and came over to us, and then sat on the ground across from me.

Joe asked, "How you feeling now James? Nervous?"

James replied, "None of us should be nervous. We're gonna be just fine."

Buck rudely said (referring to Joe) ,"Does he really need to be here?"

"Joe is a part of the family. And you two need to get over your feud. Enough is enough."

Buck said, "Sure I'll get over it, when he's dead."

Joe said, "I'm just not gonna say anything boss. It's not worth it."

"Good boy, you learned your lesson then." said Buck.

Harry tried to brighten up the mood by pulling out his banjo and saying, "Let's just sing a song, huh?" We all said ok, and I decided to pull out my harmonica. I hadn't played it in a while, and the whole gang wasn't usually together like this. Harry started plucking a tune called "Big Bad Dan." It was an uppity tune.

"The perfect song before robbing a stagecoach," I said before playing my part. Everyone started singing along, however, Joe was mumbling the words.

Big Bad Ed

In the middle of the song, Harry yelled, "C'mon Joe! I can't hear ya!" He got a little bit louder, but I could barely hear him. The chorus went something like, *"Big Bad Dan did what he could- Everybody thought he'd end up good- Now he's big and bad and mean-His way of life was to be seen."* The song was short, only lasting for a few minutes. But we all had a good time singing and playing it.

Then James said, "Hey Ed, if that song was about you, how would the lyrics go?"

I said maybe something like, *"Big Bad Ed was in his bed- then his parents wound up dead- now he's messed up in the head- so, maybe it's just better to call me Ed."*

James replied, "Fair enough. We really should get to sleep. Tomorrow is an important day. So we can't mess it up. Goodnight people." Everybody started going to their tents, and I started walking over to mine. It was a small tent, just for me. I used it for a long time, and it provided me some personal space. As I walked over, Harry came from behind and patted me on the back.

He said "You doing alright, Ed?"

I replied, "Yeah I'll be okay, just want to get this thing over with."

"I'm always here if you want to talk, don't forget that. Now get a good night's rest. You'll need it." he said.

I said back, "Thanks Harry, you too." Harry was the friendliest one in our gang. He was always looking out for all of us, even if we weren't in our best mood. We all liked Harry. He almost felt like a grandfather, or an uncle to us. I went inside my tent and fell asleep soon after. I was pretty tired at that point.

"Wake up boys! Let's go!" yelled James. The sun wasn't even out yet, but I quickly got my gear and loaded everything up on my horse, who I still called Dolly. Everyone else did the same. Before Buck got on his horse, he gave Bella a kiss goodbye.

He told her, "We'll be just fine. Trust me." Once we were all set, James started leading the way. It was going to be a decent trip before we got to the spot. And once we got there, we had to wait for the stagecoach. It took us about an hour to get to the ambush point. Once we were there, James had us get into our positions. Buck and Harry found perfect cover behind some rocks, and I was behind some trees with James and Joe.

James said, "It should take two to three hours before the stagecoach gets here. And I don't want any talking. We'll have plenty of time to talk after this is done." Time went by, and I just sat there, maintaining a calm composure. I wasn't thinking about anything during that time, just stared at the ground for the most part. James had his hand covering his forehead. He was stressed. He was the leader of this gang after all, so I know he had a lot of weight on his shoulders. He was very strict with us when it came to stick-ups. I mean, if we were joking around and having too much fun, we would have probably all gotten killed by now. So I knew this was the way to do it. We all trusted James and he didn't take that for granted. A while later, the sun had almost fully risen and we knew that the stagecoach had to be coming soon. I had two revolvers and a repeater with me. The horses started getting kind of bored, and wanted to move around. We let them move a little bit and petted them so they'd stay calm. I was just glad that they hadn't pissed our shitted right next to us. That wouldn't have been fun. A few moments later, there was still nothing but the early birds chirping. Then we heard something coming, and the three of us got on our horses, ready to do what we'd been waiting for. We saw two men on horseback in the front, behind them was the stagecoach. Then it felt like my heart dropped when I saw how many men were behind the stagecoach. I counted eight men, also on horseback. All of them had guns, and I started to think James was gonna have us back out.

I whispered to James, "It's gonna be hard killing all these men. And I got a feeling they know how to shoot."

James said, "Just relax. Buck and Harry will surprise them. And after that, there won't be many more left. You got my back, don't ya Ed?"

"Yes, of course I do." I replied. As the eight men started to pass by, Buck and Harry came up from cover and started firing. They got five or six men in just a few seconds. The rest of them started to run off as fast as they could, and the three of us got after them. Dolly was sprinting full throttle and I had my repeater in one hand, shooting it in the air along with James and Joe.

James and I started screaming, "Yeah! Woo!" We caught up to four of them behind the stage and started taking the rest out. One of them tried to shoot at us, but we were too quick. They fell off their horses and only two men in the front were left, along with the stagecoach. When I got close enough behind the stage, I took a shot at the driver's head. It looked like I just missed. James and Joe were on my left side, trying to shoot the driver as well. It was a hard shot to pull off, but I knew I had it. I concentrated, took my time with aiming, and put one right in the back of his skull. When we got up to the stage coach, we saw the last two riders running off. The three of us started shooting at them and eventually got the both of them. The people left would be whoever was in that stagecoach.

I got off my horse and walked over and yelled, "Get out of there! We might not kill you. But we'll see." Two men dressed in fancy-looking attire got out and got on their knees. It sure didn't look like they were having a good time.

One of them started saying, "The money this stagecoach is carrying is for honest hard-working folk."

"Does it look like I give a damn?" I asked. Joe and James came over and had their revolvers out. Joe had his gun pointed at both men. James took out his lock pick and went to the back, where the chest was. He was busy trying to get it open, when Harry and Buck came over on their horses. I asked them, "What do you think we should do with these poor bastards?"

Buck said, "Kill 'em, cook 'em, and eat 'em. That sounds about right to me."

We all laughed, and then that same government official asked, "What are you gonna spend all that money on anyway? Drinking and gambling? How far is that going to get you boys?"

I said, "Ah shut up." And put a bullet in his head. The other one didn't say a thing, and I figured we'd let him go.

James got the chest open and said, "This stage was carrying some real money. Boys, this was well worth it, and I'm proud of all of you." James started handing out the money to each of us to put in our satchel. We were all in a good mood, and were ready to head back.

Then I asked, "What are we doing with the last guy?"

Buck walked over to him saying, "What we always do." He pulled out his rifle and shot him square in the face. We made our way back to camp, knowing we stuck it to all of those lawmen and government officials.

Bella was excited to see us when we got back. The first thing she said was, "Where's Buck?" He quickly popped up and got off his horse. She ran over to him and gave him a big hug. She really was in love with that man. I was happy for them, but I started thinking it would be nice to have that for myself. I walked over to the log by the fireplace and sat down. Joe was in the middle of cooking up a stew he liked to make. It wasn't half bad. Over time he learned how to make it more flavorful. We all liked it, even Buck. Harry came over and sat across from me.

He said, "You look like you haven't had a good time in a while. What do you think about going into town?"

I replied, "Ah I don't know, maybe some other day. There's always time to do that stuff."

"I can tell a lot is on your mind Ed. It would do you some good." he said. I thought about it for a few seconds, and decided it wouldn't kill me.

"Yeah, sure, I'll go after I finish that stew. And let's bring Joe, not Buck. You know what it's like when Buck comes along." I said.

Harry agreed, and a few minutes later Joe shouted, "Stew's ready, help yourselves!"

Joe sat with us and I told him, "This stew of your just keeps getting better and better. Maybe it's your calling."

He replied, "I don't know. I think shooting and robbing is my calling."

"Maybe you should try making something like buffalo stew. I haven't tried that one before." said Harry.

I responded, "As long as it keeps us alive, that's all that matters." A little while later we finished everything on our plates. We even had seconds.

Then Harry got up and asked Joe, "You want to come with us into town? Just gonna have a little fun."

Joe replied, "Sure I'll go. I'm tired of being at the camp anyway." So all three of us got on our horses but just as we started to leave, James asked where we were going.

I told him, "We're just gonna be in town for a bit, nothing crazy." James nodded his head and we started riding out. We figured we wouldn't be out for that long. The nearest town wasn't too far.

It was nighttime, and when we approached the town there was something different about it. Many people were out just having a good time.

We could hear music coming from the bar, and I said, "Why don't we head down there, see what's going on." We hitched our horses on a hitching post and started walking towards the saloon.

I told Harry and Joe, "You boys know I'm not much of a drinker, so I'll probably just have one and we'll see what else happens."

"If you're looking for a lady, make sure you can afford her." said Harry. We got inside the saloon, and it was packed with people doing something called line dancing. It was simple enough for us to figure out, but Joe went to get a drink. Harry went over to the poker table and bought himself into a game. I just hoped he didn't take that much money with him. Most importantly, I hoped he wouldn't get himself in trouble. The bar was pretty big, so there was a large amount of space for people to dance around and have a good time. I went over there, and saw a woman dancing who was close to my age.

She faced me and our eyes locked. She smiled at me, but then turned away. I looked over at the musicians playing their fiddles and violins; one person was even playing a harmonica. He could sure play that thing well, even better than me. I knew I wanted to talk to that woman. She was beautiful, and there was something about her that seemed interesting.

When the song finished, I walked over to her and asked, "You from around here?"

She replied, "Yes, I just live one block down. Having some fun tonight?"

I told her, "Sure, but I need someone to teach me how to dance." She told me to get next to her, and she showed me how it's done. I couldn't have even pretended I knew what I was doing. And she knew that too. But the next song they played was slower, so it wasn't too hard following along with her.

She said, "You're not half bad at this. A fast learner I see."

I replied, "I suppose I am a fast learner." and kept dancing. I was moving my feet from side to side, swinging my arms around, and even my hips. Then I saw Joe looking at me. I almost invited him to join in, but I figured he'd be falling over and making a fool of himself anyway. After we finished the dance, I asked her if she wanted to take a walk outside. She said yes, but turned to her friend, telling her she'd be gone for a while.

Her friend gave a nasty look towards me and said, "You better go and get on outta here. Annie shouldn't be out with men like you."

I looked at her friend and said, "Well that's her choice now. Let her decide what she wants."

Annie said to her friend, "He's a good man, it'll be alright. I'll come back home by nine o' clock. I promise." Her angry friend stormed off, and we both walked out of the bar. It was a beautiful night that night, and we started walking down the street, just getting to know each other. She told me that friend of hers was like a sister. And that she was a little over protective. I told her I have friends like that too, but that they weren't what you'd call "over protective." I didn't tell her I was in a gang, just that my friends and I were travelers who liked to explore. She said she wasn't much of an explorer, along with the rest of her family, and that they stayed in town for the most part.

I told her, "That sounds interesting."

And she replied, "No, it's not. It's pretty boring actually. So it's nice to meet someone new!" She told me what her family was like, and how they'd be strict on her. But she didn't mind it. I guess that kind of life seemed nice to her. Hearing her talk about living with her family reminded me of my past. So I quickly changed the subject.

I asked, "So your name is Annie, right?"

"Oh how rude of me! Yes, I'm Annie." She shook my hand and asked for my name.

I told her, "Folks just call me Ed." She told me she would do chores all the time, and that it was nice to take a break from all of that.

Then she said, "Hey let's go to the top of that hill. It's a beautiful view up there." We got our way up, and she wasn't kidding. We could see the whole town. "Everything is just so lively tonight." she said.

I replied, "Yeah, whenever I'm around it might as well be a ghost town."

She said, "I know what you mean."

We made small talk like that for a little while, and then I asked, "Are you with a man right now?"

She chuckled and said, "Once but not anymore. Things just didn't work out between us. But you seem like a nice man."

I smiled and said, "I'm not exactly a saint, but folks 'round here treat me well, especially you." She smiled back and started to look up at the stars. I did the same thing with her.

She said, "We should lie down, this way we don't have to bend our necks to look up." We both laid down only a foot apart from each other. I wanted her. She had a real nice personality. Unlike the hookers I'd pay for. I could tell she was her own person, and that was something special. She started saying, "Most of the men around here are pretty boring. But there is something about you Ed. You seem like you're one in a million."

"Yeah, like one in a million stars I guess." I replied. She chuckled again and then she turned over facing me.

She asked, "Do you ever get lonely, Ed?"

I told her, "I feel lonely all the time." Then I turned over, facing her. We were both looking into each other's eyes.

"Well, we're here for each other at least." she said. Then we got closer, closed our eyes, and kissed. It only lasted for a few seconds, but it was amazing. We opened our eyes and looked deeply into one another.

Then I said, "I should probably get you home."

"Will you walk me down?" she asked.

Big Bad Ed

I told her, "Let's go." We held hands while walking down the hill, but she let go as soon as people were around. She told me she lived in the big white house, pointing to it. When we got down there, I asked her who she lived with.

She said, "I live with my friend you saw earlier. The one that gave you nasty looks. I'm sure she's not happy I was with you."

I replied, "Ah, that's alright, that's how people get sometimes."

Then she whispered in my ear, "Meet me on top of the hill in the afternoon tomorrow, and we can get to know each other a lot better then."

I replied, "I will. Good night Annie."

She replied, "See you tomorrow Ed." and went inside. I turned around and saw Harry and Joe far away. They were probably trying to find me. I shouted to them and they saw me.

I walked over to them, and Harry asked me, "Where the hell did you go? We were looking all over town for ya."

I replied, "I was just taking a walk; nothing to be concerned about."

"You went with that girl, didn't you?" asked Joe.

"Yes I did. Let's just get out of here. I'm feeling tired." I said.

Harry said, "So now you're becoming a lady's man!? Is she a keeper?"

I said, "I think so. But don't tell the others just yet; you too Joe."

Harry said, "We won't say nothing. Not gonna lie, I didn't have a great game tonight, had to bust out. No luck at all. I guess you're the one that got lucky Ed."

I replied "Well that's just how it is then. We better get going." I was thinking of asking Joe what he did, but I'm sure he just stood there, saying nothing to nobody. I supposed he had a good time. It didn't really matter to me. We got on our horses and headed back to camp. It had been a long day.

The next morning, I woke up excited and had myself half a can of peaches, half a can of beans. It was not a bad meal. Been having that for breakfast for a long time now. I kept a small mirror about the size of my hand that I kept in my tent. I pulled it out and took one good look at myself. It was clear I had to clean myself up. I didn't have a big beard or anything, just some facial hair that I wanted to shave off. So I got my shaving cream and a small knife, and started shaving outside near the campfire. Buck was on one side with Bella, who was still sleeping. Joe was on the other side reading the newspaper.

I got a quarter of the way done when Buck said, "You don't normally shave that early. You always let it grow out more. So that's telling me something."

"What Buck?" I replied.

"You got your own woman now. That's my boy Ed!" said Buck.

I sighed and told him, "I just met her last night, but she's not like us. She ain't a criminal; in fact she's the opposite."

Buck laughed and replied, "That won't last."

"We'll see." I said back.

Then Buck started saying, "Well if you want her to listen to you, you have to be firm. Don't let her always have her way; she'll take advantage of that. Make sure she knows who the boss is."

Then Joe jumped in saying, "He wants to build a relationship out of trust. Not out of fear Buck."

Then Buck shouted back, "I will come over there and slap you ten times harder than I did last time. And if I punch you, you won't survive that."

That woke Bella up, and I defused the situation saying, "Nobody needs to get slapped or punched. Let's just take a deep breath and try to enjoy the day. No need for us to be killing each other."

Buck shouted to Joe, "One day with God as my witness I will spit on your grave! And James can't stop me!" Bella was able to take Buck's attention away from Joe, and things settled down. I finished shaving and I thought I looked okay for a mean outlaw. I didn't smell too bad either, as long as I'd wash up at least every couple of days. I got my jacket, my hat, and mounted up on Dolly. I started riding off, eager to see Annie.

I approached the town and went straight for the hill. When I got there, I saw no one. It was early in the afternoon, so I decided to wait. I had a few apples with me, so I gave one to Dolly and one to myself. The sun was out, and there were very few clouds in the sky. It felt like the perfect day, only Annie wasn't there. I knew it was only a matter of time before I saw her. About half an hour later, I turned my head and saw Annie walking up on the left side of the hill.

I told her, "This is a good spot."

She replied, "When I was a kid, I used to play on this hill all the time with my brothers." Then she sat next to me and noticed I had shaved. She said, "You should've let it grow out more. I thought it looked good on you."

I sighed and said, "Well, you can't please everybody."

She said, "Very true." and asked, "So, where do you live?"

I said, "I share a camp with my friends, who are really my family at this point."

She replied, "Oh, that sounds fun. I've always wanted to camp out." She told me she spent the morning doing chores, and that she would normally be reading one of her books in the afternoon.

I asked her, "What kind of stuff do you like to read?"

"Just about anything, from fiction, to adventure, to mystery, so on and so forth. Do you read at all?"

I said, "I'll read a little bit, but it's not really for me." She started talking about who she lived with, which consisted of Margaret (the one that gave me nasty looks at the saloon) and everyone else in Margaret's family. In total there were six people. The rest were Margaret's husband, her two sons, and her father. Then I asked Annie if she had any family of her own.

She turned her head away, then looked back at me and said, "My parents couldn't take care of me, so they gave me to an orphanage. But eventually, a man adopted me. That man was Margaret's father."

I replied, "So, Margaret's your step-sister. How come you told me she was your friend?"

She said, "I hate saying 'step-sister.' My entire life, she's always been a best friend to me. And we'll always be there for each other. I'm sure it's like that with the friends you live with."

I replied, "Yeah, it kinda is." We talked for a while longer about our lives and what we've been doing. I told her that I liked to draw quite a bit, and she seemed very interested. She told me she tried drawing, but was terrible at it. Then she asked if I could show her some of my drawings some time. Of course I was making it all up, and drawing was one of the last things I'd be doing.

So I told her, "We'll see, maybe one day."

I thought about giving her a ride on Dolly, so I asked her, and she said, "I've only ridden horses a few times, but as the horse goes slowly, I'll be ok." I told her that Dolly was a good horse, and would go easy on her. I helped her up on the saddle, and I got Dolly to start walking.

Annie was having a good time and said, "We should move towards the brook, which was only about 100 meters away." We got down there and walked along side it. Then Annie said she was ready to get off, so I helped her down, and we sat by the stream. I had one more apple left and asked Annie if she wanted one.

She said, "I love apples, but the breakfast I had filled me up pretty good." We talked some more, and she started telling me about the things she's dreamed of doing. Her biggest one was flying in a hot air balloon. She said, "I can't even imagine what it must be like to be above the clouds. I've always believed that's where angels are. Do you believe in angels Ed?"

"A little bit, I'm not sure though." I replied.

She said back, "Well, maybe if we go up into the clouds, we'll see one." For a moment, I wondered whether my family, even my father, was up there. I didn't know for sure, so I didn't think about it for that long. A couple hours had gone by and then Annie said she should get back home. So I put her up on Dolly, and I got on the front. I rode her back to her house and then we both got off to say our goodbyes.

She gave me a hug and said, "Next time come over to the house; I'll be on the front porch. If you see someone else, just tell them you're a friend of mine." I told her I would and mounted back up on Dolly. I wasn't sure if that kiss we had that night meant much to her. It meant a lot to me. I tried to not think about it too much, but I couldn't stop thinking about it.

A few days had passed, and not much was going on with the gang. We hadn't robbed anything since the stagecoach because we already had a ton of money from it. But eventually, we would rob again, and we'd have to travel somewhere else to avoid the law. In the meantime, I thought about Annie and saddled up. James knew about her, and so did the rest of the gang. I only told them a little bit about her, and I didn't feel like it was their business anyway.

But before I was about to leave, James came over and said, "I don't think it's going to work out between you two. But if you want to see her for now, fine. Just don't tell her our names, or where we are."

I said, "I won't do that. But I might ask her to join us."

James replied, "I need to meet her first, before she can become one of us."

I replied, "I understand." Then James walked away and I got on Dolly. And with me was a drawing I made, showing the view of the town from the hill. It was my first time drawing anything, and I hoped it would impress her more than my line dancing. I got to the town, hitched Dolly, and walked down to her house with the drawing in my satchel. I felt excited, but nervous about seeing Margaret. I hoped she wouldn't try to kill me. When I got to the front porch, no one was there. So I went up to the front door and knocked. A man opened the door who I assumed was Margaret's husband.

He looked at me confused and asked, "Can I help you sir?"

I told him, "I'm a friend of Annie, is she around now?"

He replied, "I haven't seen you before. You don't look like a friend of hers."

It seemed that he wasn't too fond of me either, but I said, "We just met each other a few days ago." He turned his head back and shouted for her.

I heard someone coming down, but then he quietly said, "You best treat her right. If you do anything to her, you're dead." I nodded, and he went back inside the house. Then Annie came to the front door. She asked how I've been.

I told her, "Things are good, but it feels like I'm walking on eggshells around here." She said to not worry about it and invited me in for some coffee. She told me to leave my boots on the front porch, so I did and we went inside. The house looked beautiful with ornaments, furniture, and even paintings. The house I had with my family was nothing compared to this house. Margaret's husband was sitting on a couch in the living room, and there were also two little boys who looked to be twins. They said hello and I said hi back. Annie went into the kitchen to get coffee, and I went with her.

I told her, "There was this drawing I made a couple days ago of the town."

I started to pull it out, but she said, "Show it to me later, when we're alone."

I said, "Sure thing." And put it back in. We both took a cup of coffee and went back into the living room. Margaret's husband was staring me down. He sure didn't like the look of me. Then Annie introduced the two little boys to me.

One of them asked me, "What do you do for a living?" I wasn't sure of what to say.

So I said, "I help people." Probably the dumbest thing I could have said.

Then the boy asked, "How do you help people?"

I replied, "Well, I go up to them, and I give 'em what they need." They looked at me bewildered, and stared blankly at me for a few seconds.

Then the other boy said, "I want to be just like you when I grow up."

I said, "That's good." I drank some of the coffee, tried not to spit it out, and then asked Annie if she wanted to walk outside.

She said, "Yes, let's go."

As we started walking out, the husband shouted at me, "Remember what I said boy!"

I replied, "I will." And I walked out of the house, shaking my head. I told Annie, "Maybe next time we should meet on the top of the hill." We went over to the brook and started walking alongside it. We made some small talk for a while. It was going well, and then she asked if I had siblings. I said, "I had two brothers, but they died. One was from an accident, and the other from Tuberculosis."

She said, "I'm so sorry. What about your parents?" I paused and then took a deep breath. I only talked about it with James, and that was it. Then she put her arm around me and said, "You don't have to talk about it." We started walking slowly. Her head was resting on my shoulder, and we weren't saying anything. It was relaxing; something I needed. We walked for a while;, then she said, "I'm sorry, I should be heading back. There's some stuff I got to do." As we walked back, I asked her if she wanted to try out camping. I told her I had a tent. She said, "I'd love to. But Margaret would get angry with me if she found out I was with you. They just want me to be safe."

I replied, "Well she's not your mother. You can't let other people control your life. Sometimes you gotta live free for a bit."

She said, "Alright, a couple days from now we'll go camping somewhere, but not too far."

"Understood." I said. We got in front of the house, and I said, "Oh, I almost forgot to show you the drawing."

As I took out the drawing, she put my arm down and said, "You'll show me next time." She winked and walked back to her house. I went over to Dolly, mounted up, and rode back to the gang.

The next morning, I decided I should buy some condoms, just in case. I wasn't sure if we were going to have sex, but I sure as hell didn't want to get her pregnant. I had something for breakfast, but before I could leave, James called us all over for a meeting. Everyone was there, and I was the last one to join in. We all stood around James' tent, and he told us something big.

He said, "I've always wanted to go down south, and I'm tired of dealing with winters up in the north. I don't want to deal with the cold and the snow, it's just too much. It's too much for all of us. So this is the right move. We'll need to get a wagon if we want to make a trip. Either we'll buy it, or steal it. We'll figure it out. For the next two to three months, we'll stay here. The trip should only take a couple months. Not much longer than that. Is there anyone that opposes?" No one opposed. We all liked the idea, and James talked about how much he wanted to move down south from time to time. And the winters were tough for us. But James said that if the Indians could pull it off, we could too.

Then I asked, "Where do you want to go exactly?"

He replied, "I was thinking somewhere in Georgia. It'll be good for us." Everyone seemed to agree, and was excited for it.

The meeting went on for a little while longer, and at the end James said, "And Joe, Buck, you need to get over yourselves. We can't be working against each other. We're a family. And a family has to have each other's backs if they're going to survive." They nodded their heads and the meeting ended soon after.

I told James I had to get something from town, and James said, "Alright big man, do your thing."

Then Buck asked, "Is it for your lady friend? If you need condoms, I got plenty."

I replied, "No thanks Buck. I don't need your dirty condoms." I went to the store and got a small box. I put them in my satchel and kept them there. Two days had gone by, and I went to meet Annie at the hill again. I got there and saw no one. So I went over, sat down, and waited for Annie. Sure enough, I saw her at the bottom of the hill just a few minutes later. She waved hello and I waved back. When she came up to the top, we gave each other a hug and sat down for a bit. We talked about what the past two days were like for us. I told her a few things, but I didn't tell her I'd be leaving in a few months. Eventually, she asked if we were gonna go camping. And I pointed to Dolly, who had the tent up on her saddle. We got on Dolly, and she rode us a little ways away, over to a nice flat area. There was no one around, so it was a perfect camp spot. I showed her how I set it up and she helped me with it.

I asked her, "The people you live with won't give you a hard time, will they?"

She said, "It's not like they're gonna kick me out of the house. I haven't committed a crime or anything." It was turning to evening, so I told her we needed to make a fireplace. We searched for the materials in the woods and eventually got the fire going. Soon thereafter, it became night. We sat by our campfire and ate some canned meat and vegetables that was originally for me. I loved the stuff, but she didn't like it. We finished eating and had conversations about government, religion, stuff I never cared for. So I pretended like I gave a damn just to please her.

After we finished that conversation, she leaned on my shoulder and said, "I'm so happy I found someone like you. I feel that we relate to each other so much. I mean, we both come from broken families, and I feel like we're both just trying to figure life out."

I replied, "I think you're right... I love you." She said she loves me back, and I gave her a kiss on the forehead.

Then she said, "You have to promise me something. That one day we'll go on a hot air balloon. I dream about it all the time."

I said, "I promise it'll happen someday. Not just yet, but someday it'll happen."

She asked, "But how we gonna get a hot air balloon? Are we gonna steal it?" Clearly she was being sarcastic, but if the gang needed a getaway, something like that would come in handy.

I just told her, "We'll figure it out. Maybe we'll just 'borrow' it."

"Sounds like a good idea to me." She replied.

Then I said, "Hey, I got that drawing with me. I don't know if you want to see it, but-" I pulled out the drawing and she came right up against me to get a good look. I showed it to her and said, "Now I know it's terrible." Then she kissed me, I kissed her, and we didn't stop. We got inside the tent and started taking our clothes off. I put my condom on and we started having sex. Annie had an incredible body, and she got turned on by me pretty quickly. So we both finished around the same time, and it felt great. I was getting tired of screwing a prostitute. It was better having sex out of love, instead of just lust. After sex, we cuddled for a while and slowly drifted off to sleep. It was the best night of my life. The next morning we tore down the camp, and I took her back home. She said we could meet tomorrow in the afternoon. I told her I looked forward to it. But next time, I would tell her about the gang.

It was late morning, and soon I would head out to see Annie again. I was nervous about telling her the truth, but I felt ready for it. When I was getting ready to leave, everyone else was playing poker. It was weird seeing Buck and Joe playing together. They sat across from each other, but it was nice to see they could cooperate. We all knew they still hated each other. They stayed on their own side of the camp for so long now, that it was never going to change.

Harry asked me, "Are you sure you don't want to join in Ed?"

I declined and said, "I told Annie I would see her tomorrow, and it is tomorrow."

He replied, "Alright then, good luck."

Then Buck asked, "If you and your lady friend have a child, what are you gonna name it? 'Little Bad Ed?' Or is 'Little Bad Ed' what Annie saw last night?"

I replied, "First off, I will never become a father. Second, go to hell Buck." Everyone was laughing, except for Joe, and me. Like Joe I was also tired of

Buck's dumb jokes. He liked to tease me, and sometimes it got on my nerves. I still loved him though.

James said, "Enough is enough. Let Ed see his woman without everyone hassling him." I said bye to everyone and rode off to Annie, unsure of how it would turn out between us. When I approached the hill, I saw someone already sitting on the top. As I got closer, I saw it was Annie. It was nice to not have to wait for once. She turned her head and saw it was me. Then she got up, ran over, and gave me a hug and a kiss.

She said, "I think we should take a walk around town. I have to buy a few things. And maybe later you can introduce me to your friends."

I told her, "Let's just sit by the hill and just talk for a minute." She said ok, and we sat down and started off with small talk. Then I said, "In a few months, me and my friends will be heading down south. I know you have lived here for a long time, but do you think you might want to travel with us?"

She took a moment, and said, "I think that would be nice. I'd love to go with you."

I said, "That's great."

Then she said, "You have to be careful when travelling though. There are gangs out there that rob people. Not too long ago, a stagecoach got robbed. There were about a dozen men guarding it, and all of them were killed; even the ones that weren't armed. It makes me sick."

I replied, "Yeah I heard. It wasn't nice."

"The men that did that will eventually get what they deserve." said Annie.

Then I said "Me and my friends did it." She looked at me distraught and confused.

Then she chuckled and said, "That's not funny Ed, you really scared me."

I said, "No, I mean it. My friends and I are a gang. We kill and rob people, usually just people that work for the government. All they want is to control our lives, and we won't let them have that." She started weeping and covering her face. I added, "We're not that bad. We're fighting for the idea that man should be able to live freely without the government. I need you to understand that there isn't a simple answer, but we're fighting for the right thing here. And I want you with us."

With her tears in her eyes, she cried, "Ed I can't. I could never be a part of something like that. I-I need to go."

As she walked off, I asked, "So are you gonna tell the sheriff on me now?"

She said, "No, I won't. I love you Ed. But I can't see you anymore. You need to do something else with your life. Going on this path will lead you nowhere. And I think deep inside you know that." She walked away. I stood up, kicked the dirt, and rode back.

I spent some time alone before returning to camp. Took a ride with Dolly a bit, and fed her some oatcakes. I needed some peace and quiet and thought about travelling to Georgia. I didn't think things would be much different down there. But it seemed like it would be a nice change of pace for us. A few hours later, I picked myself up and headed back to camp. It was getting late. When I got there, it was almost nightfall. I hitched Dolly and walked over to my tent. Harry, Bella, and Buck were gathered around the fireplace.

They were all drinking, and Bella drunkenly shouted, "Hey Ed, why don't ya…come over here!"

As I sat down, Harry asked, "How are things with that girl?"

I told him, "Well, I don't think it's gonna work out anymore. I told her what I am and what we stand for. She didn't like the sound of it."

Harry replied, "Ah well, that's a damn shame. There will be plenty of beautiful women where we're going. You'll find the right one eventually."

Bella added, "To me it sounds like…she wasn't gonna really be, there for ya. You know what I mean?" She was more drunk than Buck and Harry, which didn't surprise me. That's how it usually was. Buck was sitting next to Bella. He was smoking, which always put him at ease. So he was pretty quiet.

I told Bella, "I think she wanted to be with me, but she thinks I'm on the wrong path. She was really hurt when I told her the truth."

Bella replied, "If she wants to be another sheep. Then let her. She's just like the rest then."

I said, "I really cared about Annie, and it's gonna be hard living without her."

Bella said, "Well, I don't know what to tell ya…" And drank some more.

Harry jumped in saying, "You should play some of that harmonica; it'll make you feel better." Didn't seem like a bad idea. So, I pulled it out of my pocket and started playing a song; one that we all knew. Harry, Bella, and Buck started singing. Since they were all drunk they weren't very in tune. And a lot of the words were being slurred. Playing harmonica helped everybody stay together, but that only did so much. Shortly after, James joined in. He could sing alright, and knew all the words. The only person that wasn't with us was Joe.

But soon enough, I saw him slowly coming over with the corner of my eye. He sat down and sang with us. And all of us were singing along. When the second verse came, Bella, Buck, and Harry forgot the words. They were fumbling over the melody, and everyone started laughing. I started to laugh and couldn't play harmonica. I was smiling and giggling while trying to keep singing. That was hard to do. We kept on going. And when it got to the high part, Bella stood up with her arms wide open, looking up at the night sky, and belted out the most beautiful sounding high note I'd ever heard. I think her drunkenness calmed her nerves, making it easier for her to sing like that.

Once we got to the end, we sang it loud and proud and shouted, "Hoorah!"

James said, "I think that's all I can handle for one night." I was with him on that. I was feeling good, and everyone else was, too. I knew that no matter what, family was always there. And while it may not have been perfect, I wouldn't have had it any other way.

A week passed by, and I tried to stop thinking about Annie. I was brushing Dolly at the camp. Joe and James were there, and everyone else was out. Buck and Bella rode off together and Harry went to pick something up from one of the other towns. They were gone for quite a bit, and it was nice with just the three of us. Joe came walking back to his tent with some flowers to stash away. Collecting flowers was a hobby of his. I guess he liked smelling them, and it kept him busy. James was sitting down, just finishing up his meal.

When Joe came out from the tent, James asked, "How many flowers you got in there? I kinda want to see."

Joe replied, "Not that many. As many types as I could find."

I said, "I think the reason why you like collecting flowers, is because on the inside you're a delicate flower, Joe. And I mean that in a good way."

James chuckled and said, "I think Joe is just a little more sensitive than the rest of us. And by the way, how many times have you had to brush Dolly? She seems to be dirty all the time."

I replied, "I know. It's because she always likes to get dirty. One time we were-"

"Boys! Boys!" cried out Harry. We got up and came in closer to see what was going on. Harry came up from the small hill riding his horse. Buck was lying on the back, dead. There was an arrow through his neck and his blood was dripping from his face.

James cried, "Buck! No, God! My boy..." I couldn't believe what I was seeing. I was in a state of shock.

Harry started saying, "I saw some Indians that took Bella on horseback. I think they were going back to their tribe."

"And you couldn't you stop them?!" James shouted.

Harry said, "There were too many of them. There was nothing I could do. I'm sorry. But I found Buck's body down the road, and they beat his face in with one of those Indian clubs." James and Harry got Buck's body off the horse, and put him on the ground facing up. I walked over and Buck's face was completely gone.

I said, "It looks like they killed him twice. I guess he didn't die right away from the arrow."

James shouted, "God, damn, animals!"

Harry asked, "What do you wanna do about Bella. God knows what they'll do to her."

James said, "We're gonna get her back."

James was pacing back and forth, then I said, "All of us are good shooters, but I'm not sure if we can take on a whole tribe of Indians."

James paused and said, "You're right. And if we go in shooting, they could kill Bella."

I said, "So we'll have to negotiate with them. What do you wanna do? Make a trade or something?"

James took a moment, and replied, "Yeah, we're gonna have to. Let's pack some food and medicine on one of the horses. Hopefully they don't try to kill us. If they do, we'll have to kill all of them. So boys... Get your guns. We might have to fight." We all got loaded up and put a repeater on our backs. Even if we didn't use the repeaters, they would at least intimidate the Indians.

I asked James, "Do you think they have guns?"

He replied, "I'm sure they do; probably not that much though." Once we had everything set, James called us in for one of his talks.

James started weeping and said, "Now...we all loved Buck."

"I didn't." said Joe.

"Well I did!" shouted James.

"I did too." I said.

There was a moment of silence, then James said, "But now we gotta save little Bella. They can't have her! And I won't let them hurt her!" James got up on his horse and we all did the same. We knew where the Indian camp was, and it wasn't that far. So we rode off, and rode hard.

Big Bad Ed

As we got close, James said to Harry, "I need you to find a safe spot over-looking the tribe. You'll have to keep us covered, just in case things go wrong."

I asked Harry, "How did you manage to get Buck's body up on that horse? Buck is a big guy."

He replied, "I still got some good strength in me. And I couldn't just leave him there." Before approaching the tribe, James had us stop and told Harry to find a good spot to cover us. He got off his horse and told Joe and I to do the same. We were all armed and ready for anything.

As we walked further, I asked James, "What Indian tribe is this anyway?"

James replied, "Does it matter? They're all the same." Soon we saw the whole tribe from about 400 meters. There were a lot of tepees and a lot of Indians. We had to stay tough and go in there calm. So, we kept going. James walked in the middle with me and Joe on both sides. When we got close enough, they all started noticing us and began running over. Most of them were shouting, and I couldn't understand what they were saying. We were hoping a few of them could at least speak English. There were almost a hundred of them circling around us. Some of them put their spears up, and they all kept shouting. I probably should have been scared, but I just focused on saving Bella. And I think James and Joe were doing the same thing. The shouting started to tamper down as three Indians came up to us. I figured they were the ones in charge. I was on James' right side while Joe was on his left. We could've started blowing them all away with them surrounding us. We would've easily killed most of them. But I knew we had to do this the smart way. The Indian in the middle was probably the chief, wearing a bunch of feathers on his head. The one on my side had paint on his face, and didn't look too happy to see us. The one on Joe's side didn't look much different. The presumed Indian chief started talking to his Indian friend on the left. He was the one facing me, and then he started speaking to us in English.

He said, "Why you come here? We have nothing for you."

James replied, "You have a girl. She belongs to us." The three Indians talked amongst themselves. Then the same one told us to follow, so we did. The other Indians still surrounded us, and looked like they were ready to scalp us and kill us. We followed the three Indians to a tepee, and the chief told the other Indians to back away. And they did, but only a little. The three Indians went inside, and so did we. James went in first, and before I went inside, I heard Bella breathing heavily.

Then I heard James softly say, "It's ok Bella. We're gonna get you out of here."

As I stepped in, Bella franticly looked at me and I said, "We'll be fine, just stay calm." Joe came in and said nothing. She wouldn't even look at him. I'm sure she would have preferred if he died instead of Buck. But that's just not how it turned out.

The Indian asked James, "She is yours?"

James replied, "She is. And we're taking her back home." The Indian spoke to the other two; translating what James said. Then the Indian chief spoke to the translator, saying a lot.

Then the translator said in a stern voice, "We cannot give her to you. She will be a wife, living with us."

James said, "Look, we got food, medicine, ammunition. We'll trade anything. What do you want?"

The translator talked to the chief, and looked back at us saying, "We don't want to trade. She will stay with us." I started getting nervous, thinking we'd have to shoot our way out.

Then James said, "Tell your chief that we have more than 30 men surrounding this tribe. They are all armed, and they all want Bella back. So if you don't cooperate with us, we'll kill every last one of you… What do you say?"

The translator started talking with the chief, and just a few seconds later, the translator said, "We know that you lie. You don't have 30 men. You're nothing but outlaws. Our tribe is not afraid of you."

James chuckled, and replied, "Just trust me when I say my boys can shoot pretty well, and that you'll all be dead pretty soon if you won't give her back." The translator turned to the chief and began talking, which quickly turned into arguing.

They went on for a while, until the translator faced James and said, "We have talked, and will give you back the woman. But do not come back here." Bella let out a sigh of relief, and James shook the hands of all three Indians. The four of us walked out and headed back for the horses. We walked quickly, so they wouldn't discover James' bluff before we left.

When we got to the horses, Harry came running over and said, "You boys amaze me. You really do." James put Bella on the back of his horse, and we rode back to camp. All of us got back in one piece, and then got off our horses.

James turned to Bella and said, "I'm sorry." She went over to Buck's body, fell to her knees, and began crying. The rest of us sat somewhere by ourselves. We couldn't believe what just happened.

Big Bad Ed

We buried Buck right next to the camp. There was a wooden cross and a bunch of flowers over the grave. A few days had passed, and James wanted us to leave by the end of the week. I just finished shining my boots and decided to walk over to the grave. To my surprise, I saw Joe adding another flower to the grave.

I asked him, "Are all those flowers from you Joe?"

He replied, "Not all of them, but most of them are."

I said, "So I guess you didn't hate Buck that much."

He said, "I guess not. He wasn't the best person. But neither am I. Either way he was family." I nodded and left Joe to grieve. Not sure if Buck would have done the same for him. We are a family, and we need each other. But I needed to spend some time alone. I walked away from the camp and sat down by a tree, thinking about Annie. I didn't have much time left before we'd head out. And I wanted to see her one more time. For the time being, I put my head back and rested by the tree for a while. It was nice and shady; perfect for reading a book. I fell half asleep, and it felt like I could've stayed in that spot all day long. Eventually I got up and walked around for a bit. It started to get breezy, and I didn't want it to end. I enjoyed going for walks by myself. They always put me at ease, and I could think to myself without being disturbed. I walked down the path I normally take, and everything was still the same. I enjoyed that. Even though things in life change all the time, nature doesn't change. And that's what I love about nature. It doesn't switch everything up on you. That is, unless there's a storm and then lighting strikes you. But fortunately, it doesn't storm a whole lot in Illinois; it sure does snow though. Down south it would be hot, especially in Georgia. However I preferred the heat over cold. So I was happy about making the move. Besides, we couldn't stay in the same place forever. It would've been nice to stay here. But considering what we do, it wouldn't have been smart. As time passed, I thought about going over to Annie. I went back and forth, thinking it wasn't a good idea. But I had to go back, just one more time. I got my hat on, got Dolly, and went to see her.

I walked towards the house, and hoped Annie would be the one to answer. I got to the front door and paused for a moment. I thought about turning back, but realized I couldn't. I knocked on the door, and soon enough, Annie opened the door.

As soon as she saw me, she turned away and then looked back saying, "I can't see you anymore Ed."

I replied, "I wanted to talk. I love you." She put her hand over her head and didn't know what to say. I looked away and didn't know what to say either. Then I said, "I want you to understand where I'm coming from. The government is run by evil men; men who will control just about every part of our lives. They want us to bow down as slaves, instead of living as people. Is that what you want, Annie?"

She took a breath, and said "The government and the men who run it do the best they can. It may not be a perfect system. But nothing in life is perfect. Sure, a lot of men are corrupt, but is killing and robbing people really going to make anything better? How will that solve anything?"

I replied, "If you come with me, you'll see."

"No, the problem is what you don't see. You think you're saving the world, but you can't seem to save yourself. And you have to save yourself, if you want to save the world."

I took off my hat and handed it to her saying, "I want you to take this."

She replied, "I can't Ed."

"It would mean a lot to me if you kept it. Please." I said.

She replied, "It's your hat. It looks better on you."

I sighed and said, "Annie, please. I think you should keep it."

She took the hat and said, "Please try to do better, Ed. At the end of the day, I can't really help you. Only you can." She closed the door, and I turned around and walked back to Dolly. I rode back thinking about what Annie said. But I knew she didn't have a clue of what she was saying. All of that was over. The gang needed me now more than ever. We lost Buck, and the whole gang felt torn. It was time to make something better for ourselves, and this trip would do us good. We just needed to get a wagon, and then we'd head out. Our spirits were growing. All of us were getting stronger. We couldn't stop now. It was the start of a new beginning.

PART 4

A month went by, and we had our horses, guns, and the wagon we bought. So far the weather wasn't giving us much trouble, and we were stopping off at local towns for supplies. It wasn't the same without Buck. No more obnoxious jokes or bar fights. I wanted something to fill that void, so I played a lot more harmonica. I was never that great at it, but it was something that was always there for me. Currently we were riding in Tennessee, and soon we'd cross into Georgia. We hadn't robbed anything since that stagecoach. James wanted us all to have a break, especially after dealing with the Indians. What a mess that was. There were definitely no Indians in the south. But there were a lot more racists. I heard about that KKK group. We weren't like them at all. None of us hated them for being racist. I mean, being hateful is a part of being human. But I didn't agree with them. I had no problem with colored folks; they were just like any other people. And I didn't mind if a colored man joined our gang. James and the others wouldn't care to talk about colored folks a whole lot. Their problems didn't mean much to them, but it's what my father fought for. And all that fighting was worth a lot for this country. I hoped the fighting we were going through would be worth something.

We stopped the wagon and decided we'd head into the nearest town for supplies. I got out some corn to feed Dolly, and looked at her saddle. It was getting pretty worn. And I wanted to get her a new one, same with all of our clothes, and our handbags. Everything was falling apart.

I said to James, "How much money do we even have right now?"

James replied, "Enough to keep us going. Why, you feeling the itch to go robbing?"

I said, "I don't want to bring attention towards us, but we're all looking like uncivilized reprobates. And I don't want to just have enough. There's not enough food for all of us, and I'm a man. Just having a can and a half per day isn't enough."

"Well we kind of are uncivilized reprobates. But you're right, we shouldn't drag on like this. We do need more money." said James.

"I was thinking of robbing one of those shops. They got some decent cash." I said. James didn't like the idea, especially since the last time we robbed a shop. It was some general store in an isolated town, a few months before we did the recent stagecoach job. It was me and James. We had our bandanas on, and each of us had a revolver. The plan was to wait around till we knew no one was in there besides the clerk. And then we'd get in there and take as much cash and supplies as we could carry. We knew we had to keep quiet and move quickly. I was near the general store, smoking a cigar, while James went inside to see how many folks were in there. He pretended to be a customer, buying something that didn't cost much, and met me back outside.

He said, "There are four other people in there besides the clerk, so now we wait for those people to leave. In the meantime, let's make ourselves look busy so that folks don't think we're gonna rob the place." I wasn't much of a smoker, but I went through a whole pack of cigarettes just waiting for those four people to leave. I guess they were friends with the clerk or something. Eventually, James and I saw the four of them leave. One of them passed by and glanced at me, and I quickly looked the other way. I was hoping nobody thought we looked suspicious. James told me it was time, so I threw the last cigarette on the ground, and we put our bandanas on. He was in front of me and calmly opened the door. When we got inside, James asked the clerk how he was doing.

The clerk just said, "I'm good. You boys from around here?"

Then James pulled out his gun saying, "We're not from around here, and we don't plan on coming back. Now open up the register." The clerk looked panicked as he opened it. I was about to walk around to get the money when someone opened the door. It was another customer.

I panicked and pulled out my gun, pointing it at the customer and said, "Get on the ground and don't say nothing." Then the unthinkable happened.

The customer pulled a gun out on me. And the clerk quickly pulled out a shot-gun on James. We were in a tough spot. The clerk was yelling at James to put his gun down, and James was yelling back at him to do the same. I was threat-ening the customer, saying I'd kill him if he didn't cooperate. And he was yel-ling back something I wasn't listening to. All four of us were yelling, and I'm sure the whole town heard it. Then James shot the clerk in the head, and I shot the customer dead right after.

James frantically said, "Get the money quick. And let's get out of here." So I got behind the register and took everything I saw. But as soon as I came back around the counter, James said, "Is there a back door?"

I said "No, why?"

"We got a problem." replied James. I looked out the window and saw four men out there, pointing rifles at us. One of them was taking cover behind a barrel, while the others were hiding behind a broken-down wagon. James and I got into cover. We were on each side of the door, with the customer's body right in between us. One of the men was the sheriff. Two others looked like they were also lawmen. But the third one just looked like a regular civilian. I guess he wanted to be a hero, but that wasn't the best idea. Not when dealing with the Mulligan gang.

The sheriff started saying, "We know it's just the two of you. So just give up, and go down with honor."

James replied, "Well sheriff, that's not my idea of honor. I'd rather go out fighting."

There was a long pause, and then the sheriff said, "If you surrender now, there is a chance that God might forgive you. It's never too late for that."

Then I said, "Sheriff, I think God has long forgotten about us now. We didn't want things to be like this either. Those two men should have just lis-tened to us. I don't want there to be a shootout either. So I'm asking you to listen to us. Let us go, and your lives will be spared."

The sheriff replied, "I'm afraid I can't do that. What's your name anyhow?"

I replied, "My name is Big Bad Dan. And I can shoot a gun better than all of you."

"Don't worry, I can shoot a gun pretty well too, but that won't be nec-essary." replied the sheriff.

James whispered, "Now Ed, I know you can shoot better than most. You've gotta be one of the best shooters out there. And right now, I need you to do what you do best. Pretend like you're going to step out, and then shoot 'em all down."

I replied, "I like that idea, but I'm going to do it my way."

The sheriff said, "We don't want anyone else dying. Not even you boys. So what do you think?"

I shouted, "I do want God to forgive me, sheriff."

The sheriff replied, "Surrender then, and you'll be able to think about everything you have done in a prison cell."

I said, "Oh I'll be thinking about what I've done, but not in a prison cell. I'll be thinking about it with a whiskey in my hand." I stepped out of the door and saw all four of them pointing their guns at me. It was either us, or them. And it wasn't about to be us. I quickly pulled out my revolver and started shooting like I had never shot a gun before. There was a bullet that nearly hit me, but I got all four of them.

James came out and shouted, "Go! Get on the horses!" As we ran, people were screaming and running inside. There was no one else attacking us, so had no problem getting to the hitching post. We got on our horses and got the hell out of there. We rode back to camp as fast as we could. No one was able to follow us.

As we rode, James shouted, "Well Ed, I think you just laughed at death in the face!"

All of that was behind us, but we needed money again.

I asked James, "What do you think? Should we test our luck again?"

James replied, "I don't think so. I think I have a better idea."

I said, "Hopefully it doesn't involve us getting shot at."

James said, "Probably not."

I asked, "So what's the master plan then?"

He said, "We're gonna rob a poker game. They always got those high stakes poker games in the back of bars. So for us, it's an easy target."

I nodded my head and asked, "Who are we bringing?"

"You, me, and Joe. It'll be easy; we'll pull our weapons out to scare 'em. But for once, let's try to not kill anyone. "

I replied, "I know. I won't unless I have to." We decided to do the stick up tomorrow in the evening. For now, Harry, James and I went into town to buy some more supplies. One thing we definitely needed was water. It was only getting hotter the farther down south we went. And it took some getting used to. While the three of us did that, Joe would stay with Bella. I think those two were starting to bond a little bit. They hardly ever talked to each other when Buck was around. And after that fight, Bella pretended Joe didn't even exist. But that day, I heard them say good morning to each other. So that was a start. The town we were going to was called Charlotte. I was looking forward to getting a drink as well. I needed it. James and Harry needed it. Bella used to drink quite a lot, but she was trying to slow down a little. She'd often get so sick from drinking that she'd throw up at least four times a week. I knew she changed since Buck passed. Not sure if the change was for the better. But something told me it was. Mostly she stayed quiet throughout the trip so far. We all knew it was rough for her. I wondered whether or not she'd try finding someone else. Only time would tell. Later that day, Harry started complaining about some back pains he was having, and told us he needed to rest. So it was just James and I that would go into Charlotte, which I didn't mind. I liked when it was just me and James. He always had our backs.

As the two of us started riding off, I told him, "You still owe me for getting us out of that robbery situation. So how about you pay for drinks?"

James laughed and said, "Shut up Ed. You owe me a lot more than I owe you."

I shook my head and said, "If you say so." It only took us about ten minutes to get to town. It was getting around sunset, and the town looked decent. It didn't take long for us to get supplies. We couldn't really afford a whole lot anyway.

Everything was put on the horses, and James said to me, "I think we should wait 'til after the robbery before we start drinking, because having one will turn into two, which will turn into three. So, when we get the money, then we'll celebrate."

I said, "Well after we rob this poker game, we better move out fast. Otherwise the law will be coming to the party."

James said, "Don't worry about the plan. Just do what I tell you, and everything will go fine." We rode back with what little we had, which would get us through another few months. But that time was gonna run out soon enough. At some point, we'd have to rob again. And now was the time.

That night I couldn't get any sleep. I was thinking about things going wrong. When I stepped out of the shop to kill those four men, I didn't care if I died, because it would've at least been with honor. But I lived, which meant that I had more to do in this world. I still wondered if God existed; probably not. If he did, the world wouldn't be the way it is. James told us we might all be going to heaven, if God agreed with us. I believed we were fighting for the right thing. Just not in a nice way. I also thought about my brothers, and momma. I tried to not think about them too much. My memories of them were always in the back of my mind whenever I went to sleep. I never dreamed about them or my father. Never really was a dreamer. Just didn't happen that often. If I did have a dream, it would be a small one that I half forgot about when I woke up. My main problem with not being able to fall asleep was think-ing about things. I just couldn't stop. I still thought about Annie, my father. There were also two people that I couldn't forget. I had killed both of them in the past. One person that stuck out to me was Arthur Williams. He was the first person I killed. And I was only 12 back then. I was angry, and I had the power to take his life, so I did. The memory of him stuck with me up to this point. And it wasn't going anywhere. Same with the old woman I killed from the stagecoach robbery. The one from when I was 14 and I pulled the trigger by accident, blowing her head off. I wondered what her name was, as well as her husband's name. They both could have been my grandparents. I assume by now they were buried somewhere, unless some wolves got to them first. When I killed her, I felt this painful feeling in my gut that I'd still feel at times. If I went down to hell, I hoped I wouldn't run into those people. And if hell was real, there was no question we'd be going there. I'm sure James didn't want to think about it.

Since my thoughts kept me up all night long, I wasn't able to focus in the morning. But we still had some coffee, and though I never liked the taste, it helped me out. I don't think I would've still been alive if it wasn't for drinking coffee. Once we got the coffee ready, I drank from my cup and actually enjoyed it that time. It was the small comfort I had, before risking my life yet again. I got all my bullets together, counting every single one of them. On me were two revolvers. Joe had a shotgun. And James had his revolver. While I was eat-ing some breakfast, he was cleaning his pistol. He always kept it nice and shiny. The rest of us did the same thing. But for James it had to be perfect. If it wasn't perfect, it wasn't good enough. Harry was sitting down playing his banjo (Na-poleon). He was playing a nice peaceful tune. Something that was good for the morning. Bella started singing along with it. She sang quietly, and it was a joy to listen to. It had been forever since I had seen a show or something. So hearing Bella and Harry was the only source of entertainment we had. And of course, there was me and the harmonica. I had come a long way with it. It had been there with me for a long time. And since I bought it while out with momma, I considered it a good luck charm. So I always kept it in my pocket. And playing on the streets for folks would get me a little bit of change. It would never be that much. Certainly wouldn't be able to make a living off of just that. We decided we'd head out in the afternoon. That wouldn't be too much longer. The three of us needed to have our heads on right in order to pull this off.

We waited till late afternoon and then headed into town. There was a hitching post right outside of the saloon. And once we got the money, we'd ride out of there as fast as possible. Bella and Harry would have the horses and wagon ready to leave upon our return. James found out that a poker game would be going on around this time in the back of the saloon. Most of the men in the poker game would probably be armed. But if one of them tried anything, they'd all get shot. And then we'd have to run like hell again. It was a beautiful day. There was hardly a cloud in the sky, the perfect day for a robbery. When we got to the town, it had a lot of people walking around. It made me feel a little more nervous, so I tried to just focus on getting the job done. Joe seemed alright. He was always calm anyway. He had been through a lot as well. I'm sure all of us felt nervous, but we would never show it. We hitched our horses and Joe took out his shotgun. He strapped it on his back, and we had our bandanas with us. Joe would walk in through the side door so he wouldn't be noticed, while James and I walked through the front of the saloon. James waved and said hello to the bartender.

He whispered to me, "I'm gonna distract them so we don't look suspicious. You go meet up with Joe, and I'll meet you guys at the backroom door." I said ok, and met Joe at the side door. We put our bandanas on and heard some chatter going on down the hall. We slowly walked down there and heard the chit chat getting louder.

I whispered to Joe, "Do you think its high stakes poker going on in there? Cus it better be."

Joe quietly replied, "We'll find out when we rob them." The men in there seemed to be having a good time. It kinda made me miss playing poker. I hadn't played that game in a while. A few moments later James walked towards us.

He nodded his head and whispered, "Let's do it." With James and Joe behind me, I opened the door and saw six heads turn to look at us.

The three of us pulled our guns out and I said, "Sorry, but you boys are gonna have to fold,'cus it looks like we got the better hand here."

One of the men said, "Alright, but please don't shoot us."

James said, "C'mon, let's see what you boys got. I got two angry outlaws behind me that want a decent pay day." They started putting everything they had on the table.

The money was piling up, and I told James, "I think we robbed the right poker game." I had the bag to carry the money, so I started grabbing the money and stuffing it up.

James said, "Looks like you boys were playing a high stakes poker game today." The men we were robbing were dressed up nicely, so it wasn't a surprise they had a good amount of money to spare. We had them all line up against the back wall.

One of them said, "You know you won't get away with this. The law will catch up with you." We just ignored him. But knew that all of us had to move fast in order to get away.

Once I collected all the money, James said, "Alright, I think that should do it. Thank you gentlemen; we appreciate your donation to the gang. It means a lot. And we'll be spending the money wisely." I put the bag of money over my shoulder, and we slowly walked backwards with our guns pointed at the poker players. Joe was the last one to leave. So he walked out, pointing his shotgun with one arm and closed the door with the other arm. We all went out of the side door and ran for the horses. Since we were in a rush, some people outside were staring at us as if we committed a crime. But we were able to get on our horses and get out of there. It wasn't over yet because now the Mulligan gang was on the run once again.

A little while later, we got back to our camp with everything packed and ready to go. Harry and Bella were already on the wagon.

Once they saw us, Harry asked "Did things turn out alright?"

James replied, "Things turned out just fine." Our horses were trotting, and the horses pulling the wagon were strong enough to go at a good pace. We figured we might as well run all the way to Georgia, since there was a lot of money stolen. Those folks sure were rich. I knew they'd want us hanged. We went on like that for a while and got to a more rural area surrounded by dense forest. The type of environment we were used to. At a certain point, the horses needed a rest. So we stopped by a small pasture and set up our camp.

We got several miles away from Charlotte and felt that we were safe for the time being.

Once we started getting settled, James said to us, "The law won't follow us this far. It's not like we robbed a bank. We can stay here for a few days. I kind of like it over here. The land, it's beautiful."

I replied, "I'm sure it will be even better in Georgia." Night was approaching, and we wouldn't have bothered setting up the tents if it wasn't for mosquitoes. They weren't as bad up in the north, but down here, there were just too damn many. At times I suggested to James that we find an abandoned house or barn. And a few times we had. But that wasn't easy to come across. Plus we'd always end up moving, so it was easier to camp out. It would have been nice to at least have a small house, even if we had to build it ourselves. But I knew that would never happen.

I had a hard time falling asleep, but I eventually did. Luckily, I didn't get bitten up too bad from mosquitoes. In the morning, Joe seemed to have it bad. He couldn't stop scratching his arms and legs. I think they liked his blood the most. Bella seemed to be doing better. She was a lot more talkative with us since we had been in Tennessee. She was still grieving over Buck. They had only been together for a few years, but she loved him like no one else.

I was getting myself dressed when James came up to me and said, "We did good Ed. I think tonight we're gonna celebrate how far we've come. We need it."

I replied, "Yeah, only the bugs will celebrate with us too."

"No, because we're gonna find some sweet grass. The scent keeps bugs away." said James.

"Sweet grass huh? You're always a step ahead." I replied.

"We always have to be a step ahead." said James. He told Joe and I to go and search around for some wet meadows where we would find some of those plants.

When I was ready to go, I shouted to Joe, "Let's get going! I don't want to be out looking for this stuff all day!" Joe slowly got up and went to his horse. I got on Dolly, and we both started moving out. This whole area was mostly open country. So I doubted we'd see anybody passing by. In case there was somebody, I could ask 'em if they'd seen any sweet grass. Joe and I decided to do a perimeter around the area. We stayed together and took it slow.

As we were searching, I told him, "More and more civilization is coming. With all these railroads getting built, it ain't never gonna stop. What do you think about all of it?"

Joe replied, "I don't know what to think. Who knows what life will be like twenty years from now. Or even a hundred years for now. One day this way of life won't exist. There will be nowhere for outlaws like us to run. Civilization will keep growing stronger."

I told him, "Well we'll fight while we still can. I don't think it will ever get that bad. But like you said, we'll see." We started riding a bit faster and talked about everybody in the camp.

Joe told me, "I was thinking that Bella wanted James as her new lover. I can tell by the way she looks at him."

I replied, "She looks up to him, but she's not in love with him. He still mourns over Elizabeth, even after all of these years."

Joe replied, "Yes, it's a shame."

I said, "I don't know if he'll ever get over it. That woman meant everything to him. And he is the most passionate, loyal man I know. Elizabeth will always be in his heart." Back a long time ago, Elizabeth was James' young lover. This was back when it was just the four of us. James was on his horse when he found her robbing a man on the side of the road. She turned to him pointing a gun, and he got off the horse, taking his time. With his charm and charisma, he tried convincing her to join us.

He told us she yelled, "You're just gonna take me to the sheriff! Back off or I will shoot you!" It didn't sound like she was a charmer herself.

James put his hands in the air and said, "You know, pretty lady. I think you should reconsider pointing that at James Mulligan."

She lowered her gun and said, "James Mulligan? I think I've heard that name." The two started chatting and getting along. Then they took everything left from the man, and went on their way. That's how the story went. Too bad it ended in tragedy. She got shot by a farmer while trying to steal some eggs. At the time she was with James, who started getting shot at by another farmer. He said he barely made it out alive. But Elizabeth was dead as soon as she got shot. The bullet went straight through her heart. Later that day, all of us went over there to kill all of those farmers. There were only two of them. And they were lucky they only got shot. Elizabeth's body was buried somewhere in Indiana, that poor girl.

Eventually, we saw a stream that we went down towards. Soon enough, we found some of those wet grass plants James wanted. We picked as many as we could.

Big Bad Ed

Then I asked Joe, "Do you want a girl to call your own someday?"

He answered, "Maybe. I don't know." I felt like he did, but maybe he wasn't ready for that. We figured Joe would never be a lover, but at least he had us. After we collected the plants, we rode back. It was still a beautiful day, and we all wanted to do something fun. Both of us got back to camp and pulled out all of the sweet grass we found.

James looked pleased and told us, "Good job boys. There's a town not too far away from here. I think we should head over and have ourselves a good time. But one of us has to stay and watch the horses."

Joe said, "I'll stay. I could use some quality time with the horses."

"I appreciate it Joe. We'll bring you back something special. Not sure what, but it'll be a surprise." replied James.

Joe nodded his head and said, "Sounds good." The rest of us got ourselves on the wagon and headed to the nearest town. This one was called Canvas Ridge. I'm pretty sure we had passed it on our way over to the campsite. It would take a while to get there, so I hoped it was worth it. But it's not like we had anything better to do. I didn't want to spend the whole day just sitting around, especially when we had some good money to spend. It's not like we were gonna spend that much. But we were tired of just surviving. It was important for us to live a little.

James was driving in the front and shouted, "It looks like we're finally here!" We all stood up from the wagon and looked at the town. It was smaller than Charlotte but looked nice and quiet. I just hoped there was gonna be some stuff for us to do there. James brought the wagon to the side of the rode, and we all got off.

I said to James, "Hopefully nobody tries to steal the wagon, or we're screwed!"

James replied, "In this town? That won't happen. Now let's take a look around. But remember, we ain't robbing the place. Don't want too much law on our tails." Bella suggested to us that we got our hair and beards trimmed. I didn't have much of a beard and neither did James. But Harry had his beard growing for a while, and he looked like a caveman. We all thought it looked good on him though.

We walked together down the main road, and Bella said, "There's a hair parlor right there. I don't know 'bout you boys, but my hair feels like one messy rag; too much to take care of. Who's coming with me?" James and I decided to tag along. Harry walked off somewhere else. The hair parlor was a small building. So I didn't expect to see many people in there. I was the last one to enter, and it was just us three and a small man who was the hair cutter. He was very warm and welcoming to us, saying hello and shaking our hands. The feller would have been real easy to rob.

Bella sat on the hair cutting chair first and said, "I'm tired of my hair being this long; getting way too messy. So cut it down to here. Please." The hair parlor first washed her hair and then trimmed it down. There was a lot of it. So I figured she'd take the longest.

I asked James, "You getting a fancy new haircut or what?"

He replied, "It's not like we're going to a ball. So I don't think that's necessary."

I said, "I might try out some of that pomade. I mean I don't have anyone to impress, but I always wanted to try that stuff out. I think it would look good on me."

"Then all you need is a nice-looking suit, and you might as well be a governor."

I chuckled and said, "That would be something to see." The hair cutter stepped back, and Bella turned towards us. Her hair was now halfway down her neck, and not past her shoulders. She looked real good, and I could tell it made her feel better. It wasn't doing her any favors dealing with all that hair in the hot sun. I don't know how Harry was able to do it with all of his hair, but that's the way we found him. It didn't seem like that was going to change.

James went up to the hair cutter next and said, "Just trim it down a bit. Don't need nothin' special." James always wore a hat just like me. So, hair wasn't a top priority for him. I also wore a hat most of the time. The one I had now was made out of leather. Felt more comfortable than the last one I had. That one I gave to Annie, which was made from felt; wore it for quite a number of years. But James would kill anybody trying to steal his hat. It was a simple flat crown hat, but I think he cared about it more than his own horse, who he never gave a name to. He would refer to it as "big guy" or "the big one," but normally he'd just whistle for it if he needed it to come over. He'd say he never really cared for animals much. He just saw horses tools; something that would get work done. The rest of us showed more affection to James' horse than he did. I felt like the horses were family to us. And Dolly was like my sister.

James got his hair and beard trimmed down pretty nicely.

I told him, "I gotta hand it to ya, you always were a lot more handsome than the rest of us."

James rolled his eyes and said, "Oh shut up, Ed. Are you getting your hair cut or not? And please don't get that hair pomade. Trust me, it wouldn't look right."

I said, "We'll see how it turns out." I handed my hat to James and went over to the chair.

I sat down and told the hair cutter, "I'll get a trim…and, uh, that's it I guess." I had black straight hair that went down to my ears. The hair cutter cut my hair quick, and started chattin' me up a bit.

He asked, "So, are you and your friends from 'round here?"

I said, "No, we're just travelling. We don't stay in the same place for very long. How many years have you been cutting hair?"

He replied, "Not sure exactly how many years now. It's been a long time. But you should watch out for bandits running around. I heard of one notorious group called the Mulligan gang. All of them are real nasty. They've been wanted in some of the states up north. Hopefully they don't come 'round here. If they do, well, I guess I'm screwed."

I nervously laughed and said, "I don't think that'll happen. You know what? I think I'll try some of that pomade you have."

He replied, "Sure, I can apply some. Do ya want your hair pushed back, or off to the side?" I didn't know what I wanted, so I told him to push it back and hoped it would look decent. When he finished trimming everything, he started putting on the pomade. He started saying, "I got four kids of my own. Trying to teach two of them how to do my job, so they can one day take over. The other two moved away from here. They went off to the city to be sales-men. What do ya think of that…uh, what's your name sir?"

I responded, "Ed."

He said, "Ed! That's a great name. My eldest son is named Ed. We all call him Eddy. But, Ed, do ya think being salesmen is good for 'em?"

I said, "I'm not sure. I guess they'll figure that out. At some point we all gotta figure things out."

He replied, "You're right about that. I know God is there for 'em, but in the end, it's up to them. We send each other letters, but I always pray that life will treat 'em right. I mean they have each other. So that's something."

I said, "I'm sure they'll be fine. And your other two boys will make great hair cutters as well."

He replied, "Most folks call it a barber, but you could say hair cutter if ya want. I guess you don't spend a whole lotta time in towns or cities huh?"

I replied, "Like I said, I'm a traveler. So I camp out with my buddies." He then got a small mirror and gave it to me. I looked at myself and thought "Well, I don't exactly look like a reprobate now." I got out of the chair and saw Bella sitting down.

She took one look at me and said, "Well, looks like you're ready for someone special. Is that the plan?"

I said, "Not really. Just wanted to see how I'd look."

Bella said, "Now you just need a fancy suit! We're gonna head over to the clothing shop. And don't tell me ya can't, because you gotta try on something to match that hairstyle of yours." I said I'll go, and waved goodbye to the hair cutter. He was a nice man, but I still would have robbed him. Wouldn't want to have killed him though. I didn't want to kill most people I robbed. But things went bad a lot of the time. People didn't want to just let us get away with it.

James would tell me, "That's just how it is. If someone wants to put up a fight, they're gonna die." However, the hair cutter wouldn't have put up a fight. He looked like he never shot a gun in his life. He wasn't all that wealthy either, but he did have his four boys.

I walked outside with Bella and met up with James and Harry.

James looked at me and said, "Now I think you're the handsome one."

I replied, "Well, I suppose I am." We all walked down the street to the clothing shop. As we went inside the shop, we saw all kinds of interesting looking fashions for men and women, and were excited to dress up in whatever we wanted. I said to James, "If you put on that top hat, I'm definitely making fun of you."

Harry said, "I think we're all gonna have to try that on. Whoever looks the most ridiculous in it should get to keep it." We all chuckled, and were met by the tailor.

He said, "The changing room is right around that corner. Is there a particular style any of you were looking for?"

James replied, "We'll eventually figure it out. But for now, we're just gonna have some fun with it." We all started picking whatever clothes we wanted to try on and headed to the changing rooms. I didn't think I was going to buy anything, but I figured it wouldn't hurt to try a new look. I had been wearing the same clothes for years along with the others. And this was the most fun we were having in a long time. I found a bow tie, top hat, along with trousers and a jacket. They were all much more expensive-looking than what I had. All that I needed now was a monocle. I got changed and stepped out. The Mulligan gang didn't look like a gang no more. Bella had some big fancy-lookin' hat on with flowers all over it. She was also wearing one of those big round dresses. I always thought those looked terrible. But she still looked alright with it on. I saw James and Harry across the room. The two of them just put on whatever they could find. They didn't look too bad, but none of what they were wearing matched all that well. But what did I know. I wore the same shirts, jackets, and pants for years. Not that it bothered me.

Bella came up to me and started playing with my bow tie saying, "Well looky here. Are you a city man now? Girls love a city man."

I replied, "I don't think so, just pretending to be. You look better than the rest of us." James and Harry walked over, and when I turned towards them, they started laughing.

James said, "There's a few canes they have across the room. I have to see you with one of those."

Harry added, "Yeah Ed do that; it would be priceless."

We all walked over there, and the tailor asked, "Is everything alright?"

I told him, "Don't worry about a thing."

Harry said, "I'm gonna go look around some more." and walked away I walked over to check out some of the canes with Bella and James. Bella took one and began posing with it; acting all fancy and what not. Then she started doing a little dance with it. So I grabbed one of the canes and joined her. I just followed along with whatever she was doing. She was twirling that cane around and swinging it from side to side. It was definitely more fun than line dancing.

James shook his head and said, "Now it looks like you two are from the circus."

Then I threw another cane over to James and said, "And you're gonna be our third member."

James threw the cane back at me and said, "You'll never see me walking around with that thing."

Bella said to me, "Show me how you walk, looking all rich like that. I wanna see." I put my cane up against my chest, and started struttin' my stuff. I was walking around like I owned the whole town. Then Bella told James to do the same. She gave him back the cane and grabbed his hand. They were walking across the room like they were in a royal palace. Bella was giggling, and James eventually cracked a half smile.

I began to applaud them and said, "Ladies and gentlemen, King James and her highness have arrived."

Then Harry shouted, "Are you fools almost done!?"

I replied, "I think so, just gonna change back." So I went to the changing room and changed into my normal clothes. I got myself a couple new pairs of pants and shirts. That was about it. Oh, and the fancy top hat as well. James and Bella bought some decent garments of their own. We paid for everything and went to load everything we bought on the wagon.

When we finished loading everything on there, Harry pulled out a monocle and said, "Look at this little thing. I stole it while the tailor wasn't lookin'. Any of you steal something, or am I the only real outlaw here?"

Bella pulled out a pocket watch and said, "I thought I was the only one." Then she reached into her other pocket and said, "I also got this pretty necklace." The necklace didn't look too expensive. Neither did the watch. But they wouldn't keep something worth a lot out in the open like that; especially not with the likes of us hanging about. Bella asked all three of us, "So who wants the watch? If ya'll want, I could steal another one."

James said, "Let me see it." She handed it over to him, and he gave it a good look from front to back. He said, "I'll give it to Joe. He has a few of these, and I'm sure he'll like this one."

I said to James, "We're getting drinks of course. Aren't we?"

James replied, "No, I think I'd rather give everything back that we stole from the tailor, and turn us in to the sheriff. What do you think about that?"

I replied, "The only problem James is, I don't think this town has a sheriff. Maybe there's a sheriff in the next county, but not here. So I might as well be the town's sheriff."

Harry said, "Ed's right, there is no sheriff 'round here. Guess this is supposed to be one of those peaceful towns with no trouble, at least until now."

Then James said, "Alright, let's get some drinks to bring back with us. And Harry, I need you to stock up on a few cans of whatever they got. We wanna be eating well tonight." James got the beer crate, and the three of us got ourselves as much drink as we could fit inside. It took us a while to decide what kind of drinks we wanted. Eventually we brought that back to the wagon and loaded that up.

Bella said, "Let's just look around some more. I hear some music playin' down over there." It was becoming dusk, and James didn't want to travel when it was dark. But then Bella started running off, and we chased after her. She was running towards the music, where there was only a fiddle player, trying to make some money for himself. He was at the corner of the street, under a roof, where there was plenty of shade. When James and I got over there, Bella was dancing away.

James said, "Bella, enough of this. I wanna get out of here already."

She replied, "We'll leave, in just a bit." Then Harry came over and began to dance with Bella. At that point I figured I might as well join 'em. So I did. There was only one other person watching the fiddle player, so having us around put a smile on his face. I threw a few coins in his hat for his troubles. James and Harry did the same. The four of us were swingin' along with the rhythm, having a good time. It almost made me want to buy a fiddle. But I always felt I was meant for the harmonica. When the song ended, we all clapped, and the fiddle player took a bow. He then said something in a foreign language to us; might have been Italian or something. I barely knew English, so I wasn't gonna try to guess what he was sayin'. I still knew how to read and write. All of us did. But reading and writing wasn't our biggest hobbies. The fiddle player started playing another one. But this time it was a slow song. And it sure sounded beautiful.

Harry gestured out his hand to Bella and asked, "May I take your hand for a dance m'lady?" She took his hand and they started slow dancing.

I shouted to Bella, "Next thing you'll be slow dancing with Joe!"

She replied, "Uh-huh, whatever you say."

James began to walk off and said, "I'll be at the wagon." I stayed and watched the fiddle player.

I then added a couple more coins to his hat and told him, "Good luck with it." I kinda admired him. He was out in the world just like us, tryna survive. He wasn't controlling anybody's life; just doing his own thing. This was the way things were meant to be.

A few minutes later, Harry said, "I think I'm done now. We should go see James."

Bella replied, "You do whatever you want old man."

She turned to me and said, "One more dance Ed. Please?" I took her hands, and Bella started twirling around, and then leaned backward with my arm around her. When she stood back up she hugged me, and then we started pacing back and forth with the song. Then she said, "I don't want to forget about today; how 'bout you?"

I replied, "I'll probably have a dream about it."

She said, "I'll probably dream about it every night until there's something else to dream about." After that we kept quiet and finished dancing to the song. Harry had left, and at that point it was me and Bella with the fiddle player. He put his fiddle away and gave one last bow, saying something short in Italian. I assumed it was "Goodnight."

So I said, "Have a good night." back to him and walked back with Bella. All four of us were at the wagon and we were ready to go. It was getting late, and James wanted us to get going before it was dark. We got on the wagon and rode back to camp.

It turned to nightfall halfway through the trip back. We were doin' well for ourselves, and were surely gonna be having a few drinks when we got back. James had to take the lantern out in order to see the road. We had James and Harry's horse moving the wagon. They were our two strongest horses, and we tried to not overwork them. They'd been taking the wagon all this way so far, and they were still able to go strong. We were all chit chatting on the way back with Harry yapping about how the old days was. I let Bella wear the top hat I bought. She also put on the monocle and necklace that was stolen. All she needed was a mustache and she would've made a fine gentleman. Eventually things started to look more familiar, and soon enough we saw a small fire with three horses standing by. One was lying down while the other two were standing up. All of them were sleeping. And as we approached the camp, I saw the one lying down was Dolly. She looked like she was done for the day, as well as the other horses.

As soon as James got off the wagon, he handed Joe the pocket watch saying, "We thought you might like this. So keep it somewhere safe, unless you wanna use it to scam someone. Either way, it's yours now." Him and Joe hitched up the two horses standing, and then told me to hitch up Dolly.

I said to James, "If I wake up Dolly, she'll surely make me pay for it tomorrow."

James replied, "Are you kidding Ed? That horse loves you more than anything. I don't think she'd ever buck you off." I took the horses from the wagon and hitched them up as well.

Then James said to me, "At some point, you gotta hitch Dolly up as well. I don't want anybody slippin' up on my rules." I nodded my head. It's not like we always had the horses hitched. That was usually just during nighttime. We didn't want 'em running off on us. They all knew who their family was, but James wanted us doing things a certain way and we all did as he said. He's the one that got us this far. And for that, we needed to celebrate.

We all grabbed some drinks from the wagon and sat around the campfire. We usually didn't get too carried away. But we'd gone through a lot, and the drinkin' was starting to get out of control. All of us had a few drinks of beer, whiskey, rum, you name it. We probably drank it. James got pretty loud when he was drunk. He was telling jokes and eventually started laughing at nothing. The rest of us were laughing along, even if we didn't know what we were laughing about.

James drunkenly said to me, "Hey Ed... Hey Ed..."

I said "What is it now... James."

"You gotta put... Dolly...back on the hitching post." he said. I was barely able to stand up, but was able to walk up to Dolly.

When I got to her I said, "Dolly. Get up, girl. C'mon..." She wasn't movin', so instead I ended up lying on top of her, and she didn't seem to mind. She was a lot comfier than lying on the ground.

Harry slowly came over and said, "Here. I'll help ya Ed. Here... I'll... never mind." He then walked back. I got back up and followed him back to the campfire. I was so drunk that I was wobbling around. When I came close to the campfire, I almost fell right into it.

James said, "Careful there Ed. You should...you should just sit down for a bit." I fell back, landing right on my ass. Didn't feel anything hurtin' because I was too drunk to notice. Bella was still wearing the top hat, but took it off and threw it up in the air. It landed right on my lap.

I threw it off to the side and said, "I hope I don't have to see that ugly thing again." There was another bottle next to me. So I opened it up and started drinking that one. James was sitting next to me while Harry was in the middle, and Joe was next to Bella.

Then I said, "Bella, I think you should give Joe a little kiss, huh?"

Harry added, "Yeah, he ...he needs it; been a while since that boy's made contact with any woman. Ain't that right Joe?"

Joe replied, "Well I don't think someone will ever love me like that."

James said, "That's nonsense. You're a…good-looking guy; at least right now."

We all laughed, but then Bella turned to Joe and kissed him on the lips. It lasted for about three seconds; much longer than any of us would have expected. Joe didn't react a whole lot. He was too drunk to even know what just happened. Harry stood up and began doing his impressions of us all. He would do that whenever he was drunk. He'd make funny faces and do weird voices that were supposed to sound like us. We still thought it was funny though. It was the best entertainment we had.

For Joe, he put on a grumpy lookin' mug and kept his head low saying, "I might look mean. I might look nasty. But deep down inside, I'm no tougher than a pussy cat! So watch out for these claws. They've clawed many men to death. They call me…they call me…uh, I guess they just call me Joe." Joe wasn't even paying attention. He was just trying not to pass out.

After that, Harry said, "And then there's Big Bad Ed! Or is it Big Nasty Ed?"

I replied, "Just call me Ed." Harry started to walk off, and after taking a few steps, fell flat on the ground. He was done for the night.

James shouted, "Woo-hoo! Harry finally stopped talkin'. Cheers to that." We all clinked our drinks over the fire. Joe then laid his head on the ground, and I did the same.

There was a brief moment of silence and then James said, "Buck…would be proud of us all."

I sat back up and asked, "Who's Buck again?"

James replied, "I forgot." After all of that, we passed out by the campfire and fell asleep pretty easy. I wasn't looking forward to waking up in the morning; or probably the afternoon

The next day I woke up and looked around to see everyone still asleep. It looked to be about late morning, and I had a terrible headache. I needed to get up, which wasn't easy. But I somehow found the strength to stand and not fall over. I could see things clearly and decided to leave everyone else be. Then I remembered Dolly. I looked around, but I didn't see her anywhere. My fast walking turned to running as I searched for her. It's not like she would've run away. She was always loyal to me, unless she was stolen. I ran faster, hoping that wasn't the case. As I ran further and further from camp, I began to whistle. I whistled a few times with no luck. Dolly loved to run around, so I figured she was out there but not too far. Then I saw something about a quarter of a mile away. I had a feeling it was Dolly, so I moved towards it and tried whistling louder. After the first few whistles, I saw it was a horse. And it was definitely Dolly. She was coming at me pretty fast, and I was hoping she wasn't about to kill me. When she got close enough, she slowed down just in time before running me over.

I said to her, "You're a crazy girl." I mounted up on her and rode back to the gang. It was good to see that Dolly was still in her prime. She had many more years to go. Eventually, everyone else in the gang was able to get themselves going. None of us were feeling all that great after so much drinkin', but it was worth it. We planned on moving out that day. But before we did, James told me to go into town for some horse food, as well as new brushes. I asked him, "Is it okay to go to Charlotte? I mean, we did commit a robbery there."

He said, "It's fine. They don't know who you are; just don't make yourself look suspicious." I nodded my head and started riding out.

It was a nice day out, and it was nice to be by myself for a bit. On the way to town, I thought about what the future would hold. James had talked about finding others to join our gang; saying we'd be stronger in greater numbers. Our way of life went against what most folks thought was right. But I didn't want to live my life as a sheep. I wanted to live my life as a man. We may have had a few close calls, but for the most part we were doin' just fine. Sure we lost Buck, but that wasn't under our control. I always knew that no matter where I was, all I needed was the gang, and they'd have my back. As I kept riding, the wind got stronger and almost knocked my hat off. I was wearing my normal hat. Not that silly top hat. That thing would have flown right off of my head. When the wind was too powerful, I had to keep my hand on top of my hat. Overall the ride wasn't too bad. I took it nice and easy. A while later I got to Charlotte, and there weren't many folks walking around. I got down to the main road and hitched Dolly in the same spot I hitched her in last time. I walked toward a general store when I saw something that almost made my heart stop. It was a wanted poster, with a drawing that looked like me. It was nailed up on a building, and I started reading it. It had my name, Ed Miller in big letters. Saying I was a part of the Mulligan gang. It had been a while since I read anything, so it took me some time to get through it all.

It said something like, "Ed Miller- killed both his parents and many other innocents. He is paired with James Mulligan and four to five others. They call themselves the Mulligan gang, and they won't stop til' civilization has ended. Ed is believed to be the second in command, and is wanted dead or alive." It said the reward was $1,000 just for me. I hesitated for a second, and took a deep breath. Then I ripped the wanted poster off the wall and put it in my handbag. I figured it was best for me to get out of there. So I did. I headed back to camp as fast as I could.

When I got back, James saw my worried look and asked, "Everything okay Ed?" I showed him the wanted poster and he took it without saying a word.

He started massaging his head with his thumb and whispered, "They ain't never gonna get us. Don't even bother telling the others. I don't want 'em being afraid."

I said, "Sure thing James." He was right; we knew how to play it safe. And we had seen a few wanted posters for us in the past, but this time, they knew who we were. It seemed like they were finally catching on to us. But this was wild country, and there was hardly any law to stop us. We'd been going for a long time, and knew how to play our cards right. This was our country, our time, our livelihood. They weren't gonna catch us yet.

PART 5

Four years passed since we made it to Georgia. We stayed in that state for the most part. But then traveled out to Alabama for one year and went back to Georgia. Two new men were with us. We picked them up in Alabama. They were brothers. About seven years apart from each other. They didn't have the nicest back story. Then again, none of us did. Their parents had died when they were little, and they spent most of their childhood in an orphanage. They said they couldn't take it anymore. Getting beaten almost every day wasn't what they had in mind for a decent life. So they ran away, and lived homeless for most of their lives. They started out surviving in the woods, then eventually movin' to a city. And they said it was better just livin' in the woods. I can't imagine what livin' in the city must have been like. Both of 'em had jobs that didn't pay very well, just barely getting by. At a certain point, they had enough of that. They began stealing and pulling off scams so they'd survive. At the end of the day, they were there for each other, which was something I admired about them. I always wondered if it was just me and Henry, or me and Cleet, maybe we'd be just like them. It was nice to think about that. Their names were pretty simple. The older one, Big Jack, and the younger one was called Lil' Jack. Their last name was Morrison, but they preferred to be called by their first names. James and I were the ones who first met them. And they gave us quite the first impression. The day started out with James and I in a town just buying a few things; nothing really out of the ordinary. All of a sudden we start hearing gunshots. We walked outside and saw a shootout goin' down between a sheriff, his deputy, and the two Jacks.

James asked me, "Do you think we should get the hell out of here? Or should we help 'em out?"

I replied, "Well, I only see two lawmen. Is that a good idea James?"

James said, "You make the move, or not."

I said, "Alright then." I pulled out both revolvers and put a few shots in both of those men. The sheriff was dead, but the deputy was crawling away. So I put another couple bullets in him just for good luck. He was done for after that. Jack and Jack were about 100 meters away from us. I waved to 'em, they waved back, and that's how it all started. They had been with us for almost two years. And having them made us a whole lot stronger.

We felt at home down south. In those four years, we robbed around 12 small town banks. As for stagecoaches, it was too high for me to count. Big Jack and Lil' Jack were our family, and they always served us well. Lil' Jack was about 20-years-old. He was a cocky kid who liked to get on everyone's nerves. Every now and then I had to whip him into shape.

I'd tell him, "If you were alone, you'd probably be dead by now. So don't go around thinking you're the boss or something." Eventually he'd learn to shut it every once in a while. His brother was quieter. Big Jack had a calm head on his shoulders. At first he only cared about himself and his brother; but now he cared about the rest of us just the same. At least it seemed that way to me. They had thick southern accents, and both of 'em could shoot pretty well. If they couldn't, they probably wouldn't have made it this far. Overall we liked them. They needed a family, and they finally had one.

Everyone else was still the same, except Bella was shared by me and James. I didn't love her like I loved Annie, but she was sure loyal to us. Some nights she'd sleep with me. Other nights she'd sleep with James. It was about half and half. Having her there for me was nice. She truly cared for me and wanted me to be alright. The bond between the three of us grew much stronger because of it. So much so that we started to have threesomes. Bella loved both of us just as much. We did it right in the camp too, where everybody could hear us. Lil' Jack wanted to bring a girl back to camp once just for the night.

But James would say, "If she's not loyal to us. Then she has no place being here." If the rest of the boys wanted to have a fun night, they'd go into town. Bella made it clear she wouldn't be gettin' down for anyone else but us two. One time Lil' Jack tried to make a move on her, and that didn't end well. He went up to her one morning while she was combing her hair.

He said, "How are you doing Bella? You're lookin' beautiful as always."

She replied, "Well, my hair isn't exactly what I'd call beautiful."

Lil' Jack thought he was all slick and said, "Don't worry about it Bella. You look just fine to me no matter what."

Bella replied, "Whatever you say." She was sitting on a blanket near the campfire, where we were making coffee. Then Lil' Jack sat down next to her and began to put his arm around her. I was around and saw what was going on, and didn't think much of it. She wasn't as comfortable with the two Jacks. She'd talk with Joe and Harry like they were close friends, and got along with Big Jack well enough. But I think something about Lil' Jack rubbed her the wrong way. She wasn't about to let him be all over her. As soon as he put his arm around her, Bella broke out of it, stood up, and pulled a knife on him.

She said, "Touch me again, and I'll kill you myself."

Lil' Jack started laughing and said, "You wouldn't do that. Deep down inside I know you really do love me. So please put that knife down, huh darling?"

Bella stormed off, and that's when I stepped in to have a talk with Lil' Jack.

I started walking up to him and said, "You know, she has killed men before."

He replied, "She sure is a tough one. And that's what I love about her. But one day she'll come around."

I said, "Yeah, she'll come around and slit your throat open. So just listen to me for a second. Your brother might be there for ya no matter what. And both of ya have been there for the rest of us, but try to stop annoying everybody. If James was here, he'd probably give you a beating. Did your brother ever give you a beating when you needed it?"

Lil' Jack said, "Well, sometimes he'd smack me on the head when we were young."

I replied, "He should have smacked you harder."

He said, "I'm sorry Ed, I'll do better. Just trust me." I told him to leave me be while I got my morning coffee. All of us agreed that butting heads was never a good thing. It wasn't good when Joe and Buck were at each other, and it wouldn't do us any favors now. If we wanted to live our way of life, we had to work with one another.

Over time, James convinced Bella to be more affectionate towards the other boys. One night she ended up doing it with almost the entire gang, even Lil' Jack. Everyone was inside James' tent, which had plenty of space. Everyone was there except for Joe, who sat outside staring at the ground. The rest of us were inside the tent with our clothes off. We were having one wild party in there. We went one at a time. And us boys went on for quite a while. Some of the other boys were drinking and hollering. Bella was the loudest out of all of us. She seemed to enjoy it the most.

In the middle of it I asked everyone, "What the hell could Joe possibly be thinking about out there?"

Harry replied, "He's thinking about how he'd rather get rear ended by a man." The boys were laughing, and I chuckled along.

Then I said, "Joe has never been attracted to men. I know he's not. He's thinking about something else."

James said in a playful way, "Then why don't you go join him, if that's your idea of fun."

I replied, "I can't do that. I need to show the rest of these boys how it's done."

Bella said, "Then show 'em, Ed." We continued on for a while longer. I forgot about Joe and did what I wanted with Bella. We all did.

After we finished I told Bella, "You sure can handle a lot." She nodded her head and walked away. I tried to not think about that too much.

A few days had passed since then, and things at the moment were pretty easy going. It was close to afternoon. Some of the boys were gathered 'round playing Blackjack. I was talking with James for a bit.

He told me, "Joe's been quieter than usual."

I replied, "I think he's been a little down. He told me he was doing alright. But maybe he just needs his time alone."

James said, "Maybe. What do you think life will be like 20 or 30 years from now? Do you think outlaws like us will still be around?"

I said, "Outlaws have always been around and always will be. The government knows not to mess with us. This gang has given them that message plenty of times. They want to pretend they're all tough, but on the inside, it's all hollow. And men who work for the government know this. I don't know how things will be in the future, but we'll just have to last as long as we can."

James replied, "That's it Ed... I've been trying these crackers that are sold cheap. They're actually pretty good. Not too salty like some of the others. I got some extra on me. You want to try one?"

I said, "Maybe later, just not all that hungry right now. But in the meantime I gotta take a piss."

James said, "They'll be gone soon enough. So don't take too long." I walked out to a big ol' tree and took care of everything right there. I buttoned my pants up, and saw what looked like a woman with blood all over her shirt. She was standing up, holding a double barrel shotgun. What disturbed me the most was the fact that she was staring right at me, looking like she wanted to kill me with that shotgun she was holding onto. She looked as real as anything else.

I shouted, "Hello!?" but got no response. So I stood where I was, frozen. I wondered to myself if I was having a dream, although it was more like a nightmare. She wasn't moving at all, and kept standing there. I put my hands on my knees and began to breathe heavily. I could barely stand on my own two feet. Then I tried to calm down by closing my eyes and looking at the ground. I looked back up, and she was still there. So I kept staring at the ground; and my breathing became louder and louder. I couldn't stop it.

Then I heard James running over to me saying, "What's going on over here? Is everything alright?" He put his arm over me to help me relax. But she was still there. James took me back to camp and said, "C'mon, just rest up a bit." I slowly walked with James and couldn't think straight at all. I had a feeling of wanting to vomit. That's when I realized, it was that woman I killed on the stagecoach many years ago. I didn't know whether she was real, or just an illusion. James looked around and saw nothing; same with the others. So I was the only one who saw it. I had never been one to get scared before. Even with everything I've seen and been through. But after seeing that, I was terrified.

I sat down on a chair as soon as I was brought back to camp. Everyone was confused, talking amongst each other.

Big Jack gave me some water and asked, "Should I pour that over your head?"

I replied, "No, thank you." and drank the water.

James shouted, "Give him some space! He's just been out in the sun too long." I turned around to see if the old woman was still there. And she was, standing there in the same spot. I turned back and tried not to think about it.

Then James knelt down and asked me, "What's going on Ed? Is there something that you're seeing?" I didn't know how to answer at first. I knew they'd all think I was crazy for what I saw. But I decided to just tell him anyway.

I whispered in his ear, "I see a woman out there. She's staring at me and holding a shotgun." James hesitated. He had no idea what to say.

So, he thought to himself for a moment and said to everybody else, "It needs to just be me and Ed right now. Go back to whatever you were doing." James quickly got some more water and poured it over my head and said, "So tell me what happened. You finished taking a piss and then you saw this, phantom?"

I replied, "Yeah I guess that's about right. And it's still there. Or, she's still there." James asked, "Who is she?"

I said, "A woman. A woman I killed a long time ago. I still remember what she looked like. And now I think she's real."

James said, "Well, it's a good thing you took a piss before you saw the phantom." James chuckled, but I wasn't able to laugh along with him. I didn't know whether the woman wanted to torture me, or end up killing me. Then I thought of trying to shoot it.

I stood up and said, "I'm gonna take a shot at it. I need to see if it's real." James just said, "Alright Ed." I loaded my revolver, took aim at the woman, and fired every single bullet I put in there. They all seemingly went right through her. Then I asked James if he could see it, and he still said no. I turned around and went back to my tent. It was the only place I could feel safe. I tried lying down for a while, no one bothered me. I ended up falling asleep for a little bit and woke up hearing some thunder. I got out of the tent, and the first person I saw was Harry walking by.

He came over to me and asked, "You feeling better?" And then I heard a voice I didn't recognize.

It was a man's voice saying, "You're doing alright. Yes you're ok. It's all good. Everything's fine." It wouldn't stop, just kept on going. I put my hand over my forehead and blankly stared off. I didn't know what to think of what was happening. All I knew was that I didn't have any control.

Harry said, "Ed! Are you doing ok?" The voice started getting louder, and then I heard another voice. This one wasn't so nice. It was saying the opposite.

Things like, "It's never gonna be ok. Life has always been bad, and it ain't gettin' better." Now both of those voices were going on in my head. I couldn't say anything, so I walked past him and walked over to Dolly. I needed to go somewhere alone. I didn't know what was going to happen. But part of me hoped I'd wake up and see everything was back to normal.

As I was about to ride off, James ran over and said, "Ed, where do you think you're going? It's gonna storm pretty bad!" I paused for a moment, trying to block out the two voices.

I said, "I'll come back. I promise." So I put my hat on my head, and rode into the storm.

I was riding Dolly across the fields, still hearing both voices. They started speaking less. And I was thankful for that. Hearing them was giving me a headache. The sky was covered in rain clouds. Soon enough it began to thunder. Then the rain came. I wasn't seeing the old woman, or anyone else for that matter. After riding around for a bit, I decided to head into the nearest town. I needed a drink. The town I went to was small, only having one main road with a few buildings. It was nighttime when I got there. Of course, no one was out with all the rain. It was pouring that badly, but it kept on coming. I hitched Dolly by the side street and started walking down to the bar. At that point I was soaking wet. That didn't bother me though. It hadn't rained for a while, and I kind of missed being in the rain.

Those voices were telling me things like, "Keep walking Ed. You don't know where you're going. It's time to get drunk." I thought about who the voices were, or if they were real people. I wondered if I hit my head a while ago, which could have caused all of this to start happening. Maybe they were haunting me or maybe not. I didn't know what to think. And drinking was the only thing that would help me relax a bit. I was only gonna have one anyway. I stepped into the bar, and saw about ten people in there. They all looked at me like I had been through hell. And it sure felt like I had. I slowly walked up to the bartender, and everyone else minded their own business.

The bartender said, "You look like you could use a drink there buddy. Rough day for ya?"

I replied, "Just give me a glass of whiskey." He didn't take long, and I took the whole thing in one shot. It felt like the best shot of whiskey I ever had. Then I had another, and a few more after that.

The bartender said, "I think you've had enough. You should take it easy." I felt I had had enough and decided to walk out and head back to camp. I was sure James and everybody else was getting worried. I was able to walk okay and see everything clearly. And then I realized the voices were much quieter. It felt like I could be at ease without voices constantly talking to me. It was a good feeling. I wasn't seeing any phantoms or nothing. Things almost seemed normal. It took longer than usual getting on Dolly. But I figured I'd be alright. She knew the way back. We headed off, even though it was dark out and still raining. We only traveled for a few minutes before I heard a voice. It sounded far away. And as I kept riding, it got closer and closer.

It was yelling, "Hello! Ed!" Then I heard another voice yelling the same thing but louder. It was hard to hear with all the rain. As I got close enough, I saw it was James and Joe.

James came closer to me with his horse and said, "Ed, we were worried about you. I'm glad to see you're alright."

Joe said, "We'll take care of you back at camp. It wasn't a good idea coming all the way out here."

I replied with, "Uh-huh."

Then James said, "We're all going back, let's just go slow." I followed them back and then touched the top of my head. Only to realize my hat was missing. Somehow it fell off. And now it was gone for good. It was a damn shame too, because I liked that hat a lot. However, a missing hat was the least of my problems.

Over the next two days, I tried to relax and keep a wet rag over my head. They made me some kind of tea that was supposed to calm my nerves. None of that worked. The voices weren't going to stop. There were times where they would become whispers, and other times where they'd be yelling at me. I pretended like it wasn't that bad. So everyone thought I was getting better, but I wasn't. However, I didn't see the old woman at all. I was worried if I'd see her again, or if I would see someone else. I figured I probably would, but didn't know when. Most of my day was resting inside my tent lying down. All of them came inside to talk with me at one point or another. I ended up telling them all the same thing.

"I don't know what's happening with me. But at some point I'll find out." Bella, Joe, and Harry suggested going to see a doctor, but I knew the doctor would have no idea what to do. That day I decided I was tired of lying around. So I left the tent and only saw Big Jack and Joe. They were both talking to each other, and then turned their heads towards me.

Joe asked, "How are things?"

I told him, "Just fine." Then I asked them, "Any more whiskey over here?"

Big Jack replied, "No Ed. You should probably stay off the drinking for now." Then I walked to Dolly and got on her. Big Jack came running over and said, "Hold on. You should take this before you go. You'll need it." He handed over his hat, which was old and dirty but I took it anyway. He said, "It's yours now."

I replied, "Thanks Big Jack. Tell the others they don't need to come looking for me. I can handle myself just fine." The voices in my head were getting loud again, so I rode out to the same town for more of that good ol' whiskey. I needed it now more than ever.

Later on, I stepped inside that same bar with the same bartender. There was one man sleeping over a table. Things in there were quiet. Just like everything else in that town. It was mid-day and not a whole lot was going on.

I went up to him and said, "I'll be needing some of that fine whiskey you got."

He replied, "Alright, just try to not overdo it this time." He poured me one glass and I gulled it down quick. Then I kept putting money on the counter, taking one glass after the other.

After taking one, I'd say, "C'mon, keep 'em coming."

Eventually he said, "I think you should start to slow down now."

I was already more drunk than last time and shouted, "I said give me more! Let's go!" A few glasses later, I was stumbling around the bar and talking to myself.

I started saying, "My father…was a real…son of a bitch. I guess that's why I'm a bastard."

The man sleeping woke up and said, "I guess at the end of the day, drinking solves a man's problems don't it."

I said to him, "Aw, shut up you." He chuckled to himself, and I stumbled back to the counter for one more drink.

He told me, "I think you've had enough for today."

I pulled out my gun and pointed it at him saying, "Now you're gonna give it to me. Or I'm gonna take it from ya." The other man quickly walked out of the bar, and it was just the two of us.

The bartender poured another drink while saying, "You're lucky there's no sheriff 'round here. Or you'd be going to jail." I kept the gun pointed at him, barely able to hold it straight.

Then I said, "This is how a man's meant to live. So don't go cryin' to the sheriff. There ain't nothing he can do." I took the drink with me and started to walk out.

The bartender shouted, "You forgot to pay for the last one!"

I turned my head back and replied, "Just consider yourself lucky I didn't shoot you." I drank every bit of that last bottle and threw it to the side. Since I was pretty drunk, I didn't know what I was doing. So I headed back into that bar to talk to the bartender some more. I was lucky he was nice, because if he wasn't he would have shot me by now.

As I walked in he said, "I'm all out of whiskey sir. Honest." I walked up to the wall on the other side and sat against it. I started thinking more about my father. He used to be such a strong man. I thought about him every day after what happened, but eventually I tried to forget about all of that. It was always stuck in my mind though. It wasn't going anywhere. I remembered how he talked about hearing voices and how he started drinking all the time. I was winding up the same way. It didn't seem like I had any control of it. I needed to find out exactly what was going on with me. I decided that if I saw the old woman, I'd approach her. Hopefully she wouldn't have that shotgun with her. I just wanted an answer. In the meantime, I figured I'd chat up the bartender for a bit. At least I was going to when I saw him scurry out of there. I didn't blame him, since I did yell at him and threaten him. Probably wasn't the best idea. I felt alone, confused, and didn't know what to do. I sat there by myself for a few more minutes, and then walked back to Dolly. She was the one that was always there for me.

A little while later, I got off Dolly and just laid on the grass. There were some clouds in the sky that covered the sun. As I laid there, I imagined how different my life would have been if my father hadn't done what he did, or if my brothers didn't die.

I kept hearing a voice saying, "What's done is done." That was the nicer voice talking. Drinking at the very least quieted the voices or made the bad one go away. I thought to myself, "This is as good as it's gonna get." Then a tear went down my face. Now I've cried once or twice as a boy. I will admit that. But that was the first time I ever cried as a man. It was only one tear, and I never thought that could happen. I took a few deep breaths, and ended up falling asleep right there. That lasted for a few hours. When I woke up it was night. I needed to get back to camp before the others started worrying about me. I still felt pretty tired. It's not like I had been sleeping well with the voices going on in my head. My drunkenness was feeling worse. I had no clue where I was going, so I just started riding. Several minutes had passed and I wasn't sure where I was going. Then, I heard some people singing. I got off Dolly and walked closer to the group of people. I hoped they could help me find my way. When I got close enough, I saw it was the whole gang, and felt a sigh of relief. They were singing one of those old folk songs. But when I went up to them, they ignored me and began the chorus. They sang *"Big Bad Ed was in his bed-Then both his parents wound up dead-Now he's messed up in the head-It's better off to just call him Ed."* I was standing right next to them. And in the blink of an eye, they all vanished. All I could see was grass. There was nothing but silence. I sat down, and fainted soon after.

It seemed like I woke up, but I knew I was having a dream. I just hoped it wouldn't turn into a nightmare. I was in a town. And soon I realized it was Canvas Ridge, the town where I tried out the pomade for my hair. Everything was just like I remembered. The weather was nice, and so was the town. The only difference was that I was alone. I walked down the street to see if I'd find somebody. As I walked, my body was moving slowly. Maybe it was because time slowed down, or because it felt like my heart would stop if I saw the old woman. I began hearing a fiddle being played. It was coming from the other side of town, and was playing one of those romantic songs. As I got closer, I saw Bella dancing with Joe, swaying side to side along with the fiddle. I said hello to them, but they didn't respond. It seemed like I was a ghost. I turned my head and was surprised at what I saw. It was James, slow dancing with his lost love, Elizabeth. She looked more alive than ever; and they were looking straight into each other's eyes. They didn't notice me either, so I looked around to see if I could find anyone else. I decided to walk into the hair parlor and see if that hair cutter was there. He was there alright, and cutting a man's hair. I sat down on the waiting chair and looked around the small, cluttered space. The wooden floor was creaking and the place needed some dusting. I didn't remember it being that bad in real life. However it was just a dream. The hair cutter looked the same to me. He was still a small man that almost looked like he needed a stool. He wasn't saying anything. Nor was the person getting their hair cut. I got up from my seat to take a closer look at the customer. He looked familiar. When I was only a few feet away from them, they turned their heads towards me, and I saw the customer was my father.

He said to me, "Hello Ed. Long time no see." I panicked and ran out of there. I shut the door behind me and went back to see if everyone was still dancing. When I got over there they were, but with a song that sounded different. The melody had changed slightly and was a little faster. The fiddle player started getting into it more, swaying his body along with the rhythm. The others were dancing the same way, by swaying side to side while holding each other's hands. Then I heard someone moving right behind me. So I turned around and saw an old man, dancing with the old woman. They kept on dancing as if I wasn't there, and it looked like they were having the time of their lives. There was no blood on the old woman, or her husband. I figured this at least wouldn't be a bad dream. They started dancing much more lively than everyone else. Doing arm twirls, picking her up and leaning her back as if they were young kids dancing for the first time. I just stood there and watched, and then all of a sudden, a bunch of other musicians were playing with the fiddler. There was what looked to be a bass, two violins, and of course, a harmonica. They were playing an upbeat country-style song. It sounded pretty good to me. Now everyone was doing some square dancing. Not something I really cared for, but it was fun to watch. I even began clapping along. But at the same time, I couldn't help but feel alone. Part of me wished Annie was there, and another part of me didn't. That was all over a long time ago. I just danced by myself, which was still fun to do. I was tapping my foot, moving from side to side, and shouting "Woo-hoo!" over and over again. No one else was saying anything, they just kept on dancing. I started clapping my hands with the beat and stomping my foot. I probably looked like an idiot, but it was only a dream. At a certain point, I stopped because the song wasn't ending. I didn't think it was ever going to end. But when I stopped, everyone else stopped. No one was dancing, and the musicians weren't playing. Everyone turned and looked at me, and I had no idea what was going to happen. The fiddle player took a step back. There were two musicians on his left and two on his right. They came closer to me, and I saw who they really were. It was four men I killed in the botched general store robbery with James. Then I saw a bullet hole in all of their heads. They didn't look too happy about it either. The old man and woman started walking towards me as well, with a plain expression on their faces. Then straight ahead of me, I saw Arthur Williams. He had a bunch of gunshots in his chest, looked at me confused. As if he was going to ask me something. But none of them said anything. They just kept walking closer and closer, and I started taking a few steps back. I looked towards the old couple, and saw what made me feel sicker than I had ever felt. The old man had shrapnel in his chest, and the old woman? Well I did shoot her head off, so it wasn't exactly a pretty sight. All of them had me surrounded.

And all I could do was lie down and say, "I'm sorry. I'm sorry." over and over again. I was all curled up and kept on saying that. Until I woke up saying, "I'm sorry." I stood up and could feel my heart racing. I was covered in sweat, and was eventually able to calm myself down. The only thing I heard was Dolly pouting and walking around, and I wondered if that would be the end of the voices and visions. I figured it probably wasn't the end. All of those people I killed, it wasn't my fault. It was what fate wanted. Fate is what decides who dies and who survives. I was born to be a survivor, and couldn't let those damn ghosts haunt me forever. I needed help but decided to worry about that some other time. More importantly, I had to find my way back to the gang, otherwise I wouldn't last very long by myself.

It took two days, but eventually I found 'em. They told me I was lucky. I told 'em it wasn't a big deal, and that I would ease up in the drinking. Within a few hours of being back with the gang, the voices crept up again, and I'd see Arthur Williams watching me from a distance. It was only him. He fortunately didn't have a weapon on him. He just had his arms crossed, and kept staring at me. I ignored it as best as I could. A few days passed, and it was a bright and sunny afternoon. Bella was sitting down doing some knitting. She softly hummed a tune as she knitted.

As I heard it, my voices were saying, "Absolutely beautiful. I love it. Awful! Can't stand it! Sounds like an angel." It was like listening to two brothers that couldn't agree with each other on anything. And I couldn't get 'em to shut up. Sometimes the nice voice would take control of my mind, and other times it was the other way around.

I wanted to talk to her for a bit, so I went up to her and said, "Looks like you're pretty busy there."

She replied, "Not really, just tryna pass the time. Is there something on your mind Ed?"

I said, "There's always something on my mind."

Bella put down what she was knitting and said, "Well, do ya want to talk about it?"

I replied, "That sounds good. But let's go out into the fields away from everyone else. I'm tired of sitting around in camp." We held hands and walked down the field. Eventually we found a nice spot to sit down, and I began telling her about my problems. I started off by saying, "The voices, they keep talking to me."

She asked, "What are they saying, Ed?"

I replied, "Sometimes they say good things. Other times they say bad things. It's been back and forth between the two."

Then she asked, "And how about the ghosts…or spirits…whatever they are."

I said, "I'm not sure what they are either. And I don't think I'll ever know for sure. But I'm starting to think there's something wrong with my brain or something. And I think my father had the same problem. But there was no reason for him to…do what he did."

We both took a deep breath, and then Bella asked, "What's it like? Dealing with all of that?"

I replied, "It's like, having dreams, while I'm awake."

She said, "That sounds nice."

I said to her, "It ain't."

Then Bella said, "All of us have your back. But you gotta cut down on the drinking honey. It'll end up killing ya pretty quick."

I said, "I know. I'm trying to get better with it."

She said, "I know you will. You always figure a way out of everything."

And I replied, "So it seems."

Then Bella asked me, "What do you think is gonna happen to you when you die?"

I took a moment to think, and then said, "Well, my momma believed in angels. And over the years I've stopped believing in all of that. But now with what I've been seeing, maybe angels are real. I don't know. When I was younger, I used to think my momma would come to me as an angel, and have her arms wide open. Then she'd take me someplace else. Someplace that was hopefully nicer. But now I think she'd want me burning in hell."

Bella replied, "I know she wants you to be alright, no matter what happens."

I said, "Maybe." A few moments later, we heard James calling us over. So we walked back to gather 'round with everyone else. Whenever we rallied up together, it was for something big, usually a robbery. We made loads of money with all the banks, stores, and stagecoaches we robbed. But most of that money was pissed away from gambling thanks to Harry, James, the two Jacks, and… well…the rest of us. I wasn't as much of a gambler. But I sure as hell was when it came to gunfights. I wanted to make sure the others knew I was still the best shot here, and that I wasn't losing it. I tried my best to pretend like there were no voices, and no phantoms. For the most part I did a good job with that. Everyone respected me just as much, and I wasn't about to let anybody think differently about me. We all huddled around James, and he started talking.

"Once again, we need money. And I know we all like to have fun, but we have to be a little more…conservative, with our money. Now if someone decides to be a drunken idiot, and spend all of our hard-earned money in one place, then they're gonna have a long talk with me. And if they have a problem with that…well…that won't be good for them. I do trust you all, but don't think you're gonna fool me." Then James turned to Harry, pointed his finger at him and said, "Especially you Harry. You've been our biggest problem."

Harry replied, "That's bullshit. You've been loose with money just like the rest of us."

James chuckled and said, "I know, but you get drunk, and play all them poker games, and lose it all. And now I think Ed is picking up your habits."

I told James, "I'm getting better."

Then he shouted, "Well I'm trying to keep us all going! But I need y'all to help me out here. This world ain't that nice, and if we don't get our acts together, we won't make it much longer." There was silence as James looked at all of us. We all knew he was right. We were living every day like it was our last; soon enough we'd be digging our own graves. James began saying, "Me and Big Jack have been hearing about this stagecoach. Apparently it's got a boatload of money. I'm not joking; they say it's carrying almost $1,000. This would be the richest stagecoach we'll ever rob. And I know it sounds too good to be true, but a lot of people have talked about it. They've been saying the money will be used to build more railroads. And I think we can all agree that's a wonderful thing. However, having more trains means more people, and more control from the fat greedy bastards writing the laws. And that ain't good for us. So for this one, we're all gonna go. We need as much firepower as we can get. There's an old abandoned town that the stagecoach will be passing through. It's the only good spot for us to strike. There ain't a whole lotta trees to cover us down those roads. So that town is our only option. We've got one week. Be ready for it. For now, let's just keep our heads straight. Speaking of that, how are you feeling Ed?"

I replied, "I'll be okay. Don't you worry 'bout me."

James said, "Good. I'm gonna head out to ride for a while. We're all having that deer tonight so Lil' Jack doesn't moan about not having enough meat. See y'all later." We all scattered off and I took a walk by myself for a bit.

I started hearing voices saying, "You know it ain't good. Everyone will wind up dead. Just plain dead, dead, dead!" I tried massaging my head to make it go away, and that helped a little. I couldn't let the seed of doubt get in my head. Doubt never got anybody anywhere. And the voices weren't gonna stop me, nor the phantoms. I wasn't about to let any of that get in my way.

That night we were all gathered 'round the campfire, eating some of the juiciest and tastiest deer meat I ever had. Big Jack was the one cooking it, and whoever taught him taught him well. We had some potatoes and vegetables, all on some expensive plates and silverware. There was no question we were living well, probably a little too well.

Harry was yelling at Lil' Jack saying, "You best not touch Napoleon again! The second I saw her missing I nearly fainted."

Lil' Jack replied, "You know, I think that banjo is getting to your head. How long have you had that ol' thing?"

Harry said, "Much longer than you have been alive."

Then Big Jack said, "I don't think you'll ever learn, Lil' Jacky. Never have, never will. Without me, you would've been dead a long time ago." Big Jack then drank from the beer bottle in his hand. But I don't know how he put up with him either. I'm just glad he wasn't my brother. If Buck were here, he would have been whipped right into shape. Or…he would have killed him.

Then Joe said to Lil' Jack, "Act decent, and you'll be treated decent. Plain and simple."

Lil' Jack said, "Well he really told me, didn't he?"

James said to Joe, "First Buck gave you a hard time. Now it's a kid. You just can't seem to win."

Joe replied, "I guess not." Now I had Buck on my mind. And a moment later, I saw him sitting right next to me. The Jacks, James, Bella, and Harry were sitting on chairs, while Joe and I were sitting on an old log. It wasn't the most comfortable thing to sit on, but I was used to it. So I kinda preferred it. Buck was sitting at the end of the log on my right side. He was just blankly staring into the fire. Not moving a muscle. Of course, no one else saw Buck. So I pretended he wasn't there, even though he really wasn't.

Lil' Jack said to his brother, "Tell everyone 'bout the story of you during the civil war, and how you escaped from those Union soldiers."

Big Jack sighed and said, "If y'all wanna hear it. Here it goes…It ain't the nicest campfire story. At the time, it was just me and my brother. And this wasn't too long after our parents passed. So Lil' baby Jack was in an orphanage.

I did go back for him a while later. One of the biggest mistakes I ever made. But I was on my own, helping the Confederacy. They gave me food, shelter, and protection. Those boys were good to me. They taught me how to shoot, ride a horse, and just how to be a man."

James interrupted saying, "Just get to the part when you got captured."

Big Jack said, "Alright I will. I was with a battalion encamped with the Confederate army in 1864. I would spend most of my time doing chores. They had me working all the time. And I enjoyed it. We were in a rural area with some small houses around. It was all beautiful to look at. At least until gun and canon smoke turned the sky all grey. It was summer time, and it felt like one of the hottest summers; especially with that scraggly old uniform they made me wear. It was too big for me too."

James interrupted again saying, "We don't need to hear about your life story. So you got captured, then what happened?"

Big Jack paused for a second to collect his thoughts and said, "I can't tell the story right, if you won't let me tell it from start to finish."

Lil' Jack added, "I've heard him saying the same story for years. There ain't no stopping it. So the Union army attacked and you fought 'em all by yourself. And how did ya do that exactly?"

Harry said, "He started telling 'em the most boring story he could think of and they retreated, the end."

Big Jack was getting a little frustrated and said, "Ya'll are a bunch of idiots. So, my hands were tied together and the Union soldiers were asking me questions. It's not like I was going to answer them, so the Commander got mad and started beating me, whipping me, and then threatened to break my bones if I didn't talk. The rest of 'em were alright, but that Commander was a real son of a bitch. He didn't care that I was just a kid. But it probably didn't help that I spat right in his face. He was still an evil man though. And I know Confederates weren't too nice to slaves, but neither side was perfect. Anyway, I ended up making friends with this one Union soldier that treated me well. He couldn't cut the rope off. But we talked quite a bit and had a lot of laughs. A few times he even brought me candy."

Then Harry said, "Let me guess what happened next, Lil' Jack came in to save the day right?"

James added, "With the way those boys shoot, they could've taken on the entire Union army."

Big Jack pouted and said, "In the end, I got lucky. That friend I made. I killed him. I knocked down with one good head butt. Then I started to cut myself free, but he tried to stop me. So I cut his throat open. Then I was able to sneak out during the night."

I shouted, "Now that's what I'm talking about! That's what we all wanted to hear. Not a bad story."

Big Jack said, "All the friends I had in the Confederacy died. Not one was spared. Once again, I had no one. So I went back to Lil' Jack." We all nodded our heads. Big Jack had been through a lot like the rest of us. But at least we had each other. Soon enough, Harry started cracking jokes. We didn't mind it too much, because Buck used to be the one cracking the most jokes. Now it was Harry. I wasn't even paying attention to what he was saying and kept looking at Buck, who was still sitting there. I was tempted to try touching him to see what would happen. And when I did, my hand went right through him like he was a ghost. He wouldn't move or nothing. He was no more than a lump in a log. I kept to myself and was finishing up my meal, when Buck turned his head towards me and I saw his gut wrenching, smashed in face.

I immediately dropped my plate, almost throwing up and said, "I've lost my appetite." I didn't tell anybody what I was seeing. I just told 'em I needed a few minutes alone, which turned to spending the rest of that night alone and trying to forget about Buck.

As more days passed, things weren't getting much better. The voices I could handle okay most of the time. But the visions were getting worse. I'd see bunches of people walking around that weren't there. Or sometimes I'd see spiders crawling all over my body. But I'd see Arthur and the old woman the most. When I saw the old woman, she at least had her head on her shoulders. But that could always change. There was also one other person I started seeing just as much as the other two. It was my father. I'd see him all the time. I didn't have an answer for any of it. Maybe it was a curse. Maybe the Devil was calling for me. It was nothing good, but all I could think of was getting another drink. I hadn't had one for the past few days. And James wanted me staying away from it for now. He knew it wasn't doing me any good. And I knew it too. But when no one was around, I got myself on Dolly and went over to a different town. I figured that same bartender wouldn't want to see me again. And this other town was bigger, and farther away. But that didn't matter to me. As long as they had whiskey I was going over there. It was hot and humid, like it was just about every day. I wasn't gonna have too much. And I decided I wouldn't even have whiskey, and just stick with a bottle of beer instead. I had to keep telling myself to only have one or two at the most.

The nasty voice was kicking in saying things like, "This is your fault Ed. You're gonna die from this. You'll never make it now." But I couldn't let any of that mess with my head. I had to be in control. Or at least have as much control as I could. Almost an hour later I got to the town. I didn't see any visions along the way. But I never saw visions when riding Dolly. I was seeing new visions all the time, and I tried to ready myself for what I might see. But I was never ready. I slowly walked down the street, and things were fine so far. People were walking around, work was getting done; it was just another day. I walked with my head down and tried taking deep breaths to calm my nerves. When I got closer to the saloon, I looked up and saw momma. She was far away, but I knew it was her. She had that long sleeve blue shirt, with her long skirt. And she was sweeping the ground in the middle of the street with her broomstick. Most of all, she had wide angel wings on her back. I never thought I'd see that. But that vision had been in my head since the day she died. I walked past the saloon and was getting closer to her. She kept looking at the ground and sweeping, but I felt like she was alive.

When I was a few feet away from her, I started saying, "Momma? Are you there? Is that really you? Momma!?" I got right up to her, and put my hand out to touch her face. Then I blinked, and she was gone. All I saw was a bunch of people staring at me, looking confused. They must have thought I was a crazy person, which I felt was becoming true. I was losing my mind every day, and going to the doctor seemed like a good idea. But part of me thought he would try to poison me or something. So I decided it was better to fight this alone. It was my mind, and no one knew what was going on better than me. My whole life I had been one tough son of a bitch. And I thought one day, all of this would make sense. But for now I needed a beer. The plan was to only have a quick one, and all of that was going well. I was leaning against the front counter, holding my beer. There were a few men behind me being a little loud. But I didn't worry about it. Everything was going alright until I heard one of those men talking about me.

I had my back turned against them, and I heard one of 'em say, "That's the crazy drunk. Ya'll would have been laughing so hard if you saw him. He just walked in the middle of the road moaning 'Momma! Momma! Oh momma!'"

I got angry. I wasn't about to let him make a fool of me. I slammed my beer on the counter and turned around. He looked at me right in my eyes, and I looked straight back at his.

Then I stepped right in front of him and said, "You should be careful of what you say about me." He was my height. And a little bit bigger.

He replied, "I'll say whatever the hell I wanna say. Now get outta here and go back to the street to look for your momma." After hearing that, I had enough. I tackled him to the ground and threw some good punches at him. He could take it pretty well though. The men around us were cheering and started circling around. They were in for a real good show. I got him a couple times in the face, but then he kicked me off and got back up. I kept my arms up to cover my face because if he gave me one good hit, it would be over. He started throwing some wild punches at me, striking my ribcage and stomach. They were all pretty hard. Then he shoved me into the counter, and my back went right into it. I was pinned against it as he quickly came up to me. I grabbed my beer bottle which was almost empty, and tried to smash it on his head until he blocked my arm. He kicked me towards one of the tables, and I fell back a few feet. I was still standing though. The beer bottle was now on the floor, and he picked it up from the floor as he came over to me. It was me or him, and I wasn't gonna let it be me. So I took a couple steps towards him and tried kicking him, but he grabbed my ankle with his other arm.

Now I was hopping on one foot, and he shouted, "Dance for me!" After a few seconds, he let go, and tried to hit me with the beer bottle, but I blocked with my elbow. Then he tried to grab me with his other arm, but I blocked that as well. We were trying to break each other's defense, until I kneed him in the groin. Then I quickly shoved him against a table, and got some good punches on him. Now he was bleeding and getting some nice bruises. But he stopped it by hitting me on top of the head with that beer bottle. I quickly took a few steps back, putting my hand against my forehead. Now I was bleeding a lot worse than he was. He came up to me again with his fists closed, ready to kill me. I dodged his first punch and gave him a good uppercut. He almost fell on the floor, but managed to keep himself standing. I gave him some more punches and was giving it to him pretty good. Then I grabbed him by the shirt, and threw him against the counter. I punched him in the face as hard as I could, and it knocked him out cold. I let him go and he fell to the ground. Everyone looked at me, surprised that I won. My reputation may have not been for fist fighting, but I could still hold my own against a fool like him. And a fool he was for talking crap about me. I turned towards the gate of the saloon and began to walk out.

As I walked out, I said to the bartender, "Don't worry. You won't see me here again." My head was still bleeding from that bottle. I needed to get myself cleaned up. When I got outside, I saw my old friend, Arthur Williams.

He was pointing a pistol at me and yelled, "I think you're a piece of garbage!" He shot the gun at me four times, and just like that, he was gone. I didn't care much about seeing Arthur. I just needed to get the hell out of there. When I got to Dolly, I patted her for a bit and rested my head against her.

I said to her, "Let's get out of here girl. This ain't the place for us." I got on Dolly, and she started walking. Before I left, I looked back to see if my momma was there, but she was gone. So I looked forward and gave Dolly a kick to go faster. I wasn't planning on going back to that town.

The old harmonica I had was helping me out. It made me forget about all the visions and voices, and everyone in the camp was saying I had gotten better at it. I also started washing my face whenever I woke up. For a day or two, it seemed like things were getting better. But soon we'd do that stagecoach robbery, and I wasn't sure how I felt about that. We needed that money, but we all knew it was gonna be risky. James kept telling me to focus on the gang, and not get so caught up with what was going on in my head. But no matter what, I couldn't stop it. I'd see new visions all the time. And they were only making me more afraid. I had gone to a small creek by myself to take a bath, and was at the edge scrubbing myself. Then I saw my father on the other side, and it didn't look like he was wearing any clothes.

As soon as I saw him, he asked me, "Do ya wanna go fishing?" I looked away and started scrubbing my arms. He just stayed there, staring at me.

I decided to answer, "As long as you don't go drinkin'." He wasn't saying anything, so I went about my business and then dunked my head in the water. When I came up, I saw he was gone.

I felt a sigh of relief, but then the voices kicked in saying, "This ain't a nice place. Your father is gonna drown you." I left that creek and figured I'd rather smell like shit for the rest of my life than go in there ever again. That same day, I tried to calm myself down by playing a game of checkers with Harry. And I didn't even like Checkers, but Harry said it would do me good.

We played for a little while, but I lost every time. The voices kept on talking and I couldn't concentrate at all.

Harry even said, "You gotta do better than that Ed."

And I replied, "Why don't you…get…uh, never mind." I had no idea why it what getting worse that day, but it was scary. My mind was working against me and I couldn't stop it. Later on that day, I just got up from a chair and saw Bella come up to me.

She asked, "How has everything been going Ed?" One moment, it was just her in front of me. Then in a flash I saw almost 30 people behind her, staring me down. Most of them were people I had killed. They looked normal, but also looked angry. The old woman was there holding hands with her husband. I saw my father, that brave citizen from the general store, deputies, and plenty of sheriffs. I even saw Arthur again with his arms crossed. It was intimidating to say the least.

Bella asked again, "Ed? How is everything?"

I looked at her and replied, "Ah, just fine."

She came up to me and put her hand on my shoulder saying, "I'll be there for just you tonight, no one else."

I told her, "Sounds good." and walked over to my tent and went inside. That was the only place I felt safe from all of those spirits, or imaginary people, or whatever they were. It wasn't like I could talk with them, and I didn't think anyone would understand what I was going through. If I talked with the gang about how bad it really was, they'd think I'd gone crazy. So I wouldn't talk much about it.

Dusk had set in, and I was still in my tent. The voices were getting quieter, and I could finally feel at ease. I then got on my knees, put my hands together, and began praying.

I kept my eyes closed and said, "I don't know if you're listening to me right now, but I need you to hear me for just a minute." Then I took a deep breath, knowing I had to go through with this. "I guess you know what happened to me and my family. That was a long time ago. Back then I prayed for you, but you never answered a single prayer. I had to go through it all on my own. But right now I need you more than ever. I don't know who else to turn to. You may not understand me, and I don't think I'll ever understand you. But please, help me make sense of what's happening to me. Do you think I deserve this? Are you the one causing it!? Well, are ya?" I got no answer. So I opened my eyes, stood up, and figured it was a waste of time. Though I didn't have a whole lot going on, so I went outside to get some fresh air and hoped the visions would give it a rest. I stood outside watching the sunset, and then heard someone come up from behind me.

It was Joe, saying, "Mind if I join you Ed?"

I replied, "Uh… sure, why not." He stood right beside me and we both watched the sunset.

Then he asked, "Have things been getting better?" I wasn't sure of what to say, so I took a few seconds.

Then I replied "Not exactly; not at all to be honest."

Joe said, "You know, I was thinking you should go see a doctor. He could help you out."

I said back, "I'm not sure about that. I'm just afraid of what he might do to me."

Joe replied, "What might he do to you? He can probably help you out better than anyone else can."

I replied, "He might try to hurt me or something."

Joe said, "I don't think so. Trust me, that won't happen. And you know that. You're just not thinking clearly because your own mind is getting in your way."

I replied, "Nowadays, it feels like everything is getting in my way."

Then Joe said, "Maybe it's just you."

I said, "Maybe you're right." There was a long moment of silence as we stared at the sunset getting darker and darker.

Then Joe said, "Go see a doctor, Ed. They can give you medicine or find some way to help you. Getting help ain't always a bad thing."

I replied, "I'll think on it later. But I appreciate the advice."

Joe added, "I know I've never been great at talking to people; but if you need to talk, I'll be around."

I yawned and said, "Take it easy tonight Joe." He gave me a pat on my shoulder and walked away. It was getting late, and I needed some shut eye. Part of me really did believe the doctor was gonna try to kill me, but a bigger part of me knew that was wrong. Before my problems started, I never had thoughts of a doctor trying to kill me. It was probably just my mind playing tricks on me. And I was starting to see how bad things were getting. I couldn't control what I was thinking, seeing, or hearing. Day by day, I was slowly falling apart. In the morning I decided I'd finally go and see a doctor.

The next day I woke up feeling tired, unsure whether or not I was really gonna see that doctor. It's not like I gave myself a good reputation in the last two towns I was in. SoI'd have to go off to some place farther away. What Joe said got me thinking about it.

And the voices were saying, "Now is the right time. Get going. You'll find a way Ed." It sounded like my voices agreed with Joe, especially since I wasn't hearing anything bad. I planned on leaving in the morning, since most days I'd wake up pretty early. But now all of that was different. I'd be up all night, then fall asleep for an hour, and then wake up sweating and feeling panicked. Every day was a nightmare. Currently it was late morning, so I was doing a little bit better. Later, I'd see the doctor in a nice little town known as "Old Meadow Creek." It was a town where people sold plenty of livestock, plenty of auctions, and had a piss poor excuse for a saloon. I liked being there; we all did. The people there were decent, and were easy to get along with. Eldridge might have been the one town we didn't rob. We had been in Georgia for quite some time and had seen just about all of it. Before I left, I got some eggs I kept in my basket and grabbed a pan. Anything to fill me up a little would be enough to get me through the trip. I was eating just fine a few days ago, but I was barely doing anything, apart from drinking. So I hardly ate anything. But right now, I was starving. There was a small fire going in the middle of camp with no one else around. So at least I'd have some peace and quiet. I cracked the eggs into the pan and had it right over the fire; nothing better than that. I even had some chives and pepper that I threw in there. It looked like a damn good meal to me. Then of course, Lil' Jack came over. He sat right across from me, and watched as I was cooking my eggs. I couldn't deal with him and all his nonsense. He was nothing but a pest, and just played stupid mind games all the time. I wasn't saying a word to him, and hoped he'd keep his mouth shut for once. He was just sitting there watching me and I didn't even care. It looked like the eggs were finished.

I put 'em on a plate and was about to take the first bite when he said, "Well Ed, it looks like you're doing better."

In the middle of chewing, I said, "A little bit. I need to be alone for now."

Lil' Jack replied, "Oh come on, you've hardly been talking to anyone. It ain't healthy being alone for that long. You know, me and some of the boys are doing another phony poker game. We'll make some good money off of that. You should join us."

I replied, "I got other things to do. So if ya don't leave now, I'm gonna cut you into pieces and cook you for dinner. Just gotta add some salt, and it shouldn't taste too bad."

Lil' Jack smirked and then replied, "No wonder they call you Big Bad Ed. You can be one nasty son of a bitch." I proudly said, "That's right, the nastiest of them all." Lil' Jack then asked, "So how many things do you see? And how many different voices have you heard?" I took a few more bites, pretending I didn't hear him. Once again he asked, "Um, Ed? Hello?"

I was already getting fed up with him, and calmly said, "Let me put it to you this way. You're the last thing I wanna see, and the last thing I wanna hear. So go away right now and I'll have one less problem to worry about."

Lil' Jack gave one long sigh and said, "You sure are strange."

I said, "Yep, especially nowadays." and finished my meal. A few minutes later I went over to Dolly, gave her a treat, and whispered in her ear, "We're going to the doctor today girl. Hopefully he doesn't end up trying to kill me. And hopefully I don't end up trying to kill him." I rode out, knowing it was this or nothing.

Later on I got to the town of "Old Meadow Creek." It was just like I remembered, looking all old and run down. On top of that, it smelled like cow turd. It was just how the gang and I liked it. Dolly and I walked down the dirt road and looked around at the people. They were keeping themselves busy with loading up wagons, selling chickens, and painting some of the old buildings. I saw the doctor's office on my right, and it looked like it was just built yesterday. I wasn't even sure if they had any kind of doctor last time I was here. The building for the doctor could have just been built. Or maybe it was always there and I just wasn't paying attention. Either way it didn't matter. What mattered was that I was where I needed to be. The place was so busy that there was no place to hitch Dolly. I ended up hitching her by a tree a few yards outside of the town. It's not like I was gonna be there for very long. And if someone tried to steal her, she'd kick their head in before they could even get on. That happened to one feller who didn't survive it. Couldn't say I felt sorry for him. When I hitched Dolly, I told her I'd be back soon. I walked over to the Doctor's and went right up to the front door. For a few seconds, I just stared at it. Then I took a deep breath and walked myself in. The first thing I saw was a man at the front desk.

He looked up at me and said, "Hello sir. Are you sick today?"

I replied, "I wouldn't say I'm sick, at least not physically." He told me to take a seat and that the doctor would see me shortly. I sat there waiting for a few minutes when I heard footsteps coming from the hallway. Then I saw a man who looked to be the doctor, who looked to be pretty old. All of his hair was white, and he had quite a few wrinkles. I figured if he managed to live that long, he must have done something right. He came over to me to shake my hand and introduced himself. His name was Dr. Wilson, and he seemed nice enough. I followed him back into his office. Once I got in there, it reeked of something. I didn't wanna know what.

He pushed his glasses up and asked me, "What brings you here today son?"

I told him, "Some problems I've been having. And it's not going away."

The doctor asked, "You're gonna have to be more specific than that. What kind of problems are you dealing with?"

I replied, "Problems inside my head I think. I'm pretty sure my father dealt with the same thing. And no one else can see the things I see and hear."

Dr. Wilson asked, "Seeing and hearing what exactly?"

I said, "Seeing and hearing people; people that I've known in my life. The voices are from people I don't even know. But they say things to me all the time. Some of it ain't bad. But most of what I hear ain't too nice." The doctor looked at me funny, probably thinking I was crazy. I started thinking it was a waste of time coming down here.

Then he asked, "So what are those voices saying now?"

I replied, "They're telling me that being here ain't a good idea."

Dr. Wilson said, "Are you the only one that sees these people and hears the voices?"

I said, "Yes."

Dr. Wilson took a brief moment and then said, "I'll be honest with you, that's one of the craziest things I've ever heard. Never in my life would I have thought of someone telling me something like that." He began chuckling to himself and asked, "Are you just joking with me now?"

I said back, "Does it look like I'm joking?" I was looking at him right in the eyes, and then he knew I was being serious.

He asked me, "Do you think something might have caused all of it to start happening?"

I told him, "I don't think so. It only started happening a few weeks ago. I was hoping by now I'd have an answer, but it sounds like you have no idea what I'm talking about."

Dr. Wilson said, "There could have been something that happened a long time ago that may be responsible for the problem. Did you experience any traumatic events as a child?"

I paused for a second, and then replied, "Not particularly."

He thought to himself and then said, "You seem like you must have had something bad happen to you. Was there someone you didn't get along with very well?"

I said, "There's quite a lot of folk I haven't gotten along with. So let's keep it at that."

Dr. Wilson replied, "Well I'm sorry to hear that you're going through this. My advice would be to get an adequate amount of rest, and you could try mixing some herbs with honey to calm your nerves. That's the best I can offer."

I said, "What kinda herbs?"

Then he said, "I was thinking you should try Valerian and chamomile. They are both great for relaxation and will help you keep your mind focused. You can mix 'em with honey or syrup. And make sure you heat it up for at least ten minutes. This way it'll all fuse together." I nodded my head, and he added, "You can buy those herbs from here. They might sell 'em at the general store as well. But you're better off buying them here." We walked out to the front and I bought the herbs from him. They were pretty expensive too, costing $5.00 per jar. Made me think I should have just gone to the general store. He put his hand out and said, "It'll be ten dollars for today."

I looked at him funny and said, "You really think I got all that money on me?"

Then he started laughing and said, "I'm only kidding son." He cleared his throat, making me pay only $5.00, and said, "I hope you get better soon."

I said, "Thank you." and walked out the door. I got back up to Dolly and put the herbs in my saddle bag. We had some syrup at the camp, so now I had to put it all together. I just hoped it was gonna work.

As soon as I got back, I got the campfire going. So, I sat down and began mashing up the herbs while mixing them together. All I needed was the syrup. The only other people there were Joe, James, and Bella. Jack and Jack would usually go off with each other, and now Harry was joining them quite a bit. He was almost like a third brother. James even said that we all should start calling him Old Jack.

Bella saw me mixing my herbs, so she came over and asked, "Watcha doin' there?" I wasn't in a good mood. The voices were aggravating me, and I just wanted to be alone.

I told her, "Not now Bella. I need to be alone."

She got upset with me and replied, "You know you gotta talk to people once in a while. Staying alone ain't helping with all the problems inside your head."

I said, "I know, but like I said, not now."

She sighed and then said, "I don't know how to deal with you sometimes. 'Cus you're so damn stubborn. I just can't get through to you. But fine. Go about your business. It's not like I love you or anything."

Bella started angrily walking off, when I looked back and shouted, "Hold on a moment! There's something I need help with darling!" She slowly walked back with her arms crossed and I asked, "We got some syrup around here, don't we?"

She replied, "You'll have to find it yourself." and walked off.

A few seconds later, Joe walked over and asked, "How much syrup do you need?"

I replied, "Enough to fill up this cup." He went over to the wagon to see if we had some there. Lucky for me, Joe pulled out a full jar. He handed it over, and I had all of my ingredients. I had the cup over the fire for about five minutes, and I figured that was long enough. Then I slowly started drinking the whole thing, and it wasn't as bad as I thought it would be. After drinking every last sip, I put the cup down and was feeling a little bit better. I looked over at Bella, who was washing the clothes, and wasn't too happy with me. Sooner or later she'd come around. She wasn't the kind of girl to hold grudges.

As the next several hours passed, the loud voices turned into small whispers. And I hadn't been seeing any visions since I saw that doctor. The herbs were definitely helping, and I did my best to stop thinking about the past. It was better just to let that all go. It's not like I was gonna forget everything, but my mind was much clearer than it had been in a long time. I was feeling okay, and could finally be myself again. It was about damn time. Day was turning to dusk once again, and I was walking around by myself having a smoke. All I could hear was my footsteps and the puffs of my cigarette. I wasn't too far away from the camp. Everyone was back but weren't making much noise. Then I heard James shouting, and the camp became lively with everybody gathering around.

James then shouted at me, "Ed! Get over here!" I put out the cigarette and walked right over. James was the only one standing up, and was listening to Big Jack whispering in his ear. There was some space on the log next to Bella, so I sat next to her.

I said, "You don't still hate me, do ya?"

She put her arm around me and said, "I couldn't stay mad at my big bad grizzly for that long." Bella rested her head on my shoulder and said, "Please promise me you're getting better." and I replied, "I think so. Don't worry about it too much." Then James started talking to all of us.

"Tomorrow, we'll be hitting the stagecoach. It'll be the richest one we've ever hit. And we'll all be ready for it. Though I'm not so sure about the big man over here."

James and everyone else looked at me, and I said, "I'm doing better than ever now. So don't worry about me."

James replied, "Good. That's what I want to hear." He continued saying, "The plan is simple, just like it always is. We get to the abandoned town. We sit there and wait. Then we attack the convoy as it comes through. But recently I found out there are gonna be two stagecoaches. Not like that's a big deal. But who knows? Maybe there will be more than that."

Lil' Jack shouted, "I don't care how many stagecoaches there are! The more the merrier!"

We all chuckled, and I replied, "Amen to that."

Then James said, "We'll probably leave in the late morning. So clean your guns, and make sure they're ready to get the job done." We all nodded our heads, and James sat back down. For the next couple hours, we talked about what we'd do with the money. James said we should all try to gamble a little less. But that wasn't gonna happen. We'd gamble with our money, and with our lives. At least shooting was our strong suit. As long we were one step ahead of our enemy, we'd win every time. This was no different, and we had nothing to worry about. Soon enough we all went to our tents to get some sleep for tomorrow. It was just another stagecoach robbery, and I didn't lose a wink of sleep thinking about it.

When I woke up, I could only hear a few whispers, nothing more than that. I knew that I had to keep taking that medicine to keep my mind sane. For now I was doing fine, so I'd take the medicine every other day. We had a quiet morning. There wasn't a whole lot of talking. Just thinking about getting the job done.

I was sitting around drinking coffee when James came around saying, "Just another stage, right boys?"

Big Jack was smoking a fat cigar across from me and replied, "Whatever you say, James."

Then James said to me, "Lil' Jack and Harry are still asleep. Someone's gotta wake them up." Big Jack said he would do it; then James said, "Hold on there, Jack, I got a better idea." He grabbed one of his revolvers, loaded it up, and pointed it up in the air. James started shooting and yelled, "Wake up boys! We got ourselves a robbery today!" He shot every bullet in the gun. And right after, they slowly got out of their tents to join us.

Lil' Jack said, "You really know how to get on someone's good side, don't ya, James?"

The two of them didn't look very happy, so when they came over I said, "Try some coffee, it'll do ya good."

Bella came over saying to James, "Is that really necessary? Scaring everyone isn't gonna do us any good."

James replied, "Darling, please get out of that night gown and put on something a little more fitting for robbing."

Joe also came over and asked, "Are we all having a meeting now? Or are you just shooting for the hell of it?"

James put the revolver in his holster and said to all of us, "Get yourselves ready. We'll be leaving in a few hours." Within those couple hours I fed the horses, washed my face, and just kept telling myself that it would all work out just fine. As the morning turned to afternoon, we got all of our guns loaded up on the horses, and we had bandages in case one of us got shot. But that never happened.

Soon enough we were all set, and James announced, "It's time boys, and little lady. Let's get this done with." We got on our horses and didn't even bother putting bandanas on. We'd take 'em all out before they knew what was coming. James yelled, "Let's go!" and Lil' Jack yelled, "Woohoo!" All of us rode off, and were moving fast.

Then all of a sudden, I heard voices saying, "You're gonna get killed! You're gonna get killed! Today you will die. This is it Ed." I tried to ignore it, but the voices started getting louder. Now I was a little nervous.

We were coming closer and closer to the old abandoned town, and the voices weren't going away. They were just getting louder and louder, telling me I was gonna die. This particular day was a little foggy. There were a few clouds blocking the sun, but I was still sweating. We were all moving in a pack, and Big Jack was riding right next to me.

He saw how much I was sweating, so he asked, "You doing ok there Ed? I hardly ever see you break a sweat."

I replied, "Don't worry about me." As I rode, my heartbeat kept going up. I wiped the sweat off my face and tried to focus on where I was going. The town we were heading to had been abandoned for three decades. They say that outlaws ran out the people that lived there. Then those outlaws were killed by other outlaws, and they were eventually killed by Mexicans. Now there was no one, because people were too afraid to go there. They called it "Deadman's Point." No one even knows what it was called before.

Soon enough James said, "I think we're almost there. Let's slow down a bit, and we'll find a decent spot for the horses." As we slowed down, I felt a little more at ease. I took my hat off and brushed off the sweat from my forehead. The hat I was using was the one Big Jack gave me. I kind of liked wearing it at this point, and everyone said it suited me. After getting a bunch of sweat on it, I'd be sure to give it a good wash when this was over. My body was tense, but I kept calm, and put my hat back on. As our horses were walking along the road, we saw the town from a distance. As soon as I laid eyes on it, I had a bad feeling in the pit of my stomach.

The voices were talking faster now saying, "I wouldn't go there. This'll be your grave. Get away!" They kept saying the same things over and over. I just kept pressing on because none of the voices mattered. I wasn't gonna let it be my downfall. The horses were brought over to some wooded area that was a little far off from town. We got all of our guns and walked down there. James told us the stage coach was gonna come in a few hours, and all we had to do was find good spots to position ourselves in. I grabbed the rifle and two revolvers from my horse; everyone else did the same.

Once we were loaded up, James said, "Let's get going." We kept quiet, and started to approach the town. Every building looked like it was 100-years-old. The streets were dusty and had debris scattered everywhere. Some of the buildings looked like they were blown up with dynamite. There were even a few skeletons lying around. I wondered how long they were there for; probably a long time. Most of the fog had gone away by now, but there was still a mist in the air. In the middle of the town was a big church, which was falling apart, but still in one piece. It was the best-looking thing in this town.

As we walked down the street, the voices were saying, "This isn't good Ed. You'll be dead soon. I got a bad feeling about this." I had my rifle on my back, and my revolvers tucked away in my holsters. But I didn't know what to expect, and was feeling afraid.

I told James, "I got a bad feeling about this." and James replied, "Don't worry. Just keep your head on your shoulders."

I said, "Okay." But that bad feeling kept growing inside of me. No matter what, I had to keep on going. I continued on with the gang until we got to the middle of town. I heard vultures squawking, and saw them perched on one of the buildings. Some of them were flying right above us. Then James began telling us where we'd all go. There were plenty of buildings with good cover.

Harry said, "They ain't even gonna see us." James told me I'd be behind an old stagecoach sitting across from the church. There was a wall of sandbags in front of the stagecoach that went across the entire block, made the place look like a warzone. I was trying my best to listen to what James was saying, but it was hard to with the voices going off in my head.

He kept on talking when Harry yelled, "Look!" Then a bullet whizzed along the top of my hat, knocking it right off. We started pulling our guns out when Lil' Jack got shot in the chest and dropped dead. I had my revolvers out, and was shootin' at the windows. Right after Lil' Jack was shot, Harry got shot twice and fell to the ground.

All of this was happening in a matter of seconds; then James yelled, "Get to cover!" James and I got behind the stagecoach, and Bella got behind the sandbags. Joe had gone farther to the left, and I saw Big Jack run towards his brother. Only he got shot in the arm, and started retreating while shooting back with his revolver.

Luckily he was able to make it to a building. Then I turned to James and yelled, "I knew it was gonna be a God damn trap!"

James turned to me and shouted, "Just quit yelling and start shooting!" They were everywhere; hiding in the surrounding buildings. There were also a few in the church. I was shooting back at 'em fast, but tried to be careful. We were pinned down.

I heard Joe yell, "I got one!" Then I looked around the wagon, and saw a big guy shooting at me out in the open. I squinted and saw it was Arthur Williams. If he really was in the open he would've been killed by now. So I didn't wanna waste a bullet on him. Then I looked around a second time, and he was gone, but someone was shooting from the top floor of the church. I quickly got a few shots on him, then saw him fall through the window and onto the ground. As far as I could tell the left side was clear, but there was one more in the church, and a bunch more on the right side. It was tough getting the other one in the church. He was a good shooter, and almost got me a few times. But I was able to get a fast one on him and saw him die. Then someone came to the top window of the church. It was the old woman once again. She didn't have a gun, but kept looking down on me. I shook my head and hoped it would all go away. The voices went away when all the chaos started. All I felt in that moment was adrenaline. But they started coming back. And when that happened, it was nothing I could have been prepared for. The voices were screaming at me, and there were too many of them screaming at once.

Some of the things they were yelling were, "Run away! Get yourself out of here! You should've never been born! You're gonna get yourself killed! What an idiot! Get down now!" My head began throbbing, so I dropped my guns and covered my ears.

Between all the gunshots, and the voices yelling at me, I faintly heard James shouting, "Ed! You gotta keep shooting! Ed? Ed! Dammit!" Gunshots were hurling at us nonstop.

All I could do was sit against the wagon and start yelling, "Get out of my head! Get out! Get out!" It was hurting my head so much, it felt like it was gonna kill me. My ears were still covered and my eyes were closed tight.

James shouted, "Big Ed, we need you! Get up and shoot 'em! Please Ed!" I was losing my mind, but was able to open my eyes a little bit. I looked to my left and saw Bella. She was trying her best to fight back. But without me, the rest of the gang didn't stand much of a chance. Bella was firing her repeater, and I could tell she was very afraid. As she was about to fire another shot, a bullet went through her, and she fell to the ground.

My eyes opened wide and James screamed, "Not Bella!" After seeing that, I felt something inside me that made me get up. I quickly loaded my revolvers and started firing at the rest of 'em. In that moment, I took out three more of them. There weren't too many more left, so James and Joe fired back, and I also kept on shooting. The tables had just turned, and we got most of 'em. As far as I could tell, there were three more left. Then I saw Big Jack shooting his gun from a building on the bottom floor. There were four of us and three of them. So we kept the pressure on 'em. We weren't letting them get away.

The fight went on, and soon enough there were only two left. Then there was one. And eventually there were none.

Everything was silent for a few seconds, and then James said, "I think we got 'em all." The voices had backed off, and it sounded like they were far away, instead of right next to me. I came out from cover and saw Harry on the ground. He was breathing, but looked like he was just barely alive. Lil' Jack was lying near him, and Big Jack came out with a bandage on his arm. He ran over to his dead brother. Then Joe ran over to Harry and started talking to him and taking care of his wounds. James ran towards Bella. I put my guns back in my holsters and followed him. As I got to both of them, James used his hand to put pressure on the wound. She was shot in her upper abdomen and was shaking, unable to say a word.

James picked her head up with his other arm and said, "You're gonna be alright darling. It'll be okay." She kept on shaking, making small moans, and bleeding everywhere. James was saying, "You'll be okay. Just stay strong." Then she stopped shaking, and making sounds. She was gone. He put her head down and closed her eyelids. Then he got up and started yelling in my face. This made the voices come back, and I didn't know what any of them were saying. James was shouting that it was my fault for Bella dying. And he kept going on and on.

I started screaming back, "I don't care what the hell you have to say! Don't you give me a hard time! You could have killed more of them yourself! This was your God damn idea!" Then James walked off, and I began rubbing my forehead to calm down the voices. I walked over to Harry, who was still lying on the ground. He got shot in the leg and his arm. Both of the wounds were wrapped up, and it looked like he would make it. Joe was off somewhere else, and I had my gun out in case someone else tried to shoot me. I walked over to the man I killed from the top of the church; and when got there, he looked to be a bounty hunter. He didn't have a badge on him. And he was dressed too nicely to be another outlaw. Big Jack was kneeling over his little brother with his head down. Then I saw Joe come out of one of the buildings and walked over to me.

He said, "A couple bodies have badges on them. And some others don't. I think both bounty hunters and lawmen teamed up on this one."

I replied, "That's too bad for us then. But at least we won."

Joe asked, "What about Bella? Is she okay?" I shook my head, and Joe slowly nodded his head.

Then James yelled, "Someone get me a bandage over here!" Joe and I walked over and James said "Give me the bandages." He got the bleeding to stop, and then wrapped the bandage around the wound. I figured he wanted her to look decent when she was buried. And that gunshot wound didn't look very pretty. James said, "Let's get the horses and get the hell out of here. Joe, you take Harry, Big Jack will take care of his brother, and I'll carry Bella. And Ed, get out of my way." I walked with Joe, and we picked up Harry together. We were ready to start walking back, but Big Jack was still kneeling over his brother, not saying a word. James had Bella on his shoulder and said, "Jack, c'mon." Big Jack didn't respond. He kept his head down, and James said, "We'll come back for him with the horses."

As we carried Harry, he said, "Put me on my feet. I think I can walk."

Joe asked, "Are you sure?"

He said, "I think so." We slowly got him on his feet, and he was able to stand. But he could barely walk. Both of us were holding onto him tightly. It took us a while to get to the horses. They were used to hearing gunfire at this point, so they weren't very scared. We were barely able to get Harry up on the back of Joe's horse, and then James put Bella's body on his horse. The same way Buck was put on top of Harry's horse. When we brought all the horses up to Big Jack, he was just frozen there.

James shouted, "Jack! Jack!" Still nothing. Then James got off his horse and walked over to him. He got right beside him and said, "Jack." Then he put his hand on Jack's shoulder. He said, "We ain't gonna bury him here. We're taking him home, with everybody else." Big Jack and James cleaned up Lil' Jack's wound, and they carried him back to the horses. Before I got on Dolly, I found my hat where I could see the bullet skimmed right through the top. I dusted it off and put it back on. Once we were all set, we got ourselves out of there.

As we all started riding back, Harry asked, "So I guess there was no stage-coach, huh?"

And James replied, "Forget about the damn stagecoach."

That night we buried the bodies. Both were buried near the camp. They were put on the opposite sides, since they never got along that well. We got wooden crosses for 'em and then carved their names on it. It had felt like the longest day of my life. I never thought something like that would happen. But it did.

I told James, "Next time, they could end up killing all of us."

James looked at me and said, "We'll figure things out." When all was said and done, we went to our tents, except for Big Jack. He was at Lil' Jack's grave, and would be there for a long time. I got in my tent, and all I could do was lie down. I knew I had to keep taking those herbs to make it go away as much as possible. My head couldn't take the voices anymore. At least now they were quiet, and I could just fall asleep. So I closed my eyes and fell asleep right away. Then at some point, I found myself in some dark old room. There wasn't much in there except dust and dirt. Then I walked backward and bumped into a desk behind me. I turned around and saw a razor-sharp knife on top of it, which didn't look so good. I told myself it was just another dream, but had a feeling it was gonna get ugly. The room was small, and there was one window showing it was night. Across from the window was a door, so I walked up to it and turned the knob. The door was creaking loudly, and what I saw was a long hallway going straight. It was pitch black on the other side, and I just hoped nothing would jump out at me. I began to walk down it, and as I took a few steps forward, I heard steps coming towards me. I stopped dead in my tracks, and the person coming towards me came out of the darkness. I would have rather seen the devil. Instead it was my father. He was holding a musket with a bayonet attached to it, and was wearing a civil war uniform. It was one worn by Union soldiers. As a child I had seen soldiers wearing those uniforms, but never my father. He held the musket across his body, and stared at me.

I stared at him back and then asked, "What happened to you?" There was no reply. He was several feet away from me, but there was no way around him. The hallway was too narrow. I decided to walk forward and said, "Just put the musket down. I wanna talk."

Then he shouted, "Enemy ahead! I'm loading!" He took out his cartridge and bit off the end, then began pouring powder into the musket.

I tried to stop him, saying, "Father…listen to me." He kept going and started ramming the cartridge in the barrel. Then I yelled to him, "I said stop!"

He yelled back, "Prime!" putting the cap in the musket and after doing so said, "Shoulder, arms." positioning the musket up against his shoulder.

I was getting fed up and loudly shouted, "Father!" He didn't respond to anything I was saying. No matter what I said, he wasn't going to stop doing what he was doing.

Then he yelled, "Aim!" I turned the other way and ran back to the door. It was halfway open, and I knew I had to move as quickly as I could. It was down to a matter of seconds. I just got myself through the door as he yelled, "Fire!" I slammed the door shut with my backside, and the bullet came right through the door. It created one big hole on my right side, causing pieces of wood to fall all over the floor. I didn't know how he missed that shot. But I figured I wasn't supposed to die. He was. I looked at the knife, knowing it was my only weapon. I ran over and grabbed it, holding it tightly. I quickly walked back to the door and took a deep breath. Then I peeked through the hole left by the bullet, and saw my father waiting there in a battle stance. He wasn't loading his musket, and all he had left was the bayonet. I decided now was the time to kill him before he started reloading. I slowly turned the knob, took a step back, and kicked it wide open. He was ten feet in front of me, looking like he was ready for war. We looked at each other, and I was about to say something to him, when he began charging with the bayonet pointed at me, screaming, "Charge!" I ran back into the room and closed the door behind me just in time. I was facing the door, and then looked down to see the bayonet got through the door, and partially into my stomach. It wasn't that bad, and so I backed out of it and saw I wasn't bleeding. It's as if I was a ghost, and nothing could hurt me. Before my father could pull the bayonet out from the door, I pushed the door open and he dropped it. I took advantage of that moment and used my knife on him, trying to put it into his chest. He blocked me with his arms at first, but I was stronger and was able to push through, putting it right into his heart. He slowly collapsed and took a few last breaths of air. I kept the knife in him as he fell to the ground. Then that was it. He wasn't coming back from that. On his waist was a holster, but there was no gun. I took the holster and attached it to my belt, and the knife as well. All that I saw in front of me was darkness, and I wanted to see what else I'd find. I walked past my father's corpse and didn't look back.

I kept walking down the pitch-black hall and only heard my footsteps. I could not see a thing and kept going until the hallway got brighter. There was another door at the end with the room being fully lit. I decided to open up that door, and I saw some oil lamps lit up on the walls. And there was one hanging from the ceiling. Below the hanging lamp was a large man sitting on a chair leaning back and his legs crossed on top of a desk in front of him. He had a hat on and was looking down. I wasn't sure who it was at first, but then he took off the hat and looked up at me. It was my old friend, Arthur Williams.

The first thing he said was, "Well if it isn't Big Bad Ed." Then he took his legs off the desk and got up from his chair with a revolver in his hand. He got in front of the desk and faced me from about 15 feet away. He had a mean mug on his face and said, "It's been far too long since we last met. And now I'm gonna kill you, you little bastard." He then pulled out another revolver and pointed both at me. Then he put one on the ground and kicked it over to me while holding onto the other. I was surprised, but picked it up and checked to see how many bullets were in it. There was only one. So I put it back in my holster, knowing he wanted to duel.

Then Arthur said, "Let's see if you can handle a gun like a man, and not like a child."

I said, "Let's do it then." Arthur moved his leg back, as did I. For a few seconds the room was calm. I saw a fierce look in his eyes. I focused on him, and blocked out everything else in the room. He was ready to kill me. And I was ready to kill him again.

He said, "On the count of three... Three... Two... One!" I put a bullet in his eye, and he fell down to the ground. It wasn't a good idea for him to take on a gunslinger like myself. In real life I had been in a few duels. And it's clear how it turned out for anyone who took me on. I went over to his body and picked up his gun. It also only had one bullet. So I put that gun in my holster instead, and noticed a door that was open on the other side of the room. It wasn't there before, but now it was. I walked over and saw there was a circular downward staircase, which was my only way of getting out. It didn't take long before I got to the bottom where there was another door, and a window right next to it. I looked out the window and saw it was getting brighter outside. The sun was close to rising. I opened up the door and walked into the next room. I first noticed the front entrance. So I was almost out of there. It was two large double doors in the front, and then I looked around. I realized I was now inside a bar, but it was empty. Tables were turned over, and beer bottles were scattered around. It was as if there was some kind of big brawl in there, and everybody ran out. The bar also looked pretty old, with cobwebs around the tables and walls. I didn't want to stay there any longer. Or else something bad was probably going to happen. The double doors were far away, so I walked towards them. But as I took a few steps forward, the doors were kicked open by the old woman, who fired her double barrel shotgun at me. I got behind a turned over table, and looked over it to see her face once again. Then she fired another shot at me. I ducked my head in time, and she reloaded that shotgun faster than I ever could.

She shouted, "You didn't have to kill me you son of a bitch!" I didn't know what to do. She was coming towards me and all I had was one bullet. I had to make that bullet count. There was a beer bottle right next to me, so I quickly threw it over and it hit her. That's when I cocked the revolver, and fired it at her as fast as I could. My hands were trembling, and I ended up missing. There was nothing I had left. Even the knife was gone. I waited for her to get closer. And when she got close enough, I picked the table up from the bottom and threw it at her. She fell back, still holding onto the shotgun, and I made a dash behind the counter. I was still in one piece, but I needed a weapon. She kept on coming and said, "Now you're gonna die."

I said to her, "Come and get me." I had the idea of taking my hat off and holding it up to bait her into shooting it. I just needed something long to hold my hat up. Right beside me was a loose plank, so I ripped it out and put it under my hat. She was only a few feet away from me, so when I held the bait up, she shot right at it. My hat was torn to pieces but I was okay. As she got right on the other side of the counter, I stood up and pushed the shotgun to the side before she could shoot it. She may have been an old lady, but she was strong. We struggled for that shotgun, but I pulled her close to me and slapped her, and snatched it away from her. It still had another bullet inside of it. So I pointed it at her and she screamed the same way she screamed when I killed her on that stagecoach. I didn't pull the trigger. Instead I jumped over the counter and kept the shotgun pointed at her. She fell to the ground, holding herself up with her arm and looking at me.

I looked into her eyes and told her, "You ain't ever gonna kill me you old hag." Then I blew her head off once again. She wasn't getting up from that, at least I hoped she wasn't. It seemed that it was over, so I walked to the double doors which were open, letting in the sunlight. Before I got outside the building, I dropped the shotgun and got to the front porch. I had no idea where I was, but it sure looked beautiful. I began walking forward, when I saw my own self, come up in front of me pointing a revolver at me. The gun was fired, and I woke up.

I couldn't fall asleep for the rest of the night. I tossed and turned, trying to forget about what had just happened. It was too much for me to think about, and I felt empty inside. As time passed, I decided to get up before the sun rose and lit up a cigarette. And after going through all of that, it might have been the best one I ever had. I ended up smoking a few more, which put me at ease. As I took my last few puffs, it was almost dawn, and I walked towards Bella's grave.

I got on one knee right in front of her grave and said, "I'm sorry Bella." I wanted her there with me, but it started to fully set in that she was really gone. That's when I began to feel the pain. And soon that pain turned to anger. All of us were still empty handed and needed to get money if we were going to survive. I looked over to see James sitting alone by the campfire. So I went over and sat down with him. As I sat, we didn't say anything to each other. The campfire had been put out, and both of us were calm.

A few seconds passed, and James said, "I know how we can get the money we need."

I had my head down and replied, "Not another stagecoach robbery I hope." James was hunched over, keeping his hands together. I knew it hurt him to see Bella and Lil' Jack buried. It hurt all of us.

James waited for a few seconds to reply and then said, "We'll need to hit the bank in Colestown."

I looked at him and said, "You know that's the largest town in the county, right? There's police there."

He said, "Of course, I know that. But the bank there has got a lotta money." I knew it would be dangerous, but it was our best way at making money fast.

I said to him, "Alright, but do you have a plan?"

James said, "I gotta think it through. I'm gonna head over there alone and scout the area. Everyone else needs to stay here. So don't go out drinking." Then Joe came out from his tent and joined us.

He sat across from us and said, "Morning."

James filled Joe in on the bank robbery, and then said to us both, "In three days, we'll get it done." We nodded our heads, but Joe looked unsure about it. Either way he was still gonna go along with it. Then James asked him, "So, is Harry still alive?"

Joe replied, "He's doing okay. He said it was his first time getting shot, and that he can barely move around. His body is still far too sore. But Big Jack seems to be healing up nicely."

James replied, "Well it's not Big Jack's first time getting shot, so I know he'll be fine." I hadn't seen Harry since we all got back from the gunfight.

So I got up and said, "I'm gonna give Harry a visit."

Joe replied, "I gotta warn ya, he hasn't been in the best mood. So don't be surprised if he snaps at you."

I said, "For all the times he's bothered me, I think it's only fair if I go bother him."

Joe said, "Fair enough." I walked into his tent and saw him on his bed. He was lying on his side and facing away from me.

I couldn't tell if he was awake or not, so I whispered, "Hello? Harry? Are you sleeping?"

A couple seconds later he turned over to me and said, "Yeah, I'm sleeping just fine after I got shot twice and am in God awful pain."

I replied, "You're lucky you ain't dead, so be grateful."

Harry said, "You're lucky that first bullet only shot your hat off."

I said "I know… I know." I said, "You weren't the only one that got shot. Big Jack also got shot in his arm. He can still fight though."

Harry replied, "Too bad Bella and Lil' Jack couldn't make it. "

I said, "I'm trying not to think about that right now. In a few days, me and the rest of the boys are gonna rob a bank, the one in Colestown."

Harry laughed and said, "All of you boys are gonna end up dead." Then James walked in the tent and got down on one knee to talk to Harry.

James said, "Look at me. You need to take it easy for now. I've been shot before too, and I'm a stronger man for it. They may have gotten us that one time, but I promise you, it won't happen again." Then he stood up and said to me, "Let's go outside for a bit. I think Big Jack is gonna join us." Harry was mumbling something as we walked out, and then I saw Big Jack across from Joe, standing with his foot on top of a chair. We talked about what we had to do in order to stop lawmen from catching us. If we stayed in the same spot, they were eventually gonna find us. So we had to move somewhere else after the bank robbery, somewhere far away. We didn't speak of Bella or Lil' Jack. We agreed that the past is the past, and that we had to move on.

Three days later, we knew what the plan was. James told us there weren't that many police around. All we had to do was control citizens inside the bank, open the safes, get the money, and then get out of there. It was a big bank, so there were gonna be a whole lotta people. But James taught us how to handle a crowd of scared civilians pretty well. This was gonna put us to the test. We had to keep people quiet and calm. If one man tried to stop us, there was a chance others could join him. And we couldn't afford to turn this into a massacre. Once we were ready, I put my bandana in my pocket. As for my hat, I buried it in the ground and got myself a new one. A brown slouch hat, and it was love at first sight. I hoped it wasn't gonna get shot off this time. And more importantly, I hoped none of us would get killed. We got saddled up and the four of us were ready to head out. None of us were saying much. We were all angry, except for Joe, who always had the same straight face on.

Big Jack got on his horse and said to me, "They ain't gonna get any of us. Not a single one of us. That I know."

James was on his horse and then looked back at me, saying, "I hope you had enough of that special medicine of yours. Otherwise we might be screwed like the last time."

I replied, "I took enough of that stuff to make any man want to throw up. So don't worry about me."

James looked ahead and said, "They won't be expecting us over there. So as long as we do our jobs right, we'll be rich men. Now let's go and hit 'em where it hurts!" We started making the trip over there, and kept quiet for the most part. Us boys knew what we were doing, and had a good feeling about this one.

It took us about three hours to finally get there. Colestown was even bigger since the last time I was there. Probably the biggest town I had ever seen. We slowly rode into the streets, trying to look like we were just regular folk passing by. There were plenty of wagons passing by, and most folk were dressed up pretty nice. Us boys didn't look like we'd fit in. But nobody bothered us as we went down the streets. I saw a few police officers hanging about, and some of them had horses. Even if we kept this bank heist quiet, we'd still have to get on out of there fast.

A minute later, James said, "There it is," and we took a good look at the Colestown bank. It was the biggest bank I had ever seen. I couldn't even imagine how much money was in there. We went down the road to hitch our horses. Then we got off and started walking towards the bank. No one was watching us, so we put our bandanas on as we approached the front door. It was about to be show time, and I had my revolver out, ready for anything. I was behind Joe, and James was in front.

He pushed the door open and barged right in shouting, "Everybody get on the floor! This place is getting robbed!" Immediately people did what James said and sounded frightened. I moved to the right side of the room and held my gun up in the air. Then James yelled, "As long as you don't move, we won't kill ya! We wanna do this as nicely as possible." The four of us were spread out across the room, and felt like we had control of everybody. The place wasn't too packed, but there were at least 15 people in there. I had a few people move towards the right, and Joe had another small group of people on the left side. It was easier to have everybody separated, this way they'd be less likely to fight back. But with how scared this crowd was, fighting back was out of the question. Big Jack was watching the door, and James was in front of the clerk.

He said to him, "Open the door to the safes. And do it fast."

The clerk said, "I can't…" James pointed his gun at him and cocked it back. Then the clerk swiftly moved to the door and opened it. He was covered in sweat, looking like he was about to faint.

James said to me, "Bring him in there and make him open up the safes. Try to not kill him."

I replied, "Sounds like a good time."

James shouted to Big Jack, "How's the front lookin'?" and he replied, "Okay so far. I locked the double doors already." I walked up to the clerk, grabbed, him, and threw him in the room. There were four safes in there. So I told him to start with the one closest to the door. He did exactly as I told right away. Once he got the first one open, he just started handing me the money, and I put it in my sack.

As he gave me the money, I told him, "Don't worry we're not gonna take all of it, just as much as we need."

He asked me, "How much do you need?"

I replied, "I think we're gonna need all of it." Once I got most of the money in the first safe, my sack was already filled up. I called James over to come over and help with the rest. He walked in quickly and threw me his sack. I asked, "Why am I the one that has to carry everything?"

James said, "Well that's just how it is." I pointed the clerk to the next safe, and he scurried over there like a scared little mouse.

James went back to the others, but as soon as he began opening the next safe, Big Jack yelled, " I see two policemen outside! They know something's going on."

James yelled, "C'mon Ed! Take what you have and let's get out of here!" I ran out of there and met up with the gang. James said, "Gentlemen, we're going to have to fight our way out of this one." I had the sack strapped on my shoulder, and one revolver out. I was also carrying a Winchester repeater, but I hoped I wouldn't need it. We got behind Big Jack as he took the plank out from the door handles. He then bolted out and started shooting the policemen. They dropped like flies. The rest of us got outside the bank and ran for the horses. Whistles were blowing, and people outside were running away. We ran as fast as we could, and were able to get to the horses before anyone else showed up. Then we all got on, and our horses knew to move fast. We moved through the streets close together. James led the way, and I was right behind him with Joe and Big Jack by my sides. We were about halfway out of town when four policemen came around a corner on horseback, just a few meters behind us. Our horses moved much faster, and got farther ahead of them. We went as fast as we could go, but they kept following us and then they started shooting. Joe and Big Jack fired back, killing at least one. And I pulled out my repeater and turned my torso to start shooting back. Then my voices started up again, but it wasn't as bad. I was in control of my head this time. After firing a few shots, two more fell from their horses. The last one slowed down and went back for the shot-up lawmen. We kept riding like hell, and I could still hear voices speaking so quick, I couldn't understand them. I was too busy trying to get myself out alive. All I did was look straight and focused on James. Doing that blocked out everything around me, and made it easier to do what I had to, which was to keep moving. As we went farther down I saw a dirt road, which meant we were just about out of there. We got on that road and rode our horses like we were never gonna stop. The lawmen weren't chasing after us, and we ended up getting a decent amount of money. It may have not been as much as we wanted, but it was enough for us to lay low for a while. But before we could lay low, we had to move to a different state. Things were too dangerous for us around these parts. It seemed as though we overstayed our welcome, and two members of our family were killed. None of us were gonna let that happen again. If all the lawmen out there wanted to find and destroy the rest of us, so be it. We weren't going down without a fight.

PART 6

One year passed after the bank robbery. We licked our wounds and moved all the way out to Missouri. The area was new for us, so we took our time settling in. It wasn't as warm as Georgia, and was a lot windier. But we all grew to like it. There weren't any big towns or policemen around, just farms, grass, and a few small towns that were spread out far from each other. Harry was back on his own two feet, but we lost two horses. One of them was Joe's. He had it for a long time, but it got sick and didn't make the trip. The other was an extra horse we had, but we had to kill it and eat it in order to survive. There weren't as many forests in these parts. Much of the land was just plains, which made me feel empty. Made me miss the life we had in Georgia. After living there for a couple months, Harry found a boy who ran away from home. He brought that boy back to our camp, and we accepted him into the gang. His name was Sam, and was 14-years-old. He had short brown hair along with brown eyes, and his voice wasn't finished going through puberty yet. When I first saw him he looked angry and didn't say much. After meeting him for the first time, I walked with James and told him how I felt about Sam.

I said, "You know I can't stand kids."

James replied, "Well we need someone new. Someone that's willing to learn and understand things for how they are. He'll be good for us. I know it."

I sighed and said "If you say so. I just don't know about keeping a little brat like him. We need strong men that know how to survive. This kid doesn't know the first thing about any of that. He's lucky he found us."

James replied, "You were a kid once too ya know."

I said, "Yeah, but it didn't feel like I was."

James said nothing for a few seconds, and then replied, "You'll get to know each other. He seems like a decent kid." After we finished talking, I grabbed a bucket and went to a pond to fill it up. I needed to wash the clothes because they smelled so bad, it would make the flies drop dead. Normally Bella did those kinds of chores, and she was a lot better at it than me. I had the sponge filled with soap, and began scrubbing. Sam was sitting down about ten feet away from me, reading a book. No one else was around but him, and it didn't look like he was in the mood for talking. At a certain point, I was getting bored with all the scrubbing and the washing, and Sam looked like he was real interested in that book he was reading.

I asked him, "How's that book so far?" He slowly put his book down and turned his head towards me.

Sam replied, "It's alright." Then he went right back to reading with his head buried in the pages.

I replied, "Well it looks like you're in love with it."

He replied, "Funny. Are you a jokester?"

I said, "Sometimes, but most of the time I ain't the one to be joking around. I'll get serious real fast."

Sam said, "You don't seem like the kind of feller someone should joke about... This book has got some jokes. Do you wanna read some of it?"

I thought about it for a second and said, "I can only read a little bit. It ain't for me."

Sam replied, "Oh." and kept on reading to himself. Then he said, "I could read some of it to you, if you want."

I said, "I guess it wouldn't hurt to have some kind of entertainment while doing these damn chores. What's it called anyway?"

Sam said, "It's called '*Tom and His Pet Fox*'. It ain't that bad."

I replied, "Well, start reading."

Sam said, "I'll go back a few pages. This part is pretty good." Then he cleared his throat. "*Tom was looking everywhere for his mother's lost horse named Beth. It's not like it would be hard to spot since it was all white. But darkness was setting in, and he had to find that horse before the wolves found it. Or worse, a big ol' grizzly bear. That horse was just bought too. It was said to be the best work horse in the whole county. If Tom had to look through the thick of the wilderness in the dark, he would. He had his lantern just in case. After searching for a few more hours, day-light was just about gone, and it became nighttime just like that. Tom wasn't gonna let any of that stop him. The only problem was, he had nothing to defend himself from predators. The only thing he had was a stick, and it wasn't sharp at all. He was de-termined, but it didn't look like he could harm a fly. As he slowly crept through the forest, a horse was neighing loudly a few meters west. Tom didn't hesitate to run on down there, hoping to bring Beth home. When he got there he saw Beth, but he also saw a man trying to take her away. Tom went right up to the man and told him it was his mother's horse. The man was big and round. But he was friendly to Tom, and said he'd help bring the horse back to his mother. First they had to calm Beth down. She was scared from being out in the dark. Then the man gave her a treat and patted her for a bit. Beth began easing up and the man got a rope around her so she wouldn't run away again. When that was said and done, all three of them began walking. The man's name was Billy, and they were chatting with each other quite a bit. Tom was inquisitive of Big Billy, asking him questions about what he does, and if he likes playing music. Billy said he lived a simple life, and did a lot of skinning and hunting. He espe-cially liked hunting foxes. Tom got a little worried, thinking about Bud. He decided to shrug it off and hope Bud wasn't anywhere nearby. Then Billy slowed down with Beth attached to the rope, and made a complete halt. Tom asked why he stopped walk-ing, and Billy said he'd meet Tom back at the spot they were standing at, and that he had something important to take care of first. When Tom asked what it was, Billy said to not worry about it and mounted up on Beth. The only problem was that Billy was so big, Beth couldn't handle all of his weight and bucked him right off."*

I stopped Sam and said, "You said some sort of fancy sounding word in there. I don't think I've heard folk say that word before."

Sam replied, "Are you talking 'bout the word inquisitive? I think that was the only fancy word in there."

I said, "Yeah that was it. In-quis-it-tive. Is that how you say it?"

Sam said, "That sounds right to me." and I replied, "That's a pretty long word, inquisitive. I have no idea what the hell that means, but it sounds like an interesting word."

Sam replied "I think it means to be curious, and ask a lot of questions."

I nodded my head and said, "Yeah, that sounds like Tom."

Then Sam asked, "Should I keep going?" and I said "I've heard enough. I ain't one for reading. But maybe some other time, I don't know." Sam put the book down and went over to a jar of peanuts we had lying around. I told him to not have too many, or else the others wouldn't be happy and send Sam on his way out of here.

He asked me if I was kidding, and I said, "You'll find out the hard way then."

He took a few and said, "I don't think they're gonna kill me over some peanuts."

I said, "Buck probably would."

Sam asked, "Who's Buck?" and I said, "Nobody. Just eat your peanuts." Sam was an alright kid. He wasn't a pest like many boys his age were. He reminded me of Tom a little bit. They didn't know much about the world, and Sam was still just a boy. If he was gonna be like us, he had to learn how to be a man first. That night I told Sam that I'd show him how to hunt tomorrow.

He told me he already knew how to hunt, but I said, "Then you'll have to show me what you got."

He replied, "Tomorrow sounds good to me."

I said back, "We'll go early in the morning. So get a good night's rest." Sam nodded his head and went inside of his tent. I had a feeling he wasn't gonna be a natural like I was. I could tell he didn't have it in him. He needed someone to show him how it's done.

I was up at dawn, mixing my herbs together with honey. I drank it every other day. When I finished all of it, I put the bowl on the ground.

Then Sam came over to me and asked, "What's that you're drinking?"

I replied, "Something important." He walked over to the wagon where we kept the guns, and pulled out a repeater. I went over to the wagon and said, "Grab some bullets too." I got a rifle and loaded it up. Sam did the same with his repeater, and he at least knew how to do that. But he was far too slow to survive in a shootout. I said, "Get a strap on, and get on the small horse."

Then Sam said, "I'm sorry, I never really learned how to ride."

I sighed and said, "It ain't hard. You'll learn today." Sam got the gun strapped on his shoulder, and only struggled a little bit getting on. That horse was the smallest one out of the bunch, just like Sam was. I got on Dolly, and we headed out, with our horses walking alongside each other. As Sam got more comfortable with the reins, I told him to make the horse start trotting. He felt uneasy with it, and said it would take some time getting used to. So for the time being, we trotted our way to a spot with more trees and bushes. I was hoping we'd at least find a rabbit. We slowed down and hitched the horses by a tree. I told Sam to stay low and move quietly. We had to find some bushes if we were gonna get anything. Eventually, we got ourselves behind a nice thick bush. The only thing left to do was put out the bait, which were small pieces of vegetables.

I said to Sam, "Watch me. Make sure you spread it around. Don't just put it all in one spot." After it was all laid out, I went back behind the bush with Sam. I said, "When a rabbit comes up to the bait, and cock the gun back slowly. If you do it too fast, it'll make noise and scare away the prey. And aim for the head. Shooting it in the torso will ruin the meat."

Sam said, "I'll try to not miss."

I replied, "Tell yourself you won't." I had to help Sam with holding the gun right. He was tense while holding it, and if he couldn't hit the rabbit, I would. We sat there for almost an hour until a crow swooped in and went for the bait. I nudged Sam and whispered in his ear, "It ain't a rabbit, but it's good enough." Sam aimed the repeater, and I held the back of it to keep his aim steady. The crow turned towards us and Sam fired one shot, completely missing the crow. As it started to fly up, I quickly shot it in its wing. Then I walked up to it, and it was trying to get away, so I took my knife out and slit its throat open.

Sam watched and said, "I'm sorry I missed." and I replied, "Don't ever say you're sorry... Just don't keep missing, or you'll get shot soon."

I cut the wings off and put the body in my satchel. It wasn't much, but it was at least something. Sam wanted to walk around for a bit, and I figured it wouldn't hurt. We started walking down one path and stuck to it, this way we wouldn't get lost.

As we were going, I asked Sam, "So what made you run away from home?" Sam didn't say anything for a moment and looked at the ground.

Then he said, "It's a long story."

I replied, "It's just me here with ya. I won't tell anybody else about it."

Sam said, "Alright then... I used to live in Kentucky. It was my mother and two brothers and one sister. My siblings and I fought often, especially with my mother."

I asked, "How come you and your mother didn't get along?"

He said, "I don't know. We just didn't. She kept giving me a hard time, with all of her yelling and nagging. The town I grew up in didn't treat me that well either. Eventually I grew tired of it and wanted to leave, so I did."

Then I asked, "Do ya think she misses you?"

He replied, "I doubt it." We kept walking until we got to a small cliff. Sam walked over to the edge and said, "It ain't much of a view, just some trees and rocks at the bottom." I sat down a few feet away from Sam. It felt good just to rest for a bit. Then Sam started taking a piss right off the edge of the cliff. He turned his head back and said, "I bet you can't reach the big rock down there." I got up and walked to the edge.

I saw the rock and said to Sam, "Sorry, but I'm definitely gonna win this one." I pulled out my big shooter and took aim. Not only did I hit the same rock as Sam, but then I got another rock farther down. After I finished I said, "Don't worry, you'll get there one day."

Sam said, "Yeah, eventually." We zipped up our pants and got back to the horses.

As we rode back to camp, I told Sam, "You got a lot of work to do with shooting that gun right. So keep that repeater. It's yours now." Once we got to camp, the rest of the gang was there. We sat around for a while and talked about how boring this place was. The landscape was empty with not much wildlife or folks to rob. We decided it was best to move east. In a couple days, we moved out once again.

Sam let me have the book he was reading after he finished it. He said that I'd like it, so I read it every now and then, and I was reading whole thing. Only a few weeks passed since we headed east. We stayed in Missouri, but we had to keep our heads low. Our camp ended up in the middle of the woods, like it usually did. The area kind of reminded me of "Tom and his Pet Fox" since a good part of the story takes place in the woods. Except Tom wasn't anything like me. The others thought it was funny that I was reading a whole book, but it was there for me. And it wasn't easy reading with voices in my head, but I pulled through. Sam was getting better with shooting. I had him shooting at cans, trees, bottles, just about anything. At one point he ended up killing his first rabbit. And I felt kind of proud, even if he missed his first two shots. Not too far from us was a manor house that had plenty of rich folk living there. James was planning on doing a scam there, which we all thought was a good idea. Doing that was safer than robbing banks. On one afternoon, I just got back from buying a hammer and some nails for the wagon. One of the wheels was getting loose, and we had too much for the horses to carry on their backs. I saw Sam sitting on a tree stump, practicing with loading a revolver James gave him. It was brand new too, and Sam always kept it close. He loaded it over and over again. With all that practice his speed was getting quicker. I watched him for a moment, and then took out the book from my satchel. I looked at the front cover, which was so worn you could barely see the title.

Then I looked up at Sam again and said, "You know I read the whole thing."

Sam looked up at me and said, "So…what did ya think about it?"

I replied, "Tom learned a lot about the world, friendship, and dealing with loss… That fox really helped him out with all of that."

Sam said, "I'm just happy the fox lived a long happy life, especially after everything him and Tom went through."

I asked, "But the fox was female. In the end she had the whole litter."

Sam replied, "I know it was a she fox. I wanted to see if you'd catch that… And ya did."

I said, "Of course I did."

Later in the day, I talked with James about what he was planning. He told me I wasn't gonna be a part of this one. It would just be him and Big Jack. They were gonna dress up like lawmen and pretend that they were lost out in these parts for days. Then they'd talk with the people on the manor to get some help. Of course, James was gonna give the people there a nice long sob story on how "his son and daughter" was sick and dying. And that he was low on money to buy medicine. Big Jack was gonna scold James and tell him to quit whining about it. That way they'd feel sorry for James and get angry with Big Jack for being so nasty to him. Then eventually Big Jack would leave the manor house, and hopefully by then, James would get something out of pity. I didn't think about it too much. Putting on an act wasn't my thing anyway. The both of them went out to do that the next day, and I was stuck with Harry and Joe at the camp. Sam had ridden off on Joe's horse to do what he called "exploring." Us three boys were just sitting around, talking 'bout old times. Harry recovered just fine from his gunshot wounds. He had no problems with moving around and doing what he normally did, which was mostly drinking. I would have a bottle of beer once a week. That was it. Sometimes I would try to only have half, but I couldn't stop myself from having the rest. Harry liked to drink brandy and liquor, but mostly brandy. Joe started talking about how life was simpler before the war, and that slowly America would keep on changing.

He went on saying, "This industrial age is gonna turn the world into something completely different. It makes me wonder what life is gonna be like a hundred years from now. The way of life in the South will eventually be replaced by machines and factories. Then there's all the colored folk who have to find their way in this country. And that's gonna take a long time."

Harry said, "Even back when they were slaves, they had high spirits. They're better off, but who knows what'll happen with them. For now they'll have to make the most of what they got."

Then I said, "I think you're probably right about that. But I'll be honest, if Sam was colored, I wouldn't care for him as much."

Harry said, "I understand that... You and him seem to get along well."

I said, "He's got a lot in him, and I know one day he'll be able to handle himself. It's just gonna take time."

Joe said to Harry, "You know you really should clean yourself up a bit. You're smelling worse and worse every day, and now there's flies circling around you."

Harry replied, "There's flies' flying around us all the damn time. It ain't much different than it was years ago."

Joe said, "I'm just trying to look after you. And you gotta stop with the drinking. It didn't help Ed a whole lot, just made things worse. So try laying off the Brandy at least a little bit."

Harry got up and said, "Fine. I guess I'll go drink some liquor instead." Then he walked off and picked up a bottle of liquor. Then he kept walking, and it didn't seem like he'd come back for a while.

I looked at Joe and said, "He's in a rough patch... He'll get out of it eventually."

Joe replied, "Yeah, I'm sure he will." Shortly after, Sam came riding back looking like he was ready to take on the world. He got off the horse and hitched it up like he had been riding it for years. Joe said to Sam, "She's a good one ain't she, always easy going."

I said, "Yeah, she's kind of like you. Neither of you make much of a fuss."

Then Sam turned to me and asked, "Can I ride your horse? What's her name, Dolly?"

I replied, "Me and Dolly have a special kind of bond. And she doesn't take a liking to anybody but me riding her."

Sam said, "Maybe one day she'll end up liking me. I guess that'll take time."

I grinned and said, "That ain't ever gonna happen. She'd rather go through the gates of hell with me than end up another man's horse."

Joe said, "I better go find Harry. I just hope he doesn't piss all over himself again."

I replied, "Well good luck with that." Sam came over and sat on a stool across from me. He didn't have anything to say and just sat there, staring at the ground. I asked him, "How were your adventures out there?"

He said, "There wasn't a whole lot to see. It was just trees, rocks, and a lot of thorns; far too many to count. Riding around was the only part I enjoyed. There were some open fields where I had that horse going at full speed. At least I don't think she could have gone much faster. But now I don't know what to do with myself." I didn't have a whole lot going on either.

Then I asked, "Have you ever heard of a harmonica?"

Sam thought about it, and said, "Those are the tiny instruments you play using your mouth, right?"

I replied, "Yeah it's kind of like that. I've had one for a long time, but I haven't played it in a while."

Sam said, "Well bring it out then and show me something." I went inside my tent, where I kept the old thing wrapped up in a small blanket. Then I brought it out and Sam said, "They're smaller than I thought they were." I sat down and began to play. First, I did a warm up by playing a scale going up and down. Then Sam was already looking at me amazed.

I told him, "I'll play one of my favorite songs now, and I think you're going to like this one." The song I played was called "Red River Valley," but I sped it up quite a bit. It was too easy for me to play it at the original slow boring pace. Sam was tapping his foot along with the rhythm. Then he added clapping on every beat. All of that got my adrenaline up, and I was having more fun playing than I had in a long time. But I couldn't end without doing a solo. I just made it up as I went along, and the notes were coming out like angels were singing them. All of my heart and soul went into it, which gave me a good feeling inside. A kind of feeling I hadn't felt in a while.

When the song ended Sam said, "I haven't heard anything like that before. You could probably make a living from playing that thing."

I replied, "I could, but I wouldn't make much. That harmonica is the one thing that will always be with me, no matter what."

Then Sam asked, "Why is that harmonica so special to you?"

I paused for a few seconds, and then said, "I bought this when I was with my momma a long time ago. That's one of the last memories I had of her."

Sam asked, "What was your momma like?"

I thought about it and said, "I think she was kind of like yours. She yelled at me a lot, and tried to control me as best as she could. It was the same thing with my brothers. All three of us were out of control. But I'd say I was the worst one."

Sam asked, "How come you were the worst?"

I replied, "I got angry the easiest, got into a lot of fights. I was smart in school though, but that all ended."

Then he asked, "Did you run away also?"

I replied, "I did, but my story is a little different from yours."

Sam asked, "What's your story then?"

When he asked me that question, I felt empty, and replied, "Nothing."

There was a brief moment of silence, and then Sam said, "I don't think your story is nothing. Maybe your story is that you just need to find something."

I asked "Like what?"

Sam replied, "I don't know. You'll figure it out."

Later that day, Harry and Joe came back, and Harry was hanging in there. Then a little while later, James and Big Jack walked into camp with more from that manor house than they could have asked for.

James was saying, "Those people were too easy to fool. Even one of the men there started crying."

Big Jack added, "I had to run out of there though. All of them wanted to hang me for being so nasty to James. What got 'em the most angry is when I said, 'They're just kids. They can easily be replaced.' But it was a good thing we dressed up as lawmen. Otherwise they probably would have killed me." James and Big Jack got plenty of medicine, food, and of course, some decent money. It would keep us going for a while, but we wanted to head further east. Being out near the Great Plains got boring for us pretty fast; so within two days we moved east in Missouri, close to Illinois. The trip took us almost a month, longer than we thought it would take. The main problem was the weather. It was raining pretty bad, and the wagon kept getting stuck in the mud. But we kept pushing and eventually settled down someplace that suited us well. Sam almost felt like a little brother to me. I was teaching him everything I knew about robbing, lying, cheating, and shooting like a real gunslinger. He was eager to learn, and would eventually make a damn good outlaw. That is as long as he didn't get killed. Besides doing all of that I also took him out fishing. It was his first time, so I taught him everything I knew. We didn't have a rowboat and had to stand at the edge of a pond. It was just like when my brothers and I used to fish. Sam kept asking about the kinds of fish that were in that pond. I told him that he'd have to wait and see. And after some time passed, Sam caught his first fish. It was a small one, but it was better than nothing.

At the end he said, "It ain't quite as fun as reading books. For the most part, nothing happens." and I said, "That's the fun of it." Sam kept that fish he caught, and we'd cook it for supper that night. Everyone was settling well into the new camp. There weren't as many thorns around as there were in the last place. And there was a small cliff that Sam liked to practice climbing on. This time there were plenty of big trees around, and Sam would climb on those too. The scenery was better than most of the places I had been. It felt like we were finally getting back up on our feet again. We were close to civilization, and we had to be if we were going to pull off heists. Sam was always asking me when he was gonna be part of a heist. I told him that it would probably happen soon enough, and that having a shootout was the last thing we wanted. I did get a thrill out of it, but there was always a chance anyone of us could die. And I didn't want any of us to go down any time soon. We all had a lot to live for. At least that's what I've kept telling myself.

We only spent a few days at the new camp, and Harry was stocking up on all the whiskey and liquor he could get.

James told me, "Harry's getting worse. There must be something going on with him. But I don't know what."

I said, "Drinking is just his way of dealing with his problems, just like it was for me."

James replied, "Just like it is for every other man." We both felt it was better to let Harry figure out his own problems. There were plenty of times where he'd drink a lot and smell bad, but this time it was different. I just knew it. Still, I decided to leave it be. Every man had to face their problems on their own. At least that's what I always believed. As for my problems, if I went a few days without drinking the medicine, the voices would start getting louder again. Then the same visions I had would start to come back. Though they weren't trying to kill me, but I'd see them looking at me across a distance. Sometimes it was Arthur, the old woman, and now Annie. As long as I stayed on track with taking those herbs, I'd be able to do what I normally did without any serious problems. The only thing I wasn't so sure about was fighting.

Another day passed and not much was going on with us. That was until James came back to camp with four men. He said that all of them were now a part of the gang. They all had big grizzly looking beards with decent sized beer guts. But none of them were quite as big as Harry's. James said he found them out camping in the woods. And that they used to be a part of another gang. For a while, they did what they had to do to survive. At first I wasn't sure if they could be trusted, but after talking with them I figured we'd get along well enough. They hardly had anything with them, except for the clothes on their backs and a couple revolvers. Those boys were lucky they had us now. Their names were Joel, Harris, Steve, and Cleet. All four were around the same age as Harry, and they were all ready and willing to fight hard to survive. The only thing was that they didn't come across as very smart. They'd laugh, holler, and joke around for hours. And half of what they said never made any sense. Still, James was happy to have them with us. The main thing I was worried about was the gang they were a part of. That gang was called "The Ripley Gang." It was a big group of boys, and it was said there were nearly 20 of 'em. They were also known to be nasty sons a' bitches like us. And to make matters worse, we weren't too far from their territory. James said that we wouldn't stay too long, but he wasn't gonna let us leave the nearby towns without getting a dime out of them. We were here to make money, and do so by any means necessary. If the Ripley gang wanted to take us on, it would be their greatest mistake yet.

Several days passed as the four hicks made fools out of themselves and only made me wish James never found them. He thought it was for the better. We all knew that we had to have numbers if we were going to hang in there. I was sleeping a lot better now. I wasn't having nightmares or anything like that. It felt good waking up in the morning, which was once again becoming my favorite part of the day. Then one morning, I heard yelling from James. And then I heard my name getting called to get out of my tent. So I quickly put my belt on and stepped out to see what was going on. Everyone else was sitting down on chairs around the campfire, with James standing in the middle. As I got closer, I saw everybody, except for Joe. I looked around and didn't see any sign of him. I sat down on a chair and hoped Joe was alright.

James was holding a letter in his hand, and said, "Harry found this letter by Joe's tent earlier this morning. I haven't read it yet, so I guess we're gonna find out what it says together. I just hope to God that he didn't get captured and is being held for ransom."

Harris said, "Oh I doubt it. Them cowards won't come after us. They don't really wanna fight."

James said, "If they have Joe, I don't know what we'll do." James held the letter with two hands, brought it to his face, and began reading. "*This is Joe writing. I hope you all will get to read this. I felt that it was easier to do things this way, and I hope you all listen to what I have to say. I decided it was best for me to leave the gang... I thought about it for a long time, but I didn't want to let go of what I had held onto for so long. I'm leaving because living this way isn't worth it any more. We can't stop the world from changing. The only two choices are to join it, or live in the past. And I regret the decisions I've made in the past. The only thing I can change is what I do now. I felt like this gang was the only place for me, but I always knew I could be something more. Being an outlaw will get you nothing but anger, regret, and despair. I know that probably none of you will ever change, but think about what I have said. In the end, you all know it's true. So longboys.*" James looked up at the rest of us and took one deep breath. He then started ripping the letter up, and the pieces fell into the campfire. Just like that, all of Joe's words were gone.

Then James started saying, "Now I know that all of us have been through a lot. Nowadays there's more lawmen than there once were. The industrialists are getting richer and taking out anything and everything that stands in their way. No matter what, things will always be changing. And that's a part of living. Through all the changes that have happened throughout the last decade, we made our way through all of it. Without letting anyone take advantage of us, stab us in the back, or betray us. But today, Joe betrayed the dream of living as a free man. The moment any of you forget that, you might as well bend over for men with more money, power, and greed than any man should have... It ain't about the money; it's about fighting for something. So either bow down to another man's will, or live like you have your dignity. That is all." James walked off and I followed, but he said, "Not now Ed. I need to be alone." I walked away from camp on my own, and then I saw Sam coming towards me.

He asked, "Is it alright if I join you?" and I said, "Sure. That sounds good to me."

Sam said he couldn't believe Joe was really gone. And I told him I couldn't believe it either. Joe was in the gang since the beginning. It honestly felt like a piece of me was now missing. I couldn't understand why Joe was thinking all of that. Then again, he always had a lot on his mind that he never talked much about. He may have been gone for good, but I still had Sam with me. He was telling me about a mountain not too far from camp, and that he wanted to hike up the whole thing. I said I'd join him, so we decided to go tomorrow. James and Big Jack were talking to each other a lot more now, and the hicks were as annoying as ever. Harry was too drunk and in his own head to care about what was going on. All I could think about was what Joe said, and where he'd go now. But I wasn't going anywhere. This gang was the only thing that made sense to me.

That night I tried falling asleep with voices saying, "Joe's gonna be dead. Sam's gonna be dead. It'll all be over soon." I wasn't sure if I believed that or not. So I didn't worry about it and decided to keep taking it one day at a time. Tomorrow morning, me and Sam were gonna climb that mountain, and that was about the only thing I was looking forward to.

When it was time, Sam and I set out for that mountain. I took the medicine that morning, and brought some water for the two of us. We walked a few miles just to get to the bottom of the mountain. It wasn't the biggest mountain I had ever seen, but it looked like the top of it had a pretty nice view. We both began making our way up, and Sam started asking questions again.

He asked, "When birds are chirping, are they talking or singing?"

I said, "I never thought about that one. It's not like we can ask 'em what they're doing. For all we know, they could be yelling at each other. I don't know too much about birds. But horses I know pretty well."

Sam replied, "I just wonder about the animals sometimes. And why they do what they do. I find it very interesting."

I said, "Learning about birds won't do too much good for ya; at least not as an outlaw. Back when I was around your age, I shot all kinds of birds. They make for some good target practice."

Sam replied, "I don't plan on shooting a bird I don't have to kill. I'd rather just stick with shooting bottles."

I said back, "If you don't wanna shoot a bird, then how are you gonna kill a person?"

Sam said, "If they need to be shot, I'll do what I gotta do."

I said, "I guess we'll have to wait and see." It had rained a little the night before, so the weather was all soggy and damp. Fortunately the sun was coming out from the clouds, and soon enough the day would get a whole lot brighter.

We took our time, careful not to trip over any rocks sticking out. I only tripped over myself once. Sam tripped over so many times, you'd think he drank a whole bottle of whiskey before starting the hike. He was still able to keep up with me. It's not like we were in a rush to get to the top. As we pressed on, I asked Sam what he'd do if he left the gang.

He said, "I don't know to be honest… I'd have to figure that out; and how about you?"

I replied, "I ain't ever gonna be leaving the gang."

Then Sam asked, "Was there something you wanted to be before you became an outlaw?"

I hesitated, then started saying, "There was a lot of things I thought of being. But I found the one path that worked well for me. It always made me feel like I had power. And power is something you gotta fight for in this world."

Sam said, "That sounds like something my father would have said. But he's dead now."

I replied, "I guess you're lucky then, because everyone in my family died a long time ago."

There was a moment of silence, and then Sam said, "I'm sorry to hear that. Even though I don't care for the rest of my family, I wouldn't want them to die… If I may ask, what happened?" I started telling Sam about my brothers, parents, even how I met James. As we were getting higher and higher up, I told him how each of my brothers died. Then about how my father slowly fell apart, leading to him killing momma, then himself. It was hard for Sam to hear all of that. He looked like he wanted to say something helpful, but didn't know what to say.

Then I said, "We're almost at the top now. It should be just a little bit further."

Sam replied, "All that stuff you said about your childhood. It makes me think about my own family, and that they still love me." Sam tried holding back his tears, but a few drizzled down his face. He tried to cover it up so I wouldn't see it though. A few steps later, we got through the final push, and made it to the top. All of the dark clouds had drifted away, and the sun was finally out. It felt like I had climbed up to heaven.

Then I looked at Sam and said, "I've always blamed myself for my parents dying." Sam looked at me confused. And then I said, "I've never told that to anyone."

Sam hesitated for a little while longer, and then said, "Well, you finally got that off your chest."

I said, "I guess so. How about we take a look at that view?" We were side by side, and looked down at everything we had just hiked through. I wasn't as amazed as Sam was, but it was still something to look at. As I looked across there were no houses or railroads, just Mother Nature. A lot of the time she wasn't too nice, so it was nice seeing her in all of her beauty. We looked on for a little while longer without saying anything.

Then eventually I gave Sam a pat on the shoulder and said, "We gotta head back before it gets dark. I don't want the boys to think we're leaving them too." We made our way downhill, and it was a lot easier than going up. It still took us a while to get back to camp. But Sam told me a few of his jokes along the way, which made the way back a little faster. When we did get back, everyone was just sitting around with not a whole lot going on.

I only heard a, "Hey there." from Joel, but that was it. Since it was getting late, I told Sam he should take it easy. So he went inside of his small tent that he always had, and I popped out a cigar I had with me all day. Smoking that thing cleared my mind; then I closed my eyes and all the hurt inside of me went away.

That night I was sitting by the campfire with the hicks lying down on their blankets in drunken slumber. I couldn't stand to talk to anyone of them, since they went on and on about nothing. And their breath smelled like it could kill a man that wasn't strong enough to bear it. Thankfully they weren't making a sound while sleeping. So I kicked back on a wooden chair and just tried to relax. The air was much cooler now. It wasn't cold or anything, but hanging out by the fire was a perfect way to end the day. Joel was on his blanket just a few feet away from me and was the only one tossing and turning. He eventually stopped moving and stayed put, then he let out a big ol' fart.

I smelled it right away and said, "Jesus." It was probably the worst thing I ever smelled. I couldn't imagine how bad it would've been if the others started farting too. Thinking about that made me get up and walk away to get fresh air before I passed out. For a while longer, I leaned sideways against a tree and thought about Sam. I wondered if he missed his family, or if he wanted to see them again. This gang was family now, but all of us couldn't love Sam like his mother would. I kept leaning onto that tree until I got tired of it and then walked over to my tent. I got inside, lied down on my old blanket, and fell asleep fast. It had been a long enough day, and I needed a good night sleep.

I was falling into a deeper and deeper slumber. Then as time went on, I heard a voice. It was a voice that sounded familiar, but it was fading away. I kept listening for it, and slowly everything got brighter until I saw myself in a forest. The spot I was where me and the gang camped in when I was seeing Annie. There was no one else around me. And there was no campsite, just the surrounding forest. Then I heard the voice again, and it got louder.

It was saying, "Come over here Ed!" And I realized it was Annie's voice. She then said, "Ed! Where are you?" I looked around and didn't see her. So I followed her voice and then she said, "I don't want to have to go without you!" Then I began running until I got out of the forest onto an open field. My jaw almost dropped when I saw Annie, next to a hot air balloon. She waved at me and asked, "Are we doing this thing or what?" I stood there not saying anything, amazed at how giant the hot air balloon was. Then I started walking towards Annie, and she had that same cheeky smile on her face.

When I went up to her I held her hands and said, "It's been a while."

Annie said, "You promised that one day we'd go on one of these."

I grinned and said, "I guess it's not gonna kill me, so let's go!" I got in first, and then helped Annie get in.

She said to me, "Start pulling that rope and it'll ignite the flame."

I said, "Here goes nothing." As soon as I pulled the rope, the flame grew large pretty quick. Slowly but surely, we were going up. Soon enough we were above the trees and a gentle wind carried us forward. I told Annie it wasn't high enough, and thought we could crash into a tall tree. So I tugged the rope some more, and we were soon up by more than fifty feet.

Annie told me, "I think that's enough Ed. Going up any higher is too scary."

I replied, "If you feel like throwing up, try to not get it on my boots."

Annie said, "You're such a gentleman. And you know what? It ain't really that scary. I think we should go even higher."

I replied, "Let's see what this thing can do." We soared so high to the point that we were above the mountains.

Annie's voice sounded a little nervous when she said, "I can't believe we're doing something like this."

I said, "You can always hold onto me if you want." She came closer and grabbed around my left arm with both her hands. As we stayed around the same height for a little longer, Annie got over her nerves and focused her attention towards me.

She said, "I miss those times we spent together."

I told her, "I miss them every day. There ain't any other woman like you Annie. None that is as sweet, sensitive, and thoughtful. I just wish I could have told you that."

Then Annie said, "Don't worry about any of that Ed. You know we could probably travel across the Atlantic Ocean in this thing."

I replied, "I don't know about going over oceans. This balloon ain't going that far." Annie's hands were still gripping my arm. She wasn't gonna let go, and I didn't want her to.

She looked up at me and asked, "So, where are you gonna take me?"

I shrugged and replied, "I ain't one for traveling. Staying in the same place is always what I preferred."

She said, "You live such a fast n' hard life. I doubt you could ever stay in one place for too long."

I said, "That's just how it goes. But when I hear your voice, or see your face, I feel good again." She gave me a kiss on the cheek. I turned to look at her and then Annie put her arms around the back of my neck. We shared the longest kiss I ever had with her. Then I opened my eyes and we kept looking at each other. I said, "No one will believe you when you tell 'em you were all the way up here."

She said, "I'm sure they wouldn't. But I like it up here. It's an escape from the rest of the world. It feels like our own world."

I replied, "I wouldn't have it any other way."

Annie said, "Well at some point, you have to come down."

I chuckled and said, "I'm gonna keep this thing going for as long as I can."

She said, "We'll see about that." Then she grabbed my shoulder with both of her arms and shouted, "Now wake up! C'mon Ed! Wake up! Ed! Ed!"

Then I opened my eyes and James yelled, "Ed, c'mon already!"

With my voice sounding groggy, I asked, "What the hell is it? I was having a nice dream."

James said, "Harry's missing."

Every one of us set out on foot looking through the woods for him. He had one last bottle of Brandy, and it was missing when James looked inside of his tent. We figured he must have taken it with him while he wandered out. I told James he was probably lost, and James believed he got himself hurt. To cover more ground, all eight of us spread out and kept shouting his name.

I walked with James as he told me, "There were still plenty of whiskey and liquor stashed in his tent. Last night he told me that the rest of us were welcome to take as much liquor and whiskey as we wanted. This ain't the first time he's been stuck somewhere out in the wilderness."

I replied, "I wouldn't worry so much. Harry's never too hard to find."

Later as we kept walking, James saw Sam from a far distance and shouted, "Hold on boy, I'm gonna join you!" Then said to me "Keep searching over on this side. And don't forget to look for footprints."

I replied, "Don't worry about me. I know what I'm doing." Time kept passing by, and there was still nothing. The rest of the boys weren't too far off from where I was. But I knew Harry must've gone out pretty far. I searched the grass, leaves, twigs, anything that could lead me to Harry. This forest was just too big, and there weren't enough of us. I was beginning to think he might've gone back to camp already, and that we were out here looking around for nothing. Then as I kept walking, there were some thick bushes in my way. I brushed right through them. When I looked ahead, I felt my stomach turn as I saw Harry's lifeless body hanging from a tree. Right next to that tree was his last bottle of brandy. I slowly walked closer to the bottle and saw that he drank every last sip.

I turned back towards the others and yelled, "I found him!" A few moments later, James and Sam came rushing over. The hicks along with Big Jack followed right behind them. I was still standing near Harry's body, and James only took a quick look without showing any emotion.

He walked towards Harry's body and said, "Cut him down." I took out my hunting knife and started cutting the rope. His body fell down and James put the body over his shoulder. Everyone else looked saddened and shocked Harry went down like that. He always had the strongest spirit. But slowly that must've died out. I guess that's why he stopped playing his banjo Napoleon. We buried it with him. No matter what, it always was and will forever be a part of Harry.

For the rest of that day, none of us spoke a word. Even the hicks weren't saying anything. At nighttime, I found myself sitting alone by the campfire once again. But this time, I had a bottle of whiskey.

I put it up in the air and said, "This one's for Harry." Even after drinking the entire bottle, it didn't make things any better. The whiskey only made me feel worse. I just sat there the entire night, not being able to get a wink of sleep. I wasn't thinking, nor drinking, just staring at the flames until it turned to dawn. As I was sitting leaned back with my legs crossed, Big Jack and James came out and joined me.

When they came up, I said, "Take a seat." and Big Jack sat down on my right side, with James on my left.

Big Jack started saying, "Since Lil' Jack died, I don't think I could ever be happy again." I didn't know what to say and kept my mouth shut. James did the same. Then Big Jack said, "We should've done more for Harry, but it's too late now. And I don't feel like I should be called Big Jack anymore. I never felt like Big Jack without Lil' Jack. But if you wanna still call me that, I guess it's fine. There's just been too much going on at once. First Joe left and now Harry's dead."

James said, "Forget Joe. He doesn't know who the hell he is anymore. But I know who we are, and what we're capable of. As long as we get through these hard times, we'll come out on top once again. That's life, gentlemen. It has its ups and downs." James looked up at Big Jack and said, "Don't forget who you are. You're called Big Jack for a reason, and that will always stay with you. And the same goes for you Ed. No matter what you'll always be Big Bad Ed until the end."

I nodded and said, "I know."

Then Big Jack said, "Someday we gotta have a nickname for Sam."

I replied, "If that's what Sam wants, he's gonna have to earn it." For a while longer we talked on and on. Big Jack told us another one of his stories about how he killed one of the biggest possums he had ever seen with his bare hands. He said he got bit seven times and had the scars to prove it.

Then he started saying, "Even though Lil' Jack is gone, everyone here feels like a brother to me. And I would do anything to keep ya'll safe." A short while after that, James put the fire out and told us to hang in there. We had enough people to take on a town of lawmen, and were still a force to be reckoned with. If somebody crossed one of us the wrong way, the rest of the Mulligan gang would be ready to give 'em hell.

Two more days passed by, and I was off duck hunting. Everybody else was at the camp except for Harris and Sam. They went out together to find and pick some more herbs I needed for that medicine. Harris knew a lot about where to find all different kinds of plants, and Sam had nothing else better to do. I would've taken him out with me, but I felt like spending some time alone.

I carried my repeater and walked out 'til I got to a large pond. I used the bait I had to get 'em all piled up, and got as many as I could. Of course that was all of them, so I didn't hunt the same animal too often. If everyone shot a gun like me, humans would be the only animals left. Then again, if everyone was just like me, humans wouldn't last long either. It was almost impossible for me to go on more than a month without killing someone. Whether it was a sheriff, an outlaw, or someone I didn't like, they were gonna end up dead. But with each kill, there was always a good reason behind it. And now that all those folk are gone, it makes the world a more decent place.

After shooting the ducks, I said in my own head, "Killing a man ain't even a big deal; it's just like duck hunting."

Then I started hearing voices saying, "Annie still loves you. And momma still loves you." I knew that neither of them would ever agree with how I saw the world, but I wondered if Sam did.

I brought back six of those ducks. There were a couple more I couldn't carry, so I had to leave 'em there. The ducks I had would last us for a few days. So when I got back, I dumped all of them in a large basket. Then I saw Harris and James running up to me, and I didn't see Sam. I knew something was wrong.

As they approached me, I asked, "What's going on?"

Harris stopped and had to catch his breath, then he said, "I-I was out the boy, and then two of 'em boys from Ripley gang showed up and they knew who I was right away. They were angry that I left their gang, and then one of 'em went up to the boy and smacked him in the head with the butt of his rifle. The poor kid was knocked out, and they warned me to never come around there again."

Then James started saying, "They took Sam with 'em, and told Harris they'd give him to us for $500. They said they were at the old abandoned mansion where all of 'em are held up. I'm sorry to say it, but we can't afford to make this deal. We've come too far to lose all of that money just like that. I highly doubt they'd play fair with us anyway. Even with all of us, there's just too many of 'em, and I don't want to see anyone else here die. I'm sorry Ed, the boy's a goner."

I hesitated for a moment and asked, "No one is gonna do anything about it?"

James replied, "It's for the best."

I paused a while longer, and then said, "Well I'm saving Sam." I quickly walked over to Dolly and James followed.

As I got my guns and mounted up, James said, "Ed, you're making a mistake. You'll get killed out there, and I'm not joining you."

I replied, "I can handle myself just fine."

James asked, "What about when all the voices and visions start up? You're not gonna be able to control that."

I said, "Don't worry about it. Today's a lucky day for me."

I was about ready to leave, and then James sighed and asked, "Why are you doing this?"

I replied, "Because I have to."

I rode as fast as I could, feeling the wind brushing fiercely against my face. All Dolly needed was a few good kicks and she was still one of the fastest horses out there, despite her age. There was no turning back. If I died trying to save Sam, then so be it. As I kept on riding, I only heard Sam's voice.

He was saying, "They're gonna kill you too, Ed. Don't come this way."

Then I began talking to Dolly, saying, "Keep on going at this pace girl. You'll always be a hell of a horse." I knew not to push her too hard. As fast as I wanted to get to Sam, a tired horse wasn't gonna do much good either. I had four revolvers, and my two rifles. I might as well have been a one-man army. The Ripley gang may have had numbers of men, but I had three important things, which was heart, soul, and a quicker trigger finger. This would be the greatest test of all that. Dolly and I kept pushing through all the terrain that stood in our way. I just hoped Sam was still alive. The hicks didn't say much about the old Ripley gang, but that they liked praying off the weak. It was what they looked forward to. Joel even said that they'd sometimes torture the people they captured. And back in the day, I'd use torture as a tool to get information out of somebody. One way or another, it always worked. But those cowards did it for fun. Even on women, and young boys like Sam. And they weren't as nice about it as we were. I tried not to worry about all of that.

There were still more voices in my head saying, "They're gonna skin you alive, castrate you, and pull out your intestines." In my pocket, I kept a small bottle of the herb medicine. It wasn't a lot, but I figured it would come in handy now. I had Dolly slow down and start galloping. Then I pulled out the bottle, took the cork right off, and drank it all in one shot.

It took a few minutes, but the voices were dying out, and then I looked up and said, "Please have my back momma." That old mansion wasn't too far now. The closer I got, the faster my heart started beating. Then I looked up again and said, "Henry, Cleet, you boys better have my back too." During the final stretch to get there, I slowed Dolly down even more. I didn't want any of those boys seeing me on the road, so I went off into the woods and decided it was time to get off Dolly. I walked her over to a small tree and hitched her there. Both rifles were strapped on my back, and the four revolvers were tucked in my holsters. I slowly walked down to where the mansion was. At that point it wasn't far. I had to keep quiet so I could make the first move. When I got close enough, I could hear them talking. They were talking about what would happen if a cow had sex with a chicken. It was probably one of the dumbest conversations I ever heard. But they were just as dangerous as they were stupid, especially with all the men they had. I was peaking at the mansion through some bushes, and it had more dirt and grime than anything I had ever seen. All of the windows had been shattered, and half of the front door was missing. The mansion was in the middle of nowhere, and was perfect for a bunch of fools like them. I couldn't imagine what it would be like living in there. There were five of them outside, and I heard more coming from the inside.

Then one of them started talking about Sam, saying, "I hope that boy gets comfortable. Soon enough Ripley Jr. is gonna ride him good."

Another one said, "Just wait til' you hear him screaming. That'll go on for the whole night."

I said under my breath, "You'll be the one's screaming." I moved back into the woods, trying to find the perfect cover spot. Almost all the trees close to the mansion had been cut down, and I didn't wanna put myself far back. But there was one tree stump that was tall enough and wide enough to keep me from getting shot easily. So I crept over there as carefully as I could. I was almost there, then one of 'em turned their head and spotted me.

Right away they shouted, "Someone's watching us!" And several more came outside with their revolvers out. I was tucked in good cover, but I lost the element of surprise. I took a quick peek over and saw ten of them lined up several feet across from me. I knew where they were standing, so blind firing was my only option.

One of 'em said, "I saw you creeping over there. Come out and I promise we won't kill ya, as long as you have that money with you. Don't think you're gonna take us on, because you're not gonna win."

I shouted back, "It's too bad you saw me! That's not how it was supposed to go. But let me tell you boys something... You may have seen me, but that's the last thing your ever gonna see."

I blind fired my revolver over the stump, hearing their cries and screams as I blew them away in only a few seconds. I could tell most of them were shot, but not dead. I peered out from the side of the stump and shot the ones trying to run away. There were only two I didn't get, and they ran behind a fountain. Then a few more pointed rifles out from the top and windows. They fired at the stump I was hiding behind. And I caught one with the corner of my eye running towards the woods, trying to get me on my left flank. It was one of the two men hiding behind the fountain, the one that was talking to me before I started shooting. Eventually I lost sight of him. I had both sides to watch out on, and the front had more than enough men for me to deal with, but I was in the best spot by far. So I stayed glued to that stump. And if they wanted to come to me, I'd be ready for 'em. I wasn't hearing anybody coming by, and things were starting to get quiet. They still had their guns pointed at me, and thought they were gonna pick me off like it was nothing. The silence was really setting in, and it was time for me to make the next move. I blind fired a few shots at the mansion with my revolver, giving them a jolt and causing them to shoot. But as they reloaded, I popped out and got three of them from inside the mansion. As far as I knew, there was one by the front door, and the other one by the fountain. I figured the one that ran off probably ran off for good. Still, I had an eye out for him. Two men were left, and I had to get 'em before my voices started kicking in. I tried taking out the one at the fountain quick, but he nearly got me with the rifle he was using. So I pulled out mine and made it even. The one by the door wasn't giving up either. But a few gunshots later I got both of 'em. I could hear them grunting and breathing hard. They were dying a slow death just like their friends. I waited for another minute, and all of that agonizing pain turned to silence. I looked over and saw nothing but bodies in a pool of blood. Then I got out from cover with my rifle out and looked around for the one that was still left. It seemed that they were all done for. I put the rifle on my back and pulled out the other two revolvers, just in case there were more inside the mansion. As I walked through, I saw the place was falling apart. A couple of the stairs were missing, there were holes in the wall, and dust was everywhere. I didn't hear so much as a door creak until I heard Sam trying to yell while his mouth was covered. It was coming from the door to my right, and I saw that door was closed.

I walked up to it and said, "I'm here Sam; we're getting ourselves out of here." With both revolvers in my hands, I kicked the door open. Sam was sitting right there in front of me. And he seemed fine, except for the bump on his head when he got hit with that rifle. He just had a piece of cloth tied around his mouth. I said to him, "I guess the Ripley boys thought we'd bring them the ransom money. It turned out they didn't need the money. They just needed to be put in their place." Sam kept mumbling through the cloth, so I put my guns away and untied the cloth. Then I untied the rope around his arms.

Sam said, "Did any one of our boys get shot?"

I replied, "They didn't come. It was just me."

Sam paused and then said, "Well I'm pretty sure you got all of 'em." Then I heard a revolver get cocked and the Ripley boy who ran from the fight entered the room, pointing the gun at my head. I put my hands up, and Sam had no idea what to do. It seemed our fate was in the hands of the last Ripley boy.

I told him, "I guess my luck just ran out."

He replied, "You...you are a real wild gunslinger, aren't you? You ended up killing every single man in the Ripley gang except for me."

I said, "It seems that way."

He chuckled and said, "I'll be honest, I respect you a hell lot more than anyone in the Ripley gang. I've never seen anyone take down that many men like you." Then he began to chuckle and said, "It'll sure feel good killing you anyway, and I'll take real good care of the boy." Sam got up and charged at him. As he pointed the gun at Sam, I grabbed his shooting arm and punched him in the head which made him drop it. He was knocked out cold on the floor, and I took his gun and saw there were two bullets left in there.

I pointed it at him, about to fire, but Sam said, "Just leave it be; I don't wanna see anyone else die."

I replied, "Whatever you say Sam." and put the two bullets in my revolver. It's not like he was gonna need 'em. He was no killer; he was a coward, just like the rest of his gang.

Sam told me they kept a stash of money under the bed. It was in a chest that I pulled out, and it didn't even have a lock. I opened it and saw plenty of dollar bills and coins stuffed inside.

Then I put all of it in my satchel and said, "I'm glad it ain't going to waste." There must have been at least $200 in there. It was great getting all that money, but what mattered more is that Sam was okay. We walked out of there and got to Dolly. I told Sam to get on her, and of course Dolly didn't like that.

So I petted her a few times and told her, "I promise it won't be for too long. You'll just have to deal with it. I got on the front and we started heading back towards camp.

As we were riding, I asked Sam, "What did they say they'd do to you?" and Sam replied, "I'd rather not talk about it."

Then a moment later, Sam said, "I need to go back home, back to my family."

I wasn't sure what to say, but after a brief moment I said, "There's a train station not too far from here. I'll take you there." I turned towards the other direction and we moved down there.

I did end up asking him why he wants to go back, and he told me, "For right now it's where I belong." I didn't want Sam to leave, but it was his choice, and I had to let it be. After traveling for a few miles, we got to the closest train station. It was a small one that had some houses and farms surrounding it. There was no one else but the ticket seller and two benches. I used some of the money I got from the chest to buy tickets for a train station near Kentucky, where he'd have to go on a couple other trains to finally get back home. I handed him the tickets he needed for now, and then gave him my satchel with all the money in it.

I said to him, "I know you'll need this money, so try not to spend it all in one place." Then I pulled out the oldest revolver that I had. I took it from a gunslinger I killed in a duel, and it had been special to me for a long time. I gave it to Sam, along with a good amount of bullets. I told him, "If you need to protect yourself or your family, at least you got something."

Sam stumbled on his words, and then said, "I probably won't be using this, but you're really giving me all that money?"

I replied, "Take it, it's yours." Then we sat down on the bench and Sam told me what he planned on doing with his life. He said his father worked as a doctor for fifteen years before he passed, and it's what Sam had always thought of doing. Then he talked about how he'd try harder not to let things get to him, and that things weren't always easy with his family. But he knew he could find a better way to work it out.

An hour had almost gone by since we were talking, and then Sam asked, "Do you wanna come with me?" I was shocked he asked that and stayed silent for a moment.

Then I replied, "I'm meant to be in the Mulligan gang. It'll be my family until I die. And besides, I don't think your family wants to come across an outlaw like me."

Sam nodded his head and said, "I understand that. Do what you feel is right. I just hope you stay safe. And I'll always remember you."

I put my arm around Sam and said, "I ain't gonna forget you either." As more time passed by, Sam's train eventually came, and it was time for us to part ways. He got off the bench, waved goodbye, and walked up the steps of the train. Right before he entered the train cart, he stepped off and came up to me.

He stood still and took a deep breath, and said, "Thank you, Ed." Then he turned back and got on the train. Shortly after the train started moving, I watched it leave until it was gone for good. I stood up, got on Dolly, and rode back to the only place I called home.

When I got back to camp, everyone turned and looked at me.

James took a few steps towards me and asked, "How'd it turn out?"

I began shaking my head and replied, "Sam didn't make it. They killed him before I got to him. But every last one of them is dead. I buried Sam's body already, so now he can rest in peace."

James slowly nodded his head and said, "You tried your best Ed; that was all you could do." Then James walked away, and I went to grab an apple for Dolly.

She worked pretty hard that day. And I whispered to her, "Thanks for helping me save Sam." After taking care of Dolly, I splashed some water on my face down by a creek. The water was cold, and made me feel alive. I wasn't sure what to feel. So much had happened, and I just wanted things to be the way they had always been. Sam moved on and I had to do the same. But the memories I had with him weren't gonna just go away; same with Annie. All the people I met and things that happened stuck with me. But no matter what I'd always stay true to who I was meant to be. Nothing would ever change that.

A few days went by, and we were all picking our heads up. Since I gave my satchel to Sam, I had to go out to the closest town to buy a new one. We decided to stay put where we were. The campsite we had was far away from lawmen, and we were tired of moving around so much. I was sitting by my tent, talking 'bout women with Big Jack.

He was saying, "At the end of the day, women are just a waste of time. They'll end up ripping out your heart and stomping on it 'til it turns into a puddle. Then they'll act like they didn't mean it, and end up doing the same thing all over again."

I agreed with him on that one, and told him, "I guess that's just how life is. There ain't no changing it, so it's a matter of finding a way to deal with it." Then James started walking over.

He greeted us and said, "You boys know we have another heist coming up, but this one's gonna be different… This time it'll be a train."

I replied, "It's been a while since we robbed one of those."

James said, "This will be quick and easy. I promise. It'll be carrying money and supplies for the factories heading up to Ohio, and there won't be too many guards."

I stood up, looked at him and said, "I don't know if I can do this right now. There is still a lot going on inside my head."

James said, "I know, but we'll need you. You're still the fastest gunslinger we got. And once we have that money, we'll have ourselves set for a long time."

I thought about it and said, "Alright, I'll go." James had already talked about the plan with the hicks, and then he went through it with us. We would use dynamite to blow up a bridge that the train had to cross over. The train would have no choice but to stop, and then we'd move in quick. The only problem was we didn't have the dynamite. But James said that would get taken care of soon. The hicks knew a place in town where dynamite was sold to men with the right price.

James then said, "Once we have that and some more ammo, we'll be good to go."

Big Jack asked, "How long will that be?"

James replied, "In just a few more days. So don't drink too much." I was starting to get excited about this heist. It was a big deal robbing a train. I just hoped we wouldn't stir up a whole lot more unwanted attention.

Harris and Cleet helped find and pick the herbs that I needed. It was nice of them to come around and help me out, but they could have also helped me save Sam. But at the same time, I figured it was best to let it go. They made their choice, I made mine, and Sam made his. All of that was in the past. The only thing that mattered was robbing that train without any of us dying. As time passed on, James got more than enough ammo, and more than enough dynamite. Big Jack would get the honors of setting off the dynamite, and all of us scouted the area to find the best place for an ambush. Fortunately for us, there were hills on both sides of where the train would stop. With us having the high ground, the guards on that train wouldn't stand a chance. They'd more than likely surrender instead of fighting us. Then it was just a question of letting them go or killing 'em. Either way, the law would find out about it soon enough. I was gonna wear the same bandana I had always used for the past ten years or so. The hicks had canvas sack masks that they'd always used. At nighttime Cleet put it on for show in front of the whole gang. At the very least, it covered his ugly face. But it looked like he was ready to kill an entire town of folk. I hadn't gotten into fights with them or anything like that. At the end of the day we all showed each other respect. After all we were all doing this thing together. The whole plan was set, and we felt good about it. All we had to do now was keep killing the time.

On the day of the robbery, James woke me up and asked, "Are you feeling ready for this one Ed?" and I replied, "I've been ready. It's what I was born for." We all got on our horses, and moved out in the early morning to blow up the bridge. I had my bandana on, and my guns, but I wasn't feeling excited like I was before. It was business as usual, and it was never easy. As we rode, the hicks wouldn't stop shouting and hollering. At one point James started telling them to simmer down, and they weren't very good at listening.

Eventually James yelled, "I said enough!" and they realized it wasn't a good idea to push it any further. We planned on setting off the explosion when the train would be about a mile away from the bridge. So when the conductor would hear it, he'd have plenty of time to stop the train... At least we hoped so. As we got closer we began to slow down. James told us that soon we'd dig into our positions.

Big Jack told James, "I've never blown up this much dynamite before. It's gonna be quite a show!"

James replied, "It will be. But remember that you're pushing the lever on my call."

Big Jack said, "Sure thing boss. You know what's best."

Harris was riding next to me and said, "So we're gonna be sitting next to each other, huh Big Ed?"

I replied, "Just watch that slippery trigger finger of yours. I'd rather this one go nice and smooth."

Harris said, "I can't make any promises on that one!" Then he rode ahead along with the rest of 'em. Soon I began hearing a waterfall, and knew we were near the bridge. I hitched Dolly far away from the dynamite; the same for the rest of the horses. The best we could do was covering our ears as tightly as possible and hope we wouldn't go deaf. I brought one rifle with me and two revolvers. We only needed guns to scare the guards. We figured they wouldn't have the guts to try and fight us anyway. I caught up with Harris on top of a hill on the train's left side. Then I lied down flat on my stomach, hidden in a thicket. Harris was a few feet apart from me and was busy lying on his back with his hands behind his head. I didn't worry about him that much. If one of those hicks got shot and killed, it would be from their own stupidity. At the very least they were helping to keep the Mulligan gang going. Nowadays James and Big Jack were the only ones that really mattered to me, and I'd be more than glad to take a bullet for either of them. I couldn't imagine losing Big Jack, but if James got killed, it wouldn't be the Mulligan gang anymore. At that point it wouldn't be worth calling it a gang at all. While I was set in my spot, I watched the two of them plant dynamite on the bridge. They must have had more than twenty sticks of dynamite. And all of them were connected to a spool, which connected to the lever. Once that was done, it was just a matter of waiting for that train to come. Cleet and Steve were on the other side of where the train would come. Joel was out far waiting to give us the cue for when the train was coming. For a while, we stayed put while it was nice and warm out. It was the perfect weather for a train robbery.

As I waited, I heard some disturbing whispers saying, "Step in front of the train. Go and jump off the bridge." I heard those sentences going off in my head again and again. Then it would stop for a minute, and then come back. I just had to get this over with. Down on the other side of the bridge was James and Big Jack with the dynamite. After blowing up the bridge, they'd head over to the rest of us and that's when we'd all move in.

We waited for quite a long time, until Steve saw Joel and yelled out, "The bank on wheels is approaching now boys!" Then Cleet got up and waved over to Big Jack, and I looked over to see Big Jack ready to set the dynamite off. A few more seconds went by, and I began hearing the rumble of the train. James told us it was all about timing. We were gonna have that train stop right where we wanted it. I focused on loading the first bullet in my rifle, hoping the voices would stop for good. And as I blocked out everything around me, they started drifting away.

Big Bad Ed

Then Harris said to me, "Cover your ears you damn fool, that explosions about to go off." I set aside my rifle and covered my ears as tight as possible. Big Jack was closest to the bridge, and had cotton stuffed in his ears. I was getting nervous that the explosion would be so loud that it would make everything in my head get even worse. I thought I might start hearing explosions all the time, and hearing voices was already enough. My eyes were closed shut and I had my head planted into the ground. I tried to breathe steadily, and just like that, it all went off. It sure was loud enough, but not as loud as I thought it would be. The whole time, my eyes were kept closed and the ground was shaking like it was an earthquake. All I heard was white noise as my hands covered my ears. Then a few seconds later I slowly opened my eyes and uncovered my ears. The train was slowing down and was getting close. The sound of the train grew louder and I picked up my rifle and held it steady with my finger on the trigger. We didn't know exactly how many men there were going to be, but the train wasn't that far anyway. It slowed down more and more until the front end went past me and stopped only a few meters before the bridge was cut off. There was no getting across it now.

Cleet and Steve stood up from the other side and Cleet shouted, "Get outta there, or we'll kill all of ya!"

Harris also got up and yelled, "We got our boys all over this place, so don't try anything!" Then I heard horses coming around from the other side of the bridge. It was James and Big Jack with their revolvers out. Then Joel came over on his horse from behind the train. It was over before it even began. A few men stepped out from one of the train carts with their hands in the air, looking like they were about to shit themselves. Then the conductor jumped off and surrendered. In total there were seven of them. A lot less than we thought there'd be. Steve and Cleet ran down the hill and yelled at the men to get on the ground with their hands behind their heads.

They did just as they were told, and James asked, "Which cart has the money?" and one of them said it was the second to last one. Harris and Joel went in there and James lit up a cigarette. I came down last, taking my time as I walked.

James took out a bag, threw it to me, and said, "They'll need a hand collecting all that money." Then there was a gunshot from inside the train cart.

For a second, everything was still, and then Harris shouted, "Just shootin' the lock off."

I walked in and saw five other chests, and shouted back to James, "Looks like we struck gold!" We fit everything we could in our bags; not only the money, but everything else inside that train. We took some food, letters, and even a few pictures. The hicks and I went through every cart to make sure that nothing too important was left behind. Things outside were quiet, and soon I wasn't worried at all about something going wrong. After several more minutes of looking around, we decided we were done. It was time for us to move back to camp.

Once we came out from the train carts with more than enough stuffed in our bags, James was clapping and said, "Now this is how you make a living."

Big Jack headed out to bring the rest of the horses over, and Joel asked, "What about them yellow bellies here?"

James replied, "Just leave them. They ain't gonna harm a fly." In a short while, Big Jack had all the horses with him, and we all mounted up. I tied down one sack on the back of Dolly. It was a decent amount of weight to carry. That one sack weighed almost as much as Sam. We rode off and left those men stranded there. And they should've considered themselves lucky. Nothing felt greater to me than controlling a man's fate. But it wasn't worth killing any of 'em, since none of those men had a spine to begin with. As we got farther away, I took one last look at the destroyed bridge and the train that stood right before it.

A small voice said, "Get away from the bridge because it's over now. There ain't no turning back." I moved along with the gang and they were all happy, but all I could feel was the same emptiness inside.

A few days after the train robbery, we were all at camp and enjoying ourselves. Things were looking up for the Mulligan gang. Through all the rough times we went through, we grew closer together. It was nearing the end of dusk, and I let Dolly walk around on her own for a bit. She'd hang around with Joel and Harris's horses and were always running free. We were telling stories, having a lot of laughs, but mostly bugging each other all the time. I was sitting in a circle next to James, Big Jack, and of course, the hicks. We used to have an old wooden table, but it was getting too old and falling apart. So we just got three small tables made with fresh wood. They were sturdier, and even smelled nice. One of those tables was on my left side, which I put my coffee on. James had one on his side, and the other one was still in the wagon.

Cleet wanted to try arm wrestling Big Jack on the new table, and Big Jack rolled down his sleeve saying, "Look at this forearm. Do ya think you're gonna beat all this size I got here?"

Then Steve said, "Let's see your forearm. How 'bout that?" Cleet rolled his sleeve down and we all started laughing.

After that quieted down, Big Jack said, "If you boys will excuse me, I gotta take a piss." Big Jack walked off into the bushes, and Steve kept on teasing Cleet. As that was going on, we heard Big Jack yell, "Shit!" I saw him from a far distance and he took a couple steps back, then all of us stood up. Men farther away were slowly walking closer with guns pointed at us. We had our guns pointed at them, and then one in front of Big Jack started talking.

He said, "You may have heard of me, but my name is Old Sheriff Smith. I've been a Sheriff for a long time, and I've heard a lot about you boys."

James replied back, "Well I'm sure you have. Now we were just minding our business here."

Old Sheriff Smith said, "Ya'll need to put down your guns. This is all over."

Then Big Jack said to him, "Why don't you stop hiding behind that tree, and show yourself you damn coward."

Old Sheriff Smith said, "If you wanna die, it's your call. I will give you credit though. You boys can put up a fight. You shot up all of my men at Deadman's Point."

Big Jack asked, "You knew those men?"

Old Sheriff Smith said, "I helped plan the whole thing out. It's just too bad they couldn't shoot as well as you."

Big Jack said, "My brother was killed in that fight. And you're the reason why he died... Damn you, son of a bitch!" Big Jack pulled out his revolver and started getting shot by the other men hiding in trees and bushes. I saw him collapse, and we all started shooting. I flipped the table over and took cover behind it, shooting at whatever men I could see. James did the same thing, but the hicks were out in the open, and fell one by one.

I was reloading when James shouted, "Come on Ed, this way!" I started shooting again, at least getting a few of them. And then one bullet skimmed against the arm I was shooting with. It wasn't that bad, but my better shooting arm was hurt. I made a run for it with James while turning back and shooting at the rest of them. We wouldn't be able to get on the horses without getting shot, so we had to run as fast as we could. I looked to see if Dolly was there, but she ran off along with the other two horses.

James and I kept on running, and I faintly heard Old Sheriff Smith yell, "Get after them!" We ran farther and farther into the woods until we were faced with a small cliff, and we didn't have time to go around. I remembered that Sam would climb up and down this cliff, but I was no climber.

I told James, "I ain't very good at climbing rocks." and James replied, "You're gonna have to learn fast!" He put his hands out to give me a lift up. So I stepped up and managed to get a good enough hold, and climb the rest of the way up. Once I got on top, James was already getting halfway there. I got on one knee and put my arm out for him.

I could hear the footsteps of lawmen coming closer, and I told James, "Hurry up!" Just a few seconds later, he was close enough to my hand, and then grabbed it. There were a bunch of lawmen approaching with their rifles pointed at James. As I held his hand tightly, they all began firing, and he was shot in the back several times. Blood started coming out of his mouth, and I looked right into his eyes, seeing them become lifeless. His hand slipped away, and he fell down. I had no choice but to turn the other way and keep on running. I ran through the forest as fast as I could. It was getting so dark I could barely see what was in front of me. I ran for a long time, and when I stopped to catch my breath, I didn't hear any of them chasing after me. I put my hand up against a tree and took a few more deep breaths. Everyone else was dead, except for me. And now I was all alone. I slowly walked onward, having no idea where I would go, until I heard something moving towards me fast. All the bullets I had were gone, and if it was a bear, it might as well have torn me apart. But when it got close enough, it turned out to be a horse. And not just any horse, it was Dolly.

She walked right up to me, and I gave her the biggest hug I had ever given, saying, "You found me girl. You found me." For a while we just stayed like that, and I held onto her, knowing she was the only family I had left. Then tears flowed down my face; I couldn't even control it. My eyes were closed tight as I was leaning onto Dolly. I could feel her slowly breathing, which helped soothe me. We stayed in that same spot for what seemed like forever. But eventually I wiped my face and mounted up. There was no telling what was gonna happen, but I had to keep moving. Lawmen were surely out looking for me.

Over the next few days, I rode Dolly farther out into the middle of nowhere. I was able to find food for both of us. Dolly would eat whatever I gave her. It's a good thing she was never picky about what she ate. During the afternoon I sat around with Dolly. I didn't have any medicine left, so soon enough the endless torment would start again. I had my hands covering my face, and wished I just had one bullet left. Then it would all be over… But I knew I wouldn't really do it. I made it this far, and none of the boys would've wanted me to go down like that. It may have been Harry's way, but it wasn't mine.

I put my hands on my knees and said, "Damn."

Then I heard Annie say, "Don't give up. You have a long way to go." I looked around, realizing she wasn't really there. A few seconds later, I took my time standing up and heard her say, "You've always been a strong man, and you always will be." I stood in the same spot, waiting for her to say something else. And a few moments later, she said, "You gotta do what's best. I mean you can't be alone forever." I knew that she was right about that. I went up to Dolly and was ready to do the only thing that made sense, which was to go back to Annie.

It was a long trip back to Illinois; just me and Dolly sticking with each other. I didn't have any ammo, money, or much feeling left in me. The only two things I thought about was finding Annie, and eventually killing Old Sheriff Smith. But even if I did kill him, it wouldn't change a thing. Either way, someone else would take his place. I couldn't help but think of what I would do to him if I found him. I was the one they wanted the most. After all, I did most of the killing. Thinking about James, Big Jack, and everyone else in the Mulligan gang weighed me down like weights chained to my ankles. And I didn't have any drink to wash it all away. It dwelled on me, but I had to keep moving on. Dolly and I kept going without eating or drinking anything for days. At a certain point, Dolly couldn't keep going on much further. I had no choice but to go into a local town and steal food from the marketplace. It wasn't an easy task, and was barely able to escape while getting shot at. And not only did I steal food, but I stole a revolver with a few bullets in it. The man running a marketplace pulled out his gun, threatening me for stealing fruits and vegetables. When he got close enough, I fought him for the gun, and then ran with as much as I could carry. That was enough for at least a week, but I did my best to make sure Dolly was well fed. She was the one doing all the work after all. With all the riding we did, it took us less than a month to get to Illinois. And we were getting close to Annie. I was barely hanging on by a thread and still believed this was the only way for me. If Annie was somewhere else or wound up dead, I had no idea what I'd do. As a few more days passed, we pushed through until I finally laid eyes on that old town. I remembered it was called Brookville, and looked as nice and proper as it always was; kind of like Annie. Not much had changed since I was there several years ago. The only thing was that there were a few more houses built farther away from the center of town. All those houses were big too, and looked a lot nicer to sleep in than trying to sleep in the dirt. I knew I smelled pretty bad since there was no time for bathing. I just hoped Annie wouldn't mind too much. Either way I had a feeling in my gut that she'd be there for me. It's what brought me all the way over here, and now it was time to see her again. Dolly walked me all the way up to her house. Once I was at the front, I hopped off and tried to fix my hair. My hat was left when the gang got torn to pieces, so I hoped Annie still had the hat I gave her. I slowly stepped up to the front door, stood there for a second, and then began knocking. Someone was quickly walking up to open the door, so I took a step back, and the door started opening. I was starting to feel nervous, and certainly didn't want to show it. When the door was open halfway, Annie peeped out her head. She looked at me like she didn't know who I was. Then she opened the door all the way and stepped out, with the look on her face turning from confusion to shock. I didn't know what to say, so I just stood there looking at her. She just kept looking at me, as if she was having a dream.

A few seconds later I said, "It's me, Ed." After that, Annie was about to faint. She leaned her arm against the door hinge and took a couple deep breaths. I told her, "I know it's been a while, but I had to come here. I had to see you again."

Annie looked up and replied, "I can't believe you came back here."

I said, "Everyone in that gang I was with got killed or left, but most of 'em got killed. Now it's just me, and I realized that I need you."

She said, "I always cared for you. But I couldn't live that life you lived, and now you know why."

I asked, "Is it alright if I come in?" and she replied, "I guess it's better if we talk inside." Annie let me in and I closed the door behind me. She was walking towards the kitchen and then turned around, looking upset with me.

She said, "I've heard about all the trouble you and your gang caused; about the robberies, the murders, all of it!"

I replied, "A lot of people have."

She asked, "And what was all that worth? Please tell me because I loved you since the night we met. And I didn't want you to live that way." Tears began streaming down her cheeks, and she asked, "So why Ed!? Why?"

I replied, "I don't know." Annie started walking away and then paced around the room while wiping her tears. I said, "I belong here with you, Annie. I don't know what else to do."

Then she asked, "How long is that gonna last?" I didn't say anything, and then she said, "Eventually you'll just be doing the same thing again. It's a miracle you haven't been killed yet."

I replied, "It's definitely been more than one miracle." Annie walked up to me and put her hands on my shoulders.

She looked up at me and said, "You don't look much different from when I saw you last."

I brushed her hair and said, "And you look more beautiful than ever before." She started blushing, and we held onto each other for a minute or two.

Then I asked, "So, are Margaret and her family still living here?"

She replied, "Margaret moved out with the rest of her family a while ago."

I said, "I ain't gonna complain about that."

She chuckled and said, "There was a man I was with for a few years, but he ended up cheating on me."

I replied, "I would never hurt you like that Annie, and you know that."

She said, "Yes, I do."

Then I asked, "Is anyone else living here besides you?"

She said, "A cousin of mine moved in with her mother only child. Her husband passed away, and she lost her old home. So if it wasn't for that, I would've moved out with Margaret and her family."

I said, "I see, and where's the family you're living with now?"

She replied, "They're on a camping trip. They won't be back for a few more days."

Then I asked, "Can I stay here?" She paused and looked the other way.

Then a few seconds later she said, "You can stay here. I'll have to make up a story about you, saying you're... I don't know, I'll think of something."

Then I asked, "And what about Dolly?"

Annie said, "She'll do just fine here."

For the rest of that day, Annie told me a lot about what went on with her life. And how she was a school teacher, showing children how to read. I didn't tell her much about myself. I figured it wasn't a good idea talking about that right away. We played a board game, shared a few laughs, and I finally got some decent food in my belly. The voices were still going on and off, but I tried my best to make it look like they weren't even there. All that mattered was that this was real. Annie was real. And she was still in love with me. But I knew she couldn't understand why I was the way I was. As long as she was there for me, that's what I needed. But I had no idea how things would be here on out. The Mulligan blood was still in me, and would always be a part of who I was. The whole time we sat together, I couldn't help but wonder what she was thinking. For the time being, I enjoyed the time I had to spend with her. It made the whole trip worth it. When it got dark outside, Annie told me that she needed time to herself, and preferred that I sleep in the guest room. I knew that wasn't a good sign, but I knew I was putting a lot of weight on her shoulders, and that it wasn't easy for her.

She walked me upstairs to the room, and before I went in she said, "Hold on a second." As we faced each other, she put her hand on my cheek, and we shared the sweetest goodnight kiss I ever had. She had tears in her eyes and then walked away, moving down the hall.

She said, "I love you."

Then I replied, "And I'll always love you." I went inside and closed the door. The room was small with only a bed, a dresser, and a mirror in the corner. I was very tired, hardly getting any sleep while traveling. I took off my jacket and threw it on top of the dresser. On the other side of the dresser was an oil lamp. I sat down on the bed, and then took my boots off. Then I remembered about my hat I gave to Annie. I wanted to ask her if she still had it, but decided I'd ask her about it in the morning. As I sat there on the bed, I looked up at the mirror and saw myself looking back.

I looked at myself for a moment and said, "You're getting somewhere. Just keep taking it one day at a time. Just like James always said." A short while after that, I lied down on the bed, which felt like sleeping on a cloud in heaven. The last thing I did was turn off the light, and it wasn't long before I fell right asleep.

While I was sleeping, I started hearing Annie's voice saying, "Ed… Ed… Ed…"

Then I woke up, saw six lawmen pointing guns at me, and the sheriff right in front of me said, "Ed…get up." My eyes became wide open, and I slowly got out of bed.

The sheriff told me, "Now put your hands up against the wall." I looked across at all of them, with my mouth hanging open. Then I began laughing. I was laughing real hard.

All those men were looking at each other like they were confused, and I started saying, "So you think you got me huh? You silly fools are always trying to use those damn wanted posters and hired guns to track me down. I'm sure you thought that would work. But it never has. Catching me ain't gonna happen. And you know why? It's because I'm Big Bad Ed, and I can shoot a corkscrew off a bottle of whiskey, after drinking the entire bottle. Look at you, walking around like your something special with that pretty little badge on." I tried to grab the Sheriff's badge, but his arm pushed my hand away. And that's when I realized, they were real... I stood frozen in place for a moment, taking a few uneasy breaths and sweating like I never had before.

The sheriff said, "C'mon Ed. Listen to me already." Then he tried to grab my arm and I shoved him back as hard as I could with my shoulder.

All the other men swarmed in, pinned me against the wall, and I started screaming, "Annie!" but she wasn't coming to help. They tied a rope around my hands and forced me out of the room, then down the stairs. When we got to the bottom I yelled, "Annie! Where are you!?" They pushed me forward through the front door. Right outside there was a prison carriage. A lawman grabbed each one of my arms and forced me to move up. Then I looked to my right and saw Annie with her arms crossed, and her head down. For one final time, I shouted, "Annie, help me! They found me, help! Annie I need you!" They pushed me inside and shut the door. All I saw was darkness, and shortly after the carriage began moving. This was it. I was getting locked up. There was nothing left for me, and I had no choice but to accept my fate. It was over...

THE FINALE

Ed had been taken to a penitentiary a long way from Brookville. He knew there was no getting out of this one. His hands were tied behind his back, and the carriage was well guarded with lawmen riding along on horseback. Ed kept his head faced down the entire time. It took twelve hours before they finally got to the gates of the penitentiary. The sun had just risen, and when the carriage got far enough inside it finally stopped. Lawmen came around the back and unlocked the door and told Ed to get out. There was one guard behind Ed and one in front of him as they moved forward.

The guard behind kept pushing him and telling him, "Don't slow down. Keep moving." They went inside one of the prison blocks and moved past the other prisoners. The hallway they were walking through was well kept. The prisoners had to clean almost every day. And if they didn't want to, they wouldn't get a crumb of anything.

One of the prisoners saw Ed and started shouting, "Good morning to you sir! Don't worry, you'll have a good time here!"

Another yelled, "I'll make you my lover! I promise you I will!" None of that bothered Ed. He moved along with the guards, until they came to a halt in front of an opened prison cell. The guard in front turned around and made a hand gesture for Ed to go in. All the other prison cells had beds in them, but his didn't. He had nothing but the cold, hard ground to sleep on. The only thing in there was a bucket, and he knew what that was for. Once Ed was inside, the guard slammed the cell shut and locked it.

Before he left he told Ed, "Don't worry, you won't be in there long." Ed's arms were still tied around his back. It was cold, and loud from the prisoners shouting to each other. Ed put his back against the wall and slowly skimmed down 'til he was sitting on the floor. The prisoners were talking about him, but he couldn't tell what they were saying with them shouting and the voices in his head. There was so much talking between the prisoners and Ed's head, that he couldn't make sense of what was even being said. The problems in Ed's head were the same as his father's. They had a mental disorder called Schizophrenia. This disorder wasn't diagnosed until the early 20th century, and is known to warp one's perception of reality. But Ed couldn't even think about his mental disorder, or anything for that matter. He just sat there and hoped every voice he was hearing would just go away. After a day of sitting there, the voices finally did quiet down.

The prisoners were still talking, and at a certain point, Ed had enough and shouted, "Can I just get some damn peace and quiet!" Doing so made the prisoners start shouting and banging on the bars as hard as they could. As Ed sat there longer, he started to believe that someone would save him. Or that it was all a dream he was having. But deep down inside, he knew that this was his end. He began to look back on his life and go through all the memories he had, all the conversations he could remember, the places he saw, and the people he cared about. That was all Ed had, his past. Soon he'd have to face his destiny.

Within the next few hours, a guard walked up to Ed's cell and unlocked the door. He opened it wide and grabbed Ed by the arm and forced him to stand up. He held him there and moved him through the end of the hall, and a guard opened the door from the other side. Ed looked up and saw he was in a large room with a line of chairs seating mostly men wearing elegant attire. There were also two women, both sitting next to each other. Ed had no idea who any of them were, but they took a long look at him and then looked straight ahead where Ed would be put to rest...the gallows. On top there was the noose, the lever, and a preacher. The guard moved Ed up the stairs and brought him right up to the rope. Another man started walking up the stairs. He was the sheriff that captured him. When Ed got to the top, he took the noose and put it around Ed's neck. The guard stepped to the side, and the preacher began to speak. He was reading from the bible for the most part, speaking softly and taking his time with every sentence.

After only a minute had passed, the sheriff cut him off saying, "I think that's enough. It's not like those words will change anything anyway." Then the preacher closed the bible and said to Ed, "I pray that God has mercy for your soul. If not, then you will be forever damned. God bless." He walked away with his bible and left the room. The sheriff stepped forward to talk about the kind of person Ed Miller was.

He started saying, "My name is Sheriff White, and I helped bring this poor excuse for a man to justice. His name is Ed Miller, though he's been widely known as 'Big Bad Ed' across many states. This man has killed, tortured, beaten, and stabbed good hard-working folks. Ed and his gang robbed thousands of dollars from banks, shops, stagecoaches, just about anything they could get their hands on. The rest of them were killed. And as far as we know, he's the only one left. It's time for him to go down for good. I know you all have wanted to see him hung for a long time now. I'm not sure if Ed remembers, but a long time ago he robbed a stagecoach with his gang. It was back in 1873, and all the men guarding the coach were killed, along with the men riding inside. That day was tragic for this county and tragic for all of you who knew those men. It's too bad not every family member or friend that lost a loved one from the hands of Ed Miller can watch his hanging. Hell, this room wouldn't even be able to fit that many people." Sheriff White turned to Ed and said, "That preacher was too nice. Rot in hell you scum of the earth." Then he started walking off the gallows and down the steps. Ed wasn't hearing any voices at all, but then he looked at the people sitting and watching him. He saw three sheriffs on one side, and two government officials and a banker on the other. All of them were men he had killed without any mercy. They stuck out the most to him because he looked each one of them in the eye before killing them. There were also two chairs in the middle. And in those chairs, Ed saw the old woman and Arthur Williams watching him, ready to see him swing.

Then Sheriff White shouted, "Alright, pull the lever!" But right before that happened, all the people watching Ed disappeared, and he heard someone walking to the front of the gallows. A second later he saw it was Sam, with widespread angel wings on his back. He walked in the center and looked up at Ed with gleaming eyes and a light-hearted smile.

Sam opened his arms wide, as if he was going to catch him and said, "Thank you, Ed."